WOLF HEIR

HIGHLAND WOLVES OF OLD
BOOK 3

TERRY SPEAR

PUBLISHED BY:

Wilde Ink Publishing

Wolf Heir

Discover more about Terry Spear at:

http://www.terryspear.com/

Print ISBN: 978-1-63311-119-6

Ebook ISBN: 978-1-63311-118-9

SYNOPSIS

Who would have ever expected that falling for a lovely wolf lass would put him and her in so much danger?

A crofter's son, Coinneach, wants to be a great warrior for their wolf pack, but when he meets a kitchen maid, he wants more than ever to work at the castle. But her mother is terrified that danger will befall them all if he works there.

Aisling desires for Coinneach to work on the staff as much as he does until she learns just what the deadly consequences can be.

If you enjoy underdog stories and want to see Coinneach and the woman he loves succeed, the Medieval Highlanders with a wolf's edge is the series waiting for you.

To Sue Tharp—thanks for wanting to shift and rescue me from the hospital while I was finalizing writing Wolf Heir. You are the best!!!

PROLOGUE

The storm outside was a mere murmur compared to the clamor inside Middleborough Castle. Only the bravest warriors ever crossed the threshold of its rugged stone keep, and none so formidable as Chief Hamish MacNair. Six feet four, a wall of muscle, he loomed at his mate's bedchamber door, waiting, shifting from foot to foot, the way a caged bear paced. Hamish, by all accounts, the most ruthless when killing his enemy, had never known fear. Yet tonight, on the far side of the bedchamber door, he was a man undone.

Within the bedchamber, the cries of Lady Orla—his mate, his heart, his lady—rose and fell, searing the air like a hot iron. Three days of labor had passed, an agony that would break all but the most stubborn. Orla was as stubborn as they came. She was a MacTavish by birth, a clan renowned for their spine, their wit, and the bending of men to their purpose.

But she was also a shifter, so he believed she would live. The castle's womenfolk huddled in the galleries, wringing their hands, whispering the old prayers. Even the men kept their distance, save for Hamish, who planted himself outside Orla's chamber as if his presence could ward off death by sheer force of will.

The only one who showed no fear—no respect, no awe, not even fleeting pity—was the midwife Morag. She was the same age as Orla, with the face of a mother and the mouth of a viper. She moved through the halls with the confidence of one who knows every secret passage, every loose stone, every rumor that could be turned to gold.

Morag had caught every babe born at the castle for the last four years, and she'd buried nearly as many mothers. Tonight, she wore her thick brown hair in a tidy plait, a blood-red scarf knotted at the throat. She delivered the news to Hamish each hour: another contraction, another inch dilated, another rag soaked through.

But Morag was a vessel of ambition. Orphaned at twelve after her village burned, she had honed her skills after training with another midwife who had died last year. Morag could knead life or death from a woman's body with equal ease.

On the eve of Orla's confinement, Morag had delivered her predictions with a conspirator's intimacy. "It is a hard birth, m'lord. For the bairn and the mother both. But sometimes the moon gives only one life at a time."

Hamish, ever the pragmatist, had nodded, the lines in his face like carved runes. "If it comes to a choice, save my mate," he'd said, though his voice cracked.

Morag had nodded, her own eyes softening with the gift of shared grief. "Aye, m'lord. As you wish."

But the truth was, she had no intention of letting a weakling survive. Not Orla's son, not Orla herself, not with so much at stake.

When the hour of birth arrived, the castle was alive with anticipation and dread. Servants scuttled through the corridors, bearing fresh linens, boiled water, and the calming draughts that Morag alone concocted. The warriors posted along the walls grumbled at the distraction, but even they felt the pull of destiny. The clan's future was being decided in screams and sweat and blood.

Inside the chamber, Morag stood at the foot of the bed, calmly ignoring Orla's howls. The lady's face was a mask of pain, but her eyes—gray as the northern sea—were lucid, defiant. The child was coming breech. It would be a miracle if either survived. Morag pressed down hard, forcing the issue. Orla screamed, then bit down on the leather strap, refusing to give Morag the satisfaction of a broken spirit.

The bairn slid into the world blue and limp, the cord wrapped thrice around his neck. Morag moved quickly, slicing the cord, working the tiny chest, whispering spells and curses in equal measure. As she'd expected, Orla was hemorrhaging, her life leaking onto the straw. The other women wailed, pleading for Morag to save their lady.

"She must rest," Morag snapped, and shooed them away with a flick of her hand. One of her apprentices, a mousey girl named Isla, remained, eyes wide as moonstones.

"Is he alive?" whispered Isla.

Morag barely glanced at the child. "He's a weak one. Willna last the night, most likely." She looked down at Orla, who was panting, fighting to stay conscious. There was a moment's hesitation. Then, deftly, Morag pressed her fingers to Orla's neck, just enough to render her still.

The door banged open, and Hamish strode in, his face wild with hope and fear. "Orla? The bairn?"

Morag put on the widow's mask. "She's gone, my lord. Bled out, before I could stem it. The bairn...he's alive, but only barely. I fear he's not long for this world. I did all I could."

Hamish collapsed to his knees beside the bed, gathering Orla's cooling hand in both of his. He howled, a sound so guttural and raw it might have split the stones of the keep. Morag turned away, cradling the mewling infant to her breast, her face unreadable.

And then, as the commotion raged, a rumor reached Morag's ears, borne by the scullery maids in the hallway. In the lower chamber, another woman had just delivered—a scullion, nameless even to the kitchen girls, who had birthed twins, but only one survived. The other, still and silent, was a perfect copy, a male the same age as Orla's son.

This couldn't have worked out better. She would say that the bairn died in childbirth along with his mother. She couldn't just kill the bairn right there, not when other ladies were attending Orla.

She reached down, supporting the slick, purpled weight of Orla's newborn, and passed him carefully to Blair, who at sixteen had already delivered lambs and foals but never a child. Blair, wide-eyed and trembling in her borrowed apron, cradled the infant as if she were holding a sparrow. The baby's mouth opened and closed in fishlike astonishment.

The cord, glistening and pale, trailed from his belly, and Blair's hands fumbled with the knot of twine, her cheeks flushed with pride and terror.

The baby's skin was the color of boiled shrimp, his cries thin and reedy, but his limbs flexed with a ferocious will to persist. Blair wiped his face, her fingers gentle as moth wings, then swaddled him in the towel that reeked faintly of lye and rosemary.

She pressed the baby to her chest, rocking slightly, transfixed by the sudden, hot reality of his presence. She did not notice the hush that had fallen over the room, or the way every woman's eyes slid quickly from Orla to the blood pooled beneath her hips, until the midwife's voice snapped her attention back to the birthing bed.

"Get rid of the baby," she hissed, voice a dry, thistly whisper. The words struck Blair like a sudden slap, and she recoiled, the twist of her apron nearly dropping the bundle she swaddled so tightly, as if to squeeze breath from the child's tiny lungs. Morag's knuckles were white on the oak of the table, her eyes a warning. "Now," she said with a spittle of urgency, "or you'll be dead before the sun is up." Her tone left no room for missteps or mercy.

Blair nodded, because there was nothing else to be done. Nausea pooled at the base of her throat. She looked at the baby—a boy, his hair the color of river silt, skin so pale it seemed translucent —and tried, just for a moment, to imagine what it would take to do as Morag asked.

The child had been quiet since the last feeble cry, milky lips pinched in sleep, or perhaps in the peace of not knowing what waited beyond the hem of his blanket. Blair wrapped another length of cloth around his body, as if cold was the enemy and not the woman who watched her every move.

Morag's plan was clear. She jerked her chin toward the far chamber, beyond which the night wind rattled. That door opened into the hallway and down the stairs straight into the main part of the castle. "Through there," Morag said, gesturing with her hand again, "and out the other door. The chief's eyes won't find you."

The chief was still cradling the dead Orla on the blood-spotted linen, mourning with a voice so broken it frightened even the most hard-hearted of the household. He would not notice his child's absence until morning, by which time Morag's instructions would be accomplished and the pack would be forever altered. Blair hesitated, but behind her Morag's threat hovered like a curse; she gripped the baby tighter.

The adjoining chamber was dark. Blair's sandals made no sound as she crept between the shadows, cradling the boy as if movement might shatter him. She paused at the outer door, heart hammering in her ears, and peered through the crack. The hallway was empty. She hurried down the stairs to the bottom floor and rushed to the outer doors.

She stepped into the outside air. It was colder than she had expected; the baby, sensing the sudden chill, whimpered once and then fell silent again. Blair's hands shook as she walked the length of the alley, and the child pressed hard against her ribs. She grabbed a basket and slipped the baby inside it.

At least the rain had stopped. She avoided the midden, instead winding around the back of the cookhouse, where Morag had once told her the dead were sometimes left if they were not meant to be missed.

There, behind the stacked peat blocks, she knelt. The ground was muddy, black with the recent rain, but she dug a shallow hollow with her bare hands. Clay packed beneath her nails, and after a moment she laid the baby in the earth, covering him first with his own blanket and then with a patchwork of cold, damp peat. She would not leave him there to die however.

She did not pray, but she did weep—a soundless, biting sort of weeping that left her chest aching with the effort not to scream.

When it was over, she wiped her hands on the apron and stumbled back to the door, closing it softly behind her. In the room, Morag waited, her face as unreadable as ever. She nodded once and went to tend to the chief, who was still moaning over a body that could not answer.

Blair returned to the shadows, hugging her arms to her chest, and knew time was of the essence. She needed to move the baby somewhere where he could be taken care of.

Morag leaned in so close that her breath tickled the edge of Blair's ear. "Did you do as you're told?"

"Aye, mistress."

Morag glanced at Blair's dirt-covered hands. "Go wash up, now."

"Aye." Blair raced off and headed back to the baby, uncovered him, hiding him in the basket, and took off with him.

"The baby isna breathing. Morag, what do we do?" Senga asked, one of the maids attending.

Morag hid a smile and held the dead baby swaddled in her arms as if he were the most precious thing ever. "Aye. I'll...I'll tell the chief."

"The baby died too?" Senga asked, sounding like she didn't believe it. She wiped her brow of sweat and pushed aside a strand of black hair, appearing done in by the news.

"Aye. You can see that he did." Morag straightened her posture, brushed off her gown, and had the unenviable task of informing Hamish that his beloved son was also dead. This couldn't have worked out better for her. She'd work her magic on Hamish to ensure he mated her! She had a way of making men do her bidding.

FILLED with fear of being caught with the chief's baby and distraught over Morag's threats, but not wanting to harm the healthy baby quietly sleeping, she feared she would get caught up in Morag's murderous scheme. Blair's heart beat wildly as she exited the castle, through the inner bailey, and then down the hill into the meadow.

She couldn't leave him with one of the crofters because she feared the word could get back to Morag.

She carried him to the river where she had seen some crofters fishing early in the mornings. With a heavy heart, she left the basket in the tall grass, praying someone would find the bairn soon. She knew that Morag would do anything she could to marry the chief, become the next lady of Middleborough Castle, and provide her own offspring to the chief.

Which was the reason the chief's bairn was disposable.

Blair had nowhere else to go. No other family to take her in. She was stuck working at the castle under Morag's rule, and her stomach turned at the notion. She knew that if Morag learned Blair hadn't killed the baby, Morag would murder her. But she worried that no one would find the baby.

After one last look over her shoulder at the sleeping baby in the basket, Blair vowed to check on him tomorrow, then returned to the castle with a heavy heart. She was fearful Morag would still learn the baby lived.

~

ELSPETH STRUGGLED to birth her second-born son, while her mate Magnus lifted Tamhas from the birthing blankets, cradling the slippery heft of their son with a trembling but determined reverence. He had rushed through the necessary work—tidying up, cutting the cord—a little clumsily while Elspeth had told him what to do. She was a crofter's wife, but thankfully had enough experience as a midwife for the crofter families nearby.

Magnus eased Tamhas into the old basket lined with a pelt, tucking the infant in, then promptly returned with her post-birth clothes—soft linen washed with the last of the summer soap—and a clean towel for the child. She watched him, her heart swelling with a quiet, almost painful gratitude. It was not lost on her how carefully he navigated this liminal moment. Her mate had never held a newborn before, but he wiped Tamhas gently, as if even a breath too sharp might startle the spirit from their son. He smiled at her, sheepish, one hand never leaving Tamhas's belly.

Elspeth's body still trembled from the shock of birth, the way the twins had seemed to fight to enter the world, the way the second boy had simply...failed. Elspeth wept in the nest of pelts and blood-soaked moss. Magnus hovered close but uncertain, his hands soft against her salt-wet face, gentling her in silence.

"The goddess chose to take one, but dinna fret, sweeting. We have a beautiful son to raise still."

But it was no consolation, though Elspeth tried to keep her spirits up—for Magnus and their son, Tamhas. Yet losing the twin was sometimes more than she could bear, and at the most inopportune times, she would break down and cry. Poor Magnus didn't know what to do but take Tamhas and would cradle the bairn to sleep.

Magnus worried about her state of mind. But she attempted to focus her energy on Tamhas and her mate. She had been abed too long, though it was only the day after giving birth to her twins.

Elspeth felt the compulsion to go outside, breathe the air, see the world returning. She wrapped a well-fed and sleeping Tamhas to her chest, a scarf of thick fur binding him to her skin, and shuffled out into the sunlight. His blond hair looked lighter as the rays of the sun touched the strands, making him look even more like his da. Though she was surprised he had so much hair for a newborn.

The cool air shocked her, but she drew herself up, pulled her plaid wool shawl closer, and waved at Magnus planting in the field.

He stopped for a moment, and she pointed to the river to let him know where she was going. Ever worried about her, Magnus watched her move through the pink heather in bloom until she was out of sight.

The breeze wrapped her in the smell of fishy water, kelp carried from the sea lying on the rocky bank of the river, way before she reached it, and something else. The smell of urine—human and wolf, an unfamiliar wolf shifter she hadn't smelled before. But also one who was very young. She did not hurry, not wanting to upset a mother and child.

She sauntered, her own child's breath warming her collarbone. Tamhas stirred, and his eyes opened. He cooed. She rubbed his back in a consoling way. She scanned the riverbank, the reeds, the little inlets where the locals fished.

She heard a baby crying long before she saw it, courtesy of her wolf hearing. Elspeth's scalp prickled.

The crying grew louder. Tamhas, for his part, went silent, as if he too sensed the gravity of the moment.

At the water's edge, she found him: a baby boy, wild and flailing in a reed basket, the swaddling that had bound him cast aside. His round face was framed in light brown curls as if he were older than he seemed. Yet he was a newly born babe, thin, needing sustenance.

His mouth opened and he released an angry cry, startling her. His fists battered the air. There was no scent of his mother, no warmth of recent handling. The basket's bottom was sodden with river water that could have carried him away in a few hours. The boy's lips had gone a shocking shade of blue.

"Goddess above," Elspeth whispered, all her doubts and terrors tumbling into a single note of awe. She reached for the baby, her hands steady for the first time since the previous day, and lifted him from the basket.

His skin was slick, mottled with cold, but when she pressed him to her shoulder, he shook with a living force that startled her. He was heavier than Tamhas, but softer, less substantial, as if his bones had not yet made up their mind to stay.

Elspeth scanned the riverbank—no footprints, no discarded blankets, nothing to suggest how the child had arrived. She looked at the trees, half-expecting to see a desperate mother lurking in the shadows, watching to see if her abandoned son would be found and saved. Nothing. Only wind and water and the cries of her own new son.

She pressed the stranger's cheek to Tamhas', felt the heat and hunger of both their bodies. This was what she had been denied—twins—and now, by whatever sorcery or mercy, the world had restored the balance. She felt her heart crack open, not with grief but with a terrible, impossible hope.

"Ohmigoddess, a gift from the gods," she murmured, and the words tasted sweet as honey on her tongue. Still, she couldn't quite leave the spot where the baby was until she tried to find the mother.

She called out, "Hello? Is anyone here?" Just to make sure that the mother wasn't just a stone's throw away, but the baby was so soiled, she figured he'd been there for some hours. And he was newly born, just like Tamhas.

She secured the basket to her belt.

With one baby nestled against her body in the carrier, the other cuddled against her body, hidden beneath her shawl to warm him, she tightened her grip on both babies and turned for home, her mind already racing through the practicalities—milk, warmth, shelter.

Perhaps this was a trick, an omen, or some test of her fitness as a mother. She didn't care. She would raise this stranger as her own.

As she walked, Tamhas stirred and offered a thin, wobbly cry, as if to welcome his new brother. Elspeth smiled, the first true smile since her birthing, and with both boys pressed against her, she made her way back to the croft.

Magnus was busy planting crops, but he quickly stopped when the two crying babies caught his attention.

He rushed to her aid, his feet pounding the muddy ground, and peered at the empty basket, his eyes darting to the wriggling bundle beneath her woolen shawl that wailed like a banshee. "What have ye got there?"

"A wee one left by the river's edge. The gods have answered our prayers."

Magnus's brow furrowed, but he gave a slow nod. The look in his gray-blue eyes told her everything—her happiness mattered more than his doubts. He'd welcome this child into their home and raise it alongside their own.

None of the crofters nor that of the rest of their pack that lived at the castle had reported a missing infant, which meant this gift could truly be theirs. Magnus's weathered hands would someday guide two strong backs in the fields.

He gathered Tamhas into his arms, hushing the boy's cries while the newfound babe continued its plaintive song.

"He just needs to be cleaned up and fed. He'll be fine," she assured Magnus when she entered the croft, and he followed behind.

Since she was newly in milk, she could feed both the boys. But what about shifting as wolves? Babies shifted at the same time as their mothers. But Elspeth wasn't his mother. She wondered if his mother had died in childbirth. And the babe's da couldn't care for it. Why not give him to a family to raise?

"Shifting will be an issue. Tamhas will learn to be a wolf from birth. This boy is one too, but until he's around five summers, he willna be able to shift unless his mother is still alive somewhere nearby and shifts."

"We'll worry about it later." Elspeth quickly removed all the swaddling and saw that he was a healthy boy with what she swore was a wolf's head birthmark on his shoulder. He was still crying, not liking being naked, dirty, and hungry. At least she had warmed him, and his lips were a pretty pink.

Her mate placed Tamhas in his bassinet, brought her fresh swaddling clothes, and even cleaned the new baby up. She loved how caring her mate was. Once the baby was clean, she sat on the rocking chair Magnus had made for her and began to feed the bairn. "We'll have to give him a name."

"Aye. Coinneach."

"Coinneach. That's a nice name. Handsome. He is that. We canna tell anyone we found him because we dinna know why he was abandoned."

"Aye." He observed her as she continued to feed the bairn, sucking at her nipple. He always looked so amazed and content to see her feeding their son. Now two sons, just as it was meant to be.

"That means no more celebrations with the pack."

Magnus agreed.

Once the baby unlatched from her nipple and fell asleep, Magnus burped him and put him in the cradle, which was big enough for two, since they had initially planned for twins. Then, she began to feed Tamhas.

"We have to treat them like brothers. Like they were twins from birth," she said.

"Aye."

She was so glad Magnus was agreeable. Not all men would be. Once she had them both in the cradle, he insisted she lie down and rest. He still had a half-day's work to do on sowing seeds for the crops and wanted her to get a good night's sleep. She appreciated that.

Before long, she fed both boys again, and they seemed happy to snuggle together to stay warm. When they were too big for the cradle, her mate would make a pallet for them to sleep on.

SHOCKED to see his mate return home with an abandoned baby boy, Magnus's spirits lifted to see how much she adored the newborn. He would fight to the death to keep the boy with them. He was still worried about the issue of one boy not shifting while the other could. Still, they would make do somehow and be a happy, loving family.

As the boys grew, they played with each other from sunup to sunset. Sometimes, Elspeth would shift to show her son the ropes of being a wolf, while Coinneach seemed amused and watched his brother's antics.

Once Elspeth shifted back, she told Coinneach, "You will turn into a wolf soon on your own." She had told him numerous times that he would turn wolf soon. He was nearly five, and they'd heavily anticipated his change. But still, he hadn't turned.

"He'll be all right," Magnus said quietly to his mate once the boys had fallen asleep after a hectic day. "We all shift at different ages in the beginning, once we dinna shift to our mother's change."

"I just wish it were sooner than later. I feel he'll fall behind on learning our wolf skills."

"He's very observant and watches every move we make when we're wolves. It will be instinctual once he shifts."

They finally settled down on their pallet for the night, the full moon lighting the night sky, when a woof came from the boys' bed. Not Tamhas's. They knew his whimpers, woofs, and little wolf howls.

This was different, and the next thing they knew, Tamhas had shifted and tackled Coinneach on the bed. Coinneach was now a wolf like his brother and could change at will. That meant a lot of catch-up playing, play-fighting, and showing dominance over each other.

Both mom and da loved the boys, but they could see from the beginning that Coinneach was the true alpha, more aggressive, more exploratory, and curious by nature, which sometimes got them into mischief. Both were skunked one time, and another time they came home crying, wearing porcupine quills on their muzzles. His brother was more of a follower.

As they grew older, Coinneach and his brother had done their chores and fought each other with sturdy branches they'd fashioned into wooden swords. They were always at the beck and call of the clan chief, should they have to battle invaders or neighboring clans, when riders suddenly approached, garnering their full attention.

A group of men halted their horses near the brothers fighting in the meadow, and Coinneach and Tamhas watched to see what they wanted. Their mother and da came out to see the newcomers and waved. One was a boy about their age, and he seemed intrigued by them. His dark brown hair was pulled back in a tail, his brown eyes considering their prowess.

"Chief Daire, welcome," their da said.

Coinneach and his brothers had never met the chief.

"Sup with us?" their mother asked, as if they had enough food to feed the chief and his entourage.

Were they even wolves?

The boy slid off his horse and joined them. "I'm Alasdair. Can I join you in the fight?"

Coinneach smiled. The chief and the others *were* wolves. "Aye. Do you have a stick? We can get you one. I'm Coinneach."

"I'm Tamhas," his brother said.

"We have brought a boar with us," the chief said to their parents. "We'll prepare it here since it appears my son has an important mission of his own at the moment."

Coinneach wondered if the boar was intended for the chief of Middleborough Castle and why he would feed it to them instead of someone more important, while allowing his son to play with them. But all that was forgotten when Alasdair motioned to his horse.

"I have a practice steel sword and a wooden sword, but it wouldna be fair to fight you with my steel one." Alasdair returned to his horse, pulled out his wooden sword, and rejoined them. "I have two brothers, Rory and Hans, whom I practice with. My sister, Bessetta, would, too, if we allowed her to. But you and Tamhas might challenge me further."

Coinneach fought Alasdair first, but he struggled to keep up with him. He was so used to fighting with Tamhas that he didn't expect Alasdair to so easily knock his sword away and swiftly poked him in the chest, winning time and again.

Alasdair was well-trained in the art of sword fighting, and Coinneach eagerly watched every move Alasdair made. His feinting maneuvers when he came at Coinneach, Alasdair's footwork, the power of his swings and thrusts.

Then Coinneach made a fatal mistake, thinking he had this down now, and thrust at Alasdair, but his new friend knocked the sword from his hand and sent it flying. Coinneach laughed. He hadn't had this much of a challenge ever.

As soon as Coinneach lost his makeshift sword, Alasdair fought Tamhas, but he was easier on him, sensing that Coinneach's brother was more timid, less sure of himself, which was why Coinneach needed someone more of a challenge to fight.

Coinneach retrieved his sword and observed Alasdair as he kept his feet planted apart just enough for good balance and struck at Tamhas's sword. Coinneach admired Alasdair's ability to move about—his agility and speed, throwing off the enemy who might be looking to take down a foe who would stand still for him.

Alasdair didn't strike Tamhas's sword hard enough to send it flying, though he could have. Instead, he was teaching him the rudiments of fighting. When Tamhas thrust his sword at Alasdair, their new friend swept Tamhas's sword away from him with a whack.

Coinneach glanced at Alasdair's da to see what he was doing. To his surprise, he was chatting with his da like he was an important man. At the same time, both men watched to see how the boys were faring.

Alasdair was so easy on Tamhas that it took a while before he knocked his sword out of his hand. Coinneach admired Alasdair for building his brother's confidence. Tamhas was much better at working on the farm.

Then Alasdair turned to face Coinneach. "Ready."

Coinneach smiled. "Aye." But his stance had improved this time after watching Tamhas fight his brother. He countered Alasdair's thrust, whacking his wooden sword away. He even forced Alasdair back a few times, delighting all three boys.

After an hour of fighting, it was a draw. Alasdair couldn't make Coinneach lose his sword, nor could he do that with Alasdair's. They all collapsed in the meadow.

"Do you know how to ride a horse?" Alasdair asked, watching the clouds slip across the sky.

"Nay, but I would love to," Coinneach said.

They looked at Tamhas, and he licked his lips in nervousness. "Aye."

"Good. While the boar is still cooking, we'll borrow a couple of horses from our men and ride. Oh, and Chief Daire is my uncle. My parents died when I was young, and so he has been my da." Alasdair ran off to speak with his da.

Coinneach and Tamhas walked over to join him.

"We're going to ride," Alasdair confirmed to them.

Coinneach's da raised his brows, smiling.

Then the riding lessons began. They walked the horses at first and then trotted. Coinneach had never felt such freedom and couldn't have been happier. Once the horse bounced Tamhas around, he clung to it for dear life.

They finally galloped across the field, the wind blowing Coinneach's hair over his back. He'd never felt anything like it. Exhilarating, magical. He and the horse were in sync as if they had grown up together, moving across the vast land in no time.

They slowed to a trot and then a walk until Alasdair stopped his horse. "What do you think? Do you like riding?"

Coinneach grinned. What he wouldn't give to have a horse of his own. "Walking here from the croft would have taken us forever."

Tamhas looked a little pale, but he was smiling. "'Tis great fun."

The men nearer the croft looked like tiny figures off in the distance.

"It's the only way to travel unless you run as wolves. Do you want to run as wolves?" Alasdair patted his roan.

Tamhas immediately said, "Aye."

"We will return the horses, and then you can show me your forest," Alasdair said.

"Aye, that we'll do." Coinneach was glad they could do something small in return for Alasdair after all the grand things he had shown them.

They rode at a trot back to the men, and Alasdair told his da, "We are going to run as wolves in the woods."

"Aye, but dinna tarry too long as the boar shall be ready before long, and then we'll be on our way."

The aroma of the wild boar cooking made all the boys' stomachs grumble.

"Aye, for just a little bit," Alasdair promised his da.

Then the three boys raced off to the woods, and once concealed by the undergrowth, they stripped off their clothes and shifted. Like Coinneach, Alasdair and he were of a similar build, muscular, with brown hair and eyes. Tamhas was blond, his eyes blue like those of their da and mother.

Coinneach always thought that when they looked at their reflections in the lake, he was different from the rest of his fair-haired family. Just as he was unable to shift when Tamhas had, as if something was wrong with him, though he had believed his mother was right in saying that he would change when the time was right.

For now, though, Coinneach was eager to show Alasdair the nearby waterfall. He led the way, with Alasdair following behind him. Tamhas was right on his heels on the narrow path.

Within minutes, they reached the falls. The waterfall hurled itself into the gorge with a violence that left the air quivering. Water raced down the cliff face in reckless competition, slamming into the mossy piles of stone heaped at the river's edge.

Spray leapt sideways, painting the bracken in beads of silver, so that every fern seemed to sway under the weight and blessing of the deluge. The roar of it—alive and ceaseless—drowned out the calls of songbirds and the brittle snap of twigs as animals skirted the sodden margin of the pool below.

Mist crept outward, cooling the ground and coating even distant leaves with a glassy shimmer. The sky above, a slate-gray, pressed heavily on the scene, its chill filtering through the dense canopy and settling deep into the bones of the place.

Here, time was counted in cycles of falling water, the endless resumption and renewal, each drop a promise to batter the earth until it yielded and became something new.

Alasdair just stared in awe. Coinneach was glad he could share the spectacular sight.

They drank their fill at the river and then headed back. But then Alasdair tackled Coinneach and Tamhas, and they retaliated in good-natured fun. Coinneach and Tamhas excelled at wolf fighting, as much practice as they'd had with each other.

Coinneach pinned Alasdair down so many times, he was afraid Alasdair might take offense. But Coinneach couldn't help himself. He wanted to prove he was good at something.

Then Tamhas glanced at Alasdair, and the two of them tackled Coinneach simultaneously, struggling even so to take him down. He loved it.

Someone yelled that it was time to eat, and they raced to their clothes, shifted, and dressed.

"I canna tell you how much fun I had here today. I will insist my da visit Chief Hamish more often, when before I was never interested in going."

Coinneach and his brother smiled. "We would be much pleased," Coinneach said. "Why did your brothers and sister no' come too?"

"My da is trying to teach me to be a good leader of men for when the time comes, when I will take over the pack."

That made Coinneach think that he and Tamhas were special indeed to befriend an upcoming clan chief. Though it didn't mean they would see him again. But his visit would always be something Coinneach would cherish.

They ate their fill as Chief Daire explained how Coinneach and Tamhas's da and mother had saved him when he was gravely wounded in battle.

"Your da killed the Highlander who tried to kill me," Daire said.

"And your mother nursed me back to health. I am beholden to them."

Coinneach couldn't believe it. How did his da kill a Highlander when he didn't even own a sword? And his mother, he knew, was good at taking care of injuries, though she never wanted to work at the castle and would rather be on the farm with her family. They'd never mentioned saving a chief's life.

Daire continued. "Here I was lying on my back with a wound in my side and on my sword arm, and I knew the villain was going to kill me with one more slice of his sword. But then your da was there, pitchfork in hand, and stabbing him in the neck. He pulled the pitchfork free, and the man collapsed on my legs. Your mother and da had a time pulling me out from under the brigand. My men and I had become separated, and it took them a few days before they found me."

Coinneach glanced at his da.

"I told you that you dinna need a sword to take a big man down."

Coinneach smiled. His da had said that for years when Coinneach had complained about not having a real sword, and he would never have believed it.

For years, Alasdair would return to see Coinneach and Tamhas, bringing wooden swords to share with them, ride, and play as wolves, always visiting the waterfall.

But when they saw Alasdair arrive at the croft this time, he had more of a guard force than ever. His uncle, serving as his da, wasn't with Alasdair, and Alasdair looked beleaguered.

Alasdair dismounted from his horse and embraced Tamhas and then Coinneach. "My uncle was killed in battle, and I've taken over the clan."

1

Coinneach was busy planting barley and oats near his family's croft when he noticed two women approaching with a small cart loaded with herbs and food, making their way toward Middleborough Castle. One woman seemed to be in her forties, and the other appeared to be in her twenties.

He guessed they were mother and daughter. Both women, with their striking red hair, watched him as he toiled in the field, his chest uncovered and his plaid resting low on his hips as he moved through the soil.

When he got a whiff of their scents, he realized they were wolves like him. He smiled at the two women, especially the younger one, and flexed his muscles, unable to help himself. The older woman's gaze focused on the wolf mark on his shoulder that he'd had from birth.

The next moment, her blue eyes widened, her face grew ice white, and he dashed across the field to catch her before she fell. He managed to reach her, caught her, and cradled her in his arms.

"Momma, what's wrong?" the younger woman asked, squeezing her hand, sounding shocked.

He realized he was covered in glistening sweat, and specks of dirt were splattered across his chest as he crouched and held the older woman in his arms. "Ma'am," Coinneach said. Then, he asked the younger one, "Do you have some ale?"

"Aye." She pulled a flask off her hip and gave it to him.

He dribbled a little on the older woman's lips, trying to revive her.

Suddenly, she opened her eyes wide and again stared at his shoulder, looking ready to pass out.

He rose to his feet and carried her to the croft. "My mother, da, and brother are at market. If you wish, you can lie down on my palette until you're more yourself."

"Oh yes," the younger woman said, answering for her mother.

"Nay, nay, nay, we must leave here at once," her mother said, her voice raspy and weak.

She seemed so frail that he feared she would collapse again. "I'm Coinneach." He carried her into the croft and laid her on his bed. He wasn't about to take her word for it that she was alright.

Tears pricked the woman's eyes until she was sobbing hysterically.

"Mother, what is wrong?" She turned to Coinneach and said, "I am Aisling, and this is my mother, Blair. Thanks be to thee for your help."

"I would do no less."

Her mother's sobs finally quieted, and she looked resigned to being there.

"Do you work at Middleborough Castle?" he asked, never having been there because of his farm work, but he'd always wanted to see inside the magnificent structure.

"Aye." Like her mother, Aisling had the most beautiful blue eyes. "I work in the kitchen. My mother delivers babies and cares for the wounded or ill. She never wanted me to do that job. I wanted to, though. She would never say why," Aisling said.

Her mother was again staring at the wolf's head on his shoulder. "We...we have to go," Blair said, still sniffling. She attempted to move her legs over the edge of the bed, but when she tried to stand, her legs gave out, and Coinneach caught her again.

"You will stay with us and recover. When my family returns from the market, you will eat with us. Once you feel strong enough, I'll take you to the castle." He had decided that once she couldn't stand on her own, he would take care of her until she was safely at the castle.

Appearing panicked, Blair shook her head. "You...you canna."

"Thank you. We will do that." Aisling gave her mother a reproachful look, but then her expression softened with concern.

"Good. 'Tis settled. I need to finish my chores. Will the two of you be all right?"

"Aye, thank you for your kindness."

"You're very much welcome. Just dinna let your mother leave the bed," Coinneach said sternly. "If she falls, she could hurt herself this time."

He walked to the doorway, glanced back at the two of them, and vowed to see them home safely. He also wanted to see more of the beautiful lass and ensure her mother was all right, though he was determined to know what had frightened her.

"MOTHER, WHATEVER IS WRONG?" Aisling asked, taking hold of her hands and squeezing them for reassurance. She had never seen her mother so distraught about anything.

"Dinna ask because I canna tell you," her mother said, at an attempt at making her words strong, but they lacked the strength.

Aisling had never seen her mother break down into sobs, except when Aisling's da died in battle when Aisling was ten. She shook her head. "You have to tell me what the matter is." She would help her in whatever way she could. When her mother wouldn't say, she sighed, walked over to the open door, and looked out at Coinneach as he plowed the fields.

He was so brawny, his golden muscles rippling in his back as he pushed the plow, his plaid flipping up in the breeze, showing off his muscular legs. When he turned, he caught sight of her and frowned. She smiled, indicating that her mother didn't need his assistance. She was just intrigued with him—his kindness and helpfulness, and aye, his appearance.

He smiled at her as if he knew just why she was watching him, and she loved it.

When he had first seen her before her mother had become indisposed, he had smiled at her with interest, in a way that sent delicious tingling up her spine. Their pheromones had clashed and collided, and she knew he was just as intrigued by her as she was by him.

No one at the castle interested her like he did, and she planned to make excursions past his farm any chance she got to get to know him better. Then she thought about her mother's reaction to him. Had he been violent or unkind toward her mother at some time when Aisling hadn't been with her?

She returned to check on her mother, who had finally stopped crying and was resting. "Has Coinneach ever done anything untoward to you before?"

"Nay, nay." She sounded sincere about that.

Aisling couldn't imagine what was wrong then.

"We have guests for the meal," Coinneach said to someone, and Aisling went to the doorway to see who he was talking to.

A gray-haired woman and a man, whom she assumed were his parents, and a blond-haired man who looked like the older man, but was physically smaller than Coinneach. She didn't think they bore a strong resemblance. She didn't have a sibling but had seen enough children in the pack to recognize those who favored each other.

Coinneach washed up and put on his shirt. "A lovely woman, Blair, who had become indisposed, mayhap because of the heat on this bright sunny day, and her daughter, Aisling."

They all looked at the croft door and saw Aisling standing in the doorway. She smiled, hoping that feeding her mother and her wasn't a big imposition. They might not have a lot of food to spare. She couldn't help but want to spend more time with Coinneach though.

She returned to her mom and said, "Coinneach's family has returned. Can you eat?"

"We canna stay, Aisling."

Aisling let her breath out in exasperation. "Can you walk? If you can, we'll go home." Despite wanting to stay and get to know Coinneach's family longer, she owed it to her mother to take care of her. And if her mother really couldn't eat, they might as well return to the castle. "But know this, Coinneach is taking us home, so if you collapse again, he will be there for you."

"How now," Coinneach's mother said, entering the abode first. "Welcome. Coinneach said you were feeling unwell. I am Elspeth." The dad came in after that. "And he is my mate, Magnus."

"I'm feeling better," Aisling's mother said.

"Good. Then you will eat with us, and Coinneach will take you home."

"Aye, we always have plenty of food for guests," Magnus said, smiling.

The blond-haired man entered the croft and smiled at Aisling. "I'm Tamhas."

Coinneach joined them then, bringing water for his mother to cook the fish they had brought home from the market. "I'm pleased you are looking more revived," he said to Aisling's mother.

She sat up and had her feet planted on the floor, but didn't make a move to leave Coinneach's bed. "Thank you."

"Come," their dad said to Coinneach and Tamhas. "We'll join them when the meal is done."

"I can help you, Elspeth," Aisling said. "I work as an assistant to Cook at the castle." She was eager to help Elspeth, as they now had two more mouths to feed. Besides, she had been trained to do this.

Coinneach smiled at her as he followed his da and brother out of the croft.

"Aye, that will be welcome," Elspeth said.

Aisling made the unleavened bread, while Elspeth cooked fish stew.

"It's good to have another female here who knows how to cook," Elspeth said cheerily.

"Aye. I love it." Especially when Cook wasn't getting after Aisling for doing things wrong.

Elspeth glanced back at Blair. "Are you feeling better now?"

"Aye, thank you."

"Well, a bit of food in you will make you feel even better," Elspeth said.

Once the meal was done, Elspeth called out to the men, "Supper's ready."

They were eating at an earlier hour than those who ate their meals at the castle, which meant Aisling would still be able to return in time to help prepare the meal there.

The men hurried in and sat down at the table. Blair remained on the bed, sitting over the edge to eat there. Aisling sat with her since there wasn't enough room at the table for more than four people. But Elspeth joined them, sitting opposite them on another pallet.

"My mother is a midwife at the castle," Aisling told Elspeth.

The guys were quiet, listening to the conversation between the ladies.

"Oh, that is admirable. I have some healing skills and have delivered babies," Elspeth said.

"I delivered the, uh, boys," Magnus said, smiling.

Coinneach and Tamhas's jaws dropped. Aisling realized they hadn't known their da had delivered them.

Elspeth, on the other hand, looked worried. So did Aisling's own mother. Aisling hoped her mother didn't dissolve into tears again. She reached out and touched her mother's hand.

Her mother quickly finished her fish stew and bread. "I'm ready to go home." Then she looked up at Elspeth, her eyes filled with tears, and said, "Thanks for your gracious offer of a meal. It was perfect. But they will be missing us at the castle."

"Aye, of course," Elspeth said, finishing her meal.

The men all stood.

"We dinna need your help," Blair said to Coinneach.

"I will see you to the castle," Coinneach said with fierce pride, his blue eyes as blue as the sky on a summer's day.

Aisling was glad he would walk them home. She worried about her mother's emotional and physical state.

"Aye," Magnus said. "Coinneach will make sure you get back all right." Tamhas looked hopeful he could go too, but Magnus said to him, "I have a chore for you to do since Coinneach worked the field by himself."

Outvoted, Blair submitted and rose to her feet. She managed to leave the croft on her own power, but Coinneach was right there to help her if she faltered. Aisling thought the world of him for it.

When they left the croft, Magnus said, "Come back to see us anytime."

"Aye, we insist," Elspeth said, looking straight at Aisling.

She assumed Elspeth recognized Coinneach and Aisling were intrigued with each other. Wolves could sense things like that—the considered looks, the smiles when they caught each other's gaze, the heightened scents that told everyone they were interested in each other.

"We would love to," Aisling said.

Coinneach grabbed their cart and began pulling it. It was full of herbs and mushrooms that they had harvested from the forest and produce from market. Aisling was glad to see that her mother seemed all right now and was walking as fast as she could to the castle.

Aisling smiled at Coinneach as her mother walked ahead of them. She quietly said, "I'll be back when I can."

He gave her a wicked smile. "I will look forward to it."

COINNEACH WAS SO glad his dad had put Tamhas to work and that he'd insisted Coinneach take Blair and Aisling home. He feared Blair would insist that she was fine and leave with Aisling without him. But he wanted to spend more time with Aisling and, of course, make sure that her mother didn't collapse again.

When he saw the castle up close, with its massive walls towering above him and a few guards surveying the surroundings from the top of the crenelated wall walk, he felt honored to walk inside the inner bailey. Several people were doing chores, washing clothes, caring for the horses, and feeding chickens.

Blair seemed to have improved as soon as they reached the castle and hurried to enter it without a backward glance, as if it would prove too painful to look at him again, even though his shirt covered up his wolf birthmark. On the other hand, Aisling took hold of his hand and kissed him on the cheek, bringing a smile to his lips.

"Thank you again." Then, she pulled the cart behind her as an older woman hollered at her to get into the kitchen at once.

He felt lighter than air as he headed home, vowing to see Aisling again.

2

A fter spending the day doing chores, washing himself in the lake, and getting dressed, Coinneach was prepared to call it a night and started his walk back through the meadow to his parents' croft. Suddenly, his keen wolf hearing caught a gruff man's voice saying, "We target that house first."

"*Ja,*" another man said.

Coinneach's heart thundered like an ominous drum echoing through the darkened landscape, a relentless rhythm of dread and fury. The modest stone-and-thatch dwelling that served as his family's haven now stood vulnerable in the path of the marauding Vikings.

Shadows flickered grotesquely against the sky, their eerie dance created by flames from torches clutched in rough, battle-hardened hands. As the bitter chill of rage crept through his veins, Coinneach's eyes narrowed into slits of determination.

From his concealed vantage point in the tall meadow grasses, he observed the raiders with their wild hair and beards glinting gold in the firelight. There were eight in total—an ominous number that whispered unspeakable devastation. Their low laughter and brief conversations were coarse and foreign, promising nothing but chaos and destruction. They gestured among themselves, pointing towards his family's croft with greedy anticipation.

Coinneach knew he had to act swiftly. His pulse quickening with every heartbeat, he slipped through the shadows like a wraith, every step measured yet desperate. Keeping a careful distance from the flickering pools of torchlight that threatened to reveal him, he maneuvered towards the small croft—a sanctuary of love and memories now under siege.

His mind raced with strategies, each plan dissolving into the next in feverish succession. Was there time to warn their neighboring clansmen? Could he distract the Vikings long enough for his family to escape? Every second counted, and with each breathless moment, Coinneach's resolve solidified into ironclad determination.

He reached the edge of their land, hidden from view by thickets so familiar that even in darkness they guided him silently forward. He paused for a moment behind an ancient oak tree that's gnarled branches had witnessed countless seasons pass.

The flickering lights grew closer as the Vikings' footsteps moved through the meadow. Coinneach raced to the croft, far enough away from their torchlight so they couldn't see him.

His heart racing, he rushed inside the home through the back door, startling his mother, da, and Tamhas, who were getting ready for bed.

"Eight Viking raiders are headed this way." Usually, his da would tell them what to do if there was trouble like that, but Coinneach was impatient and already taking charge. "Shift. And I'll join you. I'll make sure the other crofters get to safety."

His mother removed her nightshirt and transformed into her wolf, and his dad was doing the same. "Be safe," his da said before he shifted.

"Aye." Coinneach glanced at his brother, silently telling him to look after their parents.

Tamhas nodded, finished undressing, and shifted. The three of them ran out the back door.

With only a rudimentary sword that Coinneach had tried to fashion himself without the tools or metals for the job—he was not a blacksmith trained—he raced out after his family and headed to where the other families lived. As wolves, he hoped everyone would fade into the forest and never be found.

The castle gates were already closed for the night, so they couldn't take refuge there.

He swore he had never run as fast as he had done this night, only pausing to howl in his human form to alert the castle guards and the other crofters of the danger. The croft, situated farthest from his family's, also had the most vulnerable family because they had four bairns that were only a few days old.

As soon as he threw the door open to their new parents' croft, he startled the mother and da. They jumped off their pallet in their nightshirts, looking shocked and worried.

"Viking raiders. Shift. I'll carry the little ones." Coinneach knew the mom was still recovering from having given birth. He wanted the father to take care of her while Coinneach tended to the wolf pups.

The da and mother quickly removed their clothes, and they pulled the swaddling clothes off the babies. Then she shifted, and so did her babies, both turning into little wolf pups. The da shifted after that. Each of the parents took a pup in their mouths.

"Go!" Coinneach said. "I'll be right behind you." He lifted the last two wolf pups, carrying them in his arms, and raced after the parents to the forest, keeping the pups close to his body, warming them.

Once they found a safe place to hide in the thick, tall bracken in the forest, Coinneach fully intended to shift into his wolf and offer his protection when he smelled Aisling's scent nearby. He placed the pups at their mother's belly for nourishment and warmth while the other two supped at her teats.

"Stay here," Coinneach told the parents.

He couldn't help the way he felt about Aisling. Every time she was near, he wanted to see more of her. But he wondered what she'd been doing out there so late that she had been locked out of the castle, and he worried about her. He removed his clothes, shifted, and raced to find her.

So intent on finding her, Coinneach nearly ran headlong into a Viking warrior creeping through the trees, the breeze blowing his scent away from Coinneach, or he would have smelled him earlier. As soon as the large man dressed in furs and war paint raised an arrow to his bow, Coinneach knew he couldn't dodge the arrow in time, even as a wolf.

Then, to Coinneach's shock, Aisling in her gray wolf form raced out of the bracken, leaped at the man's throat, and bit him hard, killing him instantly before he could cry out and warn the others.

As the man dropped onto the ground in death, Coinneach nuzzled Aisling, thanking her for saving his life, her muzzle covered in blood. Their hearts were beating hard as Aisling licked his cheek, telling him she was glad to save him.

They heard other Vikings moving through the woods, the bracken rustling, giving away their movement. Coinneach eyed the dead Viking's beautiful sword, the hilt covered in serpentine motifs. He grabbed it with his teeth and moved deeper into the woods.

He dug a shallow pit for it and quickly buried it. As a crofter's son, he couldn't afford to purchase such a beautiful weapon. Aisling followed and watched him while they listened to the other men moving through the woods.

Coinneach wanted his brother to have a weapon too, though it was risky to return to the dead man. He shifted. "Stay hidden. I'll be right back." He shifted into his wolf.

She shook her head and stuck right beside him, not surprising him. It appeared she was willful when she wanted to be, which appealed to him all the more. When they reached the dead Viking, Coinneach shifted and pulled a short sword from the Viking's belt, the hilt made of hardwood and bone. To his amusement, Aisling grabbed the Viking's yew bow and yanked at it, trying to free it.

"I've got them." As a naked human, he carried the weapons at a run, jumping over fallen trees in his path, winding through the bracken while she ran beside him as a wolf. When they reached the spot where the sword was buried, he shifted into his wolf form. They dug more shallow graves to hide the Viking's weapons so they could put them to good use later.

"Ivor, where are ye, brother?" a man called out in a hushed voice.

Coinneach and Aisling moved deeper into the woods to stay hidden.

"Ivor, nay, brother!" the man cried out, having discovered the body, his upset palpable.

"What happened to him, Holgar?" another man asked in a low, gruff voice.

"A man didna kill him," Holgar said. "A wild beast did. See the wound on his throat?"

"*Ja.* Come, we must join the others. We'll carry him back with us. The people here have been alerted. No one is in any of the crofts. We canna take any slaves with us like we planned."

"Wait, where are Ivor's weapons? They are no' here. We have to bury them with him."

The men rustled through the bracken, looking for the weapons, but couldn't find them.

"We have to leave, or our brethren will leave without us."

"He willna go to Valhalla," Holgar said, sounding disappointed.

"*Ja.* He didn't battle anyone for the honor. He will go to Hel."

Which, as Coinneach had heard, was a place misty and cold for those who didn't die in battle—not a place of punishment.

"A wild beast couldna have carried off his weapons," Holgar said.

"We canna find them. Come, we have to go."

"If someone has them, I will kill him," Holgar said.

Then the men moved off. In the semi-dark, the wolves could hear, smell, and see them. The Vikings, being human, could not sense the wolves nearby.

3

A isling and Coinneach followed the Viking raiders, staying hidden and watching where they went to ensure they left their territory. She'd finally gotten her bag of herbs that evening, but the castle gates were locked by the time she had found everything she needed that they hadn't located on their first trip foraging for them for the morning meal. Then she heard the Vikings were headed for the crofts.

She'd only had time to remove her clothes in the forest and then shift. Before she could howl a warning, she heard another wolf howl. She hadn't recognized who it was. Then she saw wolves racing into the forest, seeking safety. Coinneach's mother, father, and brother were nearby, but Coinneach hadn't been with them.

She began searching for him when she saw him facing the Viking down. Even as a wolf, Coinneach couldn't have moved from where he was standing before the Viking shot him with his arrow. As dangerous as it was, she had sprung, not thinking of the peril to herself, only knowing that she could not let it end like this. She hadn't hesitated to rip into the man's throat to save Coinneach.

Now, she and Coinneach were shrouded beneath the towering canopy of the ancient forest, their presence camouflaged by the dense bracken. The echoes of distant crunching leaves betrayed the Vikings ahead, guiding their stealthy pursuit through the woodland. Each sure-footed step was a whisper against the forest floor, their breaths synchronized with the rustling wind that enveloped them, ruffling their fur like an unseen guide, as she and he followed the Vikings.

As they neared the jagged edge of the cliffs, their anticipation swelled with each glimpse of moonlight piercing through the thinning trees. The mighty ocean roared below, a symphony of waves crashing against stone echoed up to meet them.

From this vantage point, they spied upon the Viking warriors who skillfully descended the craggy face of the cliffside—a deftness honed by years spent upon their seafaring quests. It was a sight both awe-inspiring and ominous, as the figures moved with a purpose that hinted at ages-old traditions and unyielding resolve.

Reaching the precipice, she and Coinneach exchanged a silent glance, understanding passing wordlessly between them, hearts beating in tandem with excitement and trepidation. The expanse opened before them—a breathtaking panorama that revealed the foggy shoreline below.

There, nestled within a secluded inlet, lay a majestic longship —its formidable silhouette casting an elongated shadow upon the lapping waves. The ship rode silently at anchor, swaying gently with the rhythm of the sea.

With eyes fixed on this scene of raw power and potential fury, she wondered what tales those warriors might spin upon returning to distant lands, what myths would be born from their ventures across this realm where a sky-kissed sea and legends took shape. Would they speak of victory or loss? Change the narrative to one that made them seem more braw?

Coinneach's nuzzling her face brought her back to reality, a gesture both grounding and encouraging, reminding her that they had not come merely to observe what the Vikings were doing. They needed to let the others know that the Vikings were leaving.

From the cliff above, they observed the raiders reach the pebbled shore while carrying their dead comrade, and then wasted no time reaching their longboat. A carved dragon sat at the helm, the red and white striped sails beckoning them in the wind to hurry and climb aboard the Viking ship moored in the inlet before it was too late.

Before long, the men had reached the ship and taken hold of the oars, knifing them into the foamy water, their muscles straining to push on.

She wished she and Coinneach could destroy the Vikings and their ship, but they would have needed more help to accomplish it.

She nuzzled Coinneach's face and returned to the forest where she had left her clothes. He stayed by her side, then she shifted and dressed. She grabbed her bag of herbs and followed him to where he had ditched his clothes. Once he was dressed, they dug up the Viking's weapons and carried them to Coinneach's home.

He howled to let the others, both the crofters and the castle guards, know the danger had passed.

Soon, Coinneach's parents and his brother were running beside them as wolves.

"You'll stay with us the night," Coinneach said to Aisling, his voice firm, protective of her.

"If 'tis no' an inconvenience."

"Nay. You can have my pallet."

She smiled at Coinneach. He was so sweet. She howled to let her mother know she was okay; otherwise, her mother would worry about Aisling being beyond the castle walls that night.

When they reached the croft, Coinneach's family shifted, then dressed.

"You can sleep with me on the pallet," Aisling said to Coinneach, not wanting him to give up his bed when he would have to work hard in the morning like she had to and would need a good night's sleep.

He smiled at her, a little evilly, and she smiled back. She was serious. She had never slept with a male wolf before, but with him, she was ready. Though they had just met, he was someone special, and she wanted him in her life.

His mom and dad were smiling as they climbed onto their pallet. Tamhas's mouth was gaping while he waited to see what Coinneach would say.

"I'll be comfortable on the floor if I wear my wolf coat."

She took hold of Coinneach's hand and pulled him to his pallet. "I'm tired. Let's sleep."

Coinneach smiled. "Your wish is my command. Oh, and, Tamhas, I have a short sword for you."

Tamhas's eyes grew round, and his mouth gaped again as he took the sword and turned it in his hands. "You took this off a Viking?"

"Aye, 'tis yours now."

"Thank you, brother."

"You should..." Coinneach started to say.

"Get some good use out of it." Aisling cast Coinneach a warning glance. She didn't want Coinneach to tell anyone she had killed the Viking herself in the event they would think less of her.

Coinneach seemed to get her message. "Aye, to help you stay safe when you're no' in your wolf coat."

Then he joined her on his pallet. Tamhas took the short sword with him to bed.

As the moonlight gently filtered through the small, dust-laden window, Coinneach and Aisling drew closer together on the narrow confines of his modest pallet. The old frame beneath them creaked softly, almost as if it were a living thing, attempting to accommodate the two bodies nestled against each other.

Coinneach pulled a wool blanket over them. Their limbs

tangled naturally, as if they had always been together in this way, entwined in an embrace forged from equal parts passion and solace.

She rested her head lightly on his chest, rising and falling with each steady breath he took. His heartbeat was a rhythm both comforting and constant beneath her ear—a reminder that this moment was real, not some fleeting dream to be scattered by morning light after what they'd been through.

She cherished this time with him. He gently nuzzled her ear with his lips and kissed her. She returned the kiss with equal passion. Everything felt so perfect with him. It would have been even better if they'd had more privacy, but she was glad to end the day in this way.

He wrapped his arm protectively around her, pulling her even closer until there was no space left between them. As he did so, she marveled at how seamlessly he fit against her.

Just as they were surrendering fully to this peaceful proximity, allowing their eyes to flutter closed in mutual surrender to sleep's gentle pull, a soft sigh escaped from her. She was as close to heaven as she would ever come.

Then she realized that her mother would smell him on her and be all upset again.

THE NEXT MORNING, Aisling smiled at Coinneach, not wanting to leave the pallet. Everyone was stirring, and she got up and said to Elspeth, "I'll help you make breakfast before I return to the castle. I canna be late to the kitchen where I'll be helping to prepare the meal."

"Aye," Elspeth said.

Coinneach kissed Aisling. "We'll be outside planting seeds. After we break our fast, I'll walk you back to the castle."

"I would like that."

Then the men went outside to work on the crops, Coinneach winking at Aisling as he left the croft.

She smiled and saw Elspeth watching them. "You know he has never been interested in a she-wolf like he's intrigued with you." Elspeth prepared oats.

"The feeling is mutual."

Elspeth sighed.

Aisling realized his mother might be worried that she was leading him astray and might break his heart. But she had genuine feelings for him. She knew he felt the same way about her.

She sliced the rye bread. Then Elspeth left the croft and brought in five eggs and boiled them.

Once they were finished, Aisling called out to the men that it was time to break their fast. She was beginning to feel anxious because she needed to arrive at the castle on time. She served up honeyed mead, and they all sat down to eat.

"Were the long sword, bow, and arrows from the same Viking you had killed?" Tamhas asked Coinneach.

"Aye," Aisling said. "But the bow and arrows are mine."

Tamhas smiled at her and raised his brows at Coinneach. He was busy eating his bread and reached over to squeeze Aisling's hand. Once they were done eating, she grabbed her bag of herbs, then seized his hand and pulled him out of the croft, saying, "Thanks," to his parents and brother.

Then she walked as fast as she could while she held his hand, loving the intimacy between them.

"I wish we could prolong this between us, but I know you're anxious to get back to the castle."

"Aye. I canna afford to lose my job."

COINNEACH WANTED to enjoy the walk through the meadow with Aisling at a slower pace, but he knew she worried that she might be late. "You didna want me to tell my family that you killed the Viking?"

"Nay. What would everyone think of me?" She looked serious when she glanced at him.

"That you are a great warrior wolf."

"That's all right for a male wolf, not a she-wolf."

"No' in my estimation. If you hadna killed him, I wouldna be alive."

"I couldna have allowed that."

"I was lucky you were there when I needed you."

"Aye, you were." She smiled at him.

He loved her quick-wittedness. Sleeping with her last night had been the highlight of his life.

"About last night..." she said.

He hoped she didn't regret that they had slept together. Not that they had mated, but even so, sleeping with an unmated she-wolf wasn't usually done.

"I was glad for it. I have never slept so well in my life." She squeezed his hand.

"Me either. What were you doing outside the castle walls at night?"

"I didn't want to wake up so early to gather the herbs before the morning meal. I thought I could get what we needed and return before the castle gates were closed."

He nodded. "Your mother, will she be worried that you were outside the walls when the raiders came?"

"Aye. She will no doubt be upset with me for worrying her so."

"Has she told you what upset her when she saw me?"

"Nay. I still dinna know what the matter was, but I keep asking and I will eventually get the truth out of her."

They finally reached the gates of the castle, now open, and

Coinneach brushed Aisling's soft red hair out of her blue eyes and cradled her face as he kissed her mouth. "When will I see you again?"

"Oh, whenever I have the chance, I'll meet you in the meadow near your croft. I'll just give a little wolf howl to let you know that I'm there." Then she howled in her human form, and the sound of her howl captivated him.

WITH A BACKWARD WAVE TO COINNEACH, Aisling rushed into the outer bailey and then into the inner bailey. Her mother was just coming out of the castle and raced to take her in her arms.

"Why were you beyond the castle walls? I didna learn about it until it was too late," her mother said.

"I thought I would gather the herbs in time. I need to get these to the kitchen."

"You have his smell on you," her mother accused her, probably believing that's why Aisling had been locked out of the castle that night.

"Aye. I stayed with Coinneach and his family. He offered his pallet to me."

"You smell of a human's blood. What did you do?"

"I killed a Viking raider before he eliminated Coinneach."

"Och, Aisling." Her mother looked at the bow and arrows she was carrying. "You took his bow?"

"Aye, and I'll learn to use it. I must go, Mother, or lose my position in the kitchen."

"We will talk more later."

Aisling knew her mother would question her further, but she didn't want anyone else to know what she had done.

4
_____

After weeks of rendezvousing with each other, Coinneach found Aisling already waiting in the meadow for him, her body a dark silhouette against the riot of wildflowers. He settled beside her in the tall grass, watching the purple thistles and yellow buttercups bend with each whisper of wind. Above them, the sky played hide-and-seek—brilliant blue one moment, then veiled by clouds drifting like scattered sheep.

The chill in the air meant fall was on its way.

"I still dinna know why your mother is so afraid of me." He had pondered it for far too long.

Aisling rolled over atop him and rested her chin on his chest, her fingers lazily toying with his hair. "Maybe she is afraid you will marry me and leave her alone."

"I _will_ marry you. But family being family, I want her to feel the joy in our union and not leave her out in the cold."

Aisling sighed. "I've asked her numerous times what she's so afraid of concerning you, but she refuses to answer me."

"I'm going to work at Middleborough Castle," Coinneach said decisively.

"I would love that. My mother wouldna."

He swept his hands through her long red tresses. "I canna stay away from you, and Tamhas needs the croft to call his own when our parents can no longer manage it. He'll marry, and he'll be content."

"But you? You are too alpha to want to continue to till the soil until you are old and gray. What would you do at the castle though? Most everyone there has been trained since they were wee lads and lasses to fit a particular role."

"A fighter."

"YOU HAVE NO FORMAL TRAINING." Aisling rested her cheek against Coinneach's chest and listened to his strong heartbeat. She smelled his wolfish scent that she loved so much and absorbed the heat of his body on this late summer's day. She had no doubt he could do anything he put his mind to, but that didn't mean the chief would agree to add an untrained warrior to his ranks.

"I practice." He patted the Viking sword he carried with him just in case he encountered trouble.

"Against your brother. But we're talking about warriors who are strong and muscular, who have the skill with a sword. They would love to show you how poorly you can compete and make fun of you. You know how men can be."

"Aye." Coinneach gave her one of his lopsided little smiles. "While you're watching, I'll best them all."

Aisling scoffed. "They will knock you on your arse."

"And I will get back up and take them on again. I'm no' afraid of a challenge."

"Have you talked to your family about this?" She wondered if they would be all right with him leaving them to work the farm on their own.

"I have. Tamhas is eager to take over the farm when our da can no longer manage, though if I ever have a chance to leave, I will talk it over with them again to make sure they are ready for me to work somewhere else."

"But you will come to work at Middleborough Castle, aye? You willna be going somewhere else," Aisling said.

"At any time, I could have worked for Alasdair if I had wanted to. He is the chief of Ghealach Castle."

"Ooh, you know a chief."

"We are best of friends."

"But?"

"I want to work at Middleborough Castle so I can be close to you. And to my family, should they need me."

"That's what I want to hear."

They began to kiss, and he pressed his hand against her breast.

She moaned against his mouth. "We should just mate," she said. "My mother will come around."

"My family wants to celebrate our union with your mother's consent."

"We may never get it."

He sighed and kissed her forehead. "If she doesna agree in a fortnight, we will mate anyway."

She smiled. "I'm glad, but I will try to convince her before then."

"If you can think of anything I can do to help, just let me know."

"Aye."

Then, with the gentle breeze caressing them and the flowers swaying around them, she climbed on top of him, and they kissed again when they heard horses approaching.

Coinneach sat up abruptly. "That is Alasdair."

"Aye, I've seen him at Middleborough before. He has an alliance with Chief Hamish. Wolves need to stick together."

"I agree."

Coinneach pulled Aisling up from the grass, and they stood. He waved at Alasdair to let him know where he was.

When Alasdair rode his horse across the meadow to join them, he looked surprised that Coinneach was with a lass.

"How now!" Alasdair greeted Coinneach, his smile broadening as he glanced Aisling's way. "It seems you have been busy while I've been away."

Coinneach smiled. "I would marry Aisling in a heartbeat, but her mother objects."

Aisling's cheeks flushed. "We dinna ken why. He is always so kind to my mother and treats me with the same kind of respect and kindness."

"Mayhap I can convince her that he is of good heart," Alasdair said.

"Nay. She willna tell me why, only to say it could be the death of us."

Alasdair looked at Coinneach to gauge his reaction.

He shrugged. "She willna discuss what worries her. I've tried everything I can think of."

"Coinneach, Aisling, come with us. We'll show Aisling's mother that we are friends and allies. Mayhap that will help," Alasdair said.

Coinneach couldn't have a better friend than Alasdair. "Aye, if you think it will be all right with Chief Hamish."

Alasdair slapped him on the back. "You will have to sit at a lower table."

"To be closer to Aisling, I would do anything. I've always wanted to see the inside of the castle also."

"I am Cook's assistant, and I'll be serving the meals. I'll sit in the kitchen and eat after the laird and everyone else eats. Otherwise, I would ensure I could sit with you at the meal." She sounded so disappointed, and he knew exactly how she felt.

Alasdair cleared his throat. "Maybe in the future, I could help to change your circumstances, but for now, I'll be visiting with Chief Hamish. We brought barrels of wine to celebrate the occasion."

"Was Chief Hamish angry when your da had gone to visit him when we were younger and we ate the boar?"

"Nay, we had wine that time too, and he was much pleased." Alasdair motioned to one of the spare horses they had brought with them this time. "Yours and your lady's to ride. I dinna know you would have a companion."

She was hoisted onto Coinneach's lap and whispered, "Do you know how to ride?"

"Alasdair taught Tamhas and me when we were younger." Coinneach held her close.

"He is a good friend indeed."

"Aye."

"Let me tell my family where I'll be," Coinneach said.

"Aye. We'll head toward Middleborough Castle, and you can catch up," Alasdair said.

Coinneach inclined his head and galloped toward the croft.

"'Tis exhilarating and frightening at the same time," she said.

"See the distance we cover in such a short time?"

"Aye. Much quicker than walking."

As soon as he reached the croft, he called out to his family to let them know they had visitors and told Aisling, "I'll be right back."

Magnus walked out of the croft with Tamhas right behind them, while Elspeth wiped her hands off on a cloth as she joined them.

"Alasdair has invited me to dine with him at the castle," Coinneach said.

His da smiled. "Good. Mayhap Aisling's mother will see you differently then."

"Aye, she's the one for you." Elspeth waved at Aisling, who smiled and waved back.

"I'm off then before Alasdair reaches the castle and I canna gain entrance."

"Aye, go," Magnus said.

Coinneach hugged his mom and kissed her forehead, then hurried to climb back on the horse and leave. He galloped off to catch up to Alasdair and his men.

They were getting close when Aisling said, "I worry about my mother, though. She will be angry when you join us for the meal."

Alasdair overheard her and drew his horse closer. "She canna be angry with him when she sees Coinneach is our guest. I didna tell you, Coinneach, but we always have sword fights between our packs to display strength and prowess when we visit with your pack. You will have to do it also."

Coinneach wasn't sure he could fight against well-trained men, not when he had only fought against Alasdair and Tamhas over the years and knew all their moves.

"You can do it. I have every faith in you that you'll best half the men there." Alasdair was always great at offering encouraging words.

"Aye, I will give it my best."

"That's all any of us can do," Alasdair said.

"If you dinna get yourself killed," Aisling said.

When they arrived at the castle gates, the guards greeted them warmly. Coinneach could see that Alasdair and his pack had a good working relationship with Hamish's pack. Coinneach was glad for that because, for the first time since escorting Aisling home, he was treated with respect as well.

On occasion, they would have celebrations of one sort or another at the castle, but his mother always said that their place was on the farm and their da always agreed with her. He wondered if they had some trouble with the people in their clan who lived in the castle, but when he'd asked, his mother and da had shared looks, but neither had said anything.

Now, that was in the back of Coinneach's mind as he got ready to fight one of the warriors.

"We fight and then feast," Alasdair said.

Warriors from both sides were gearing up to fight in the inner bailey.

Aisling said, "I can stay for just a short while and watch you, and then I must help Cook with the meal. Dinna let anyone get the best of you."

Coinneach dismounted, helped her off the horse, and gave her a spontaneous hug and kiss. "Aye. As you wish."

She quickly hugged and kissed him back.

Then he pulled off his shirt, just like the other men did, preparing himself to fight.

No one looked eager to take on the biggest man, his solid muscles glistening in the sunlight, his intimidating, fierce scowl directed at Coinneach, as if challenging him to fight him. Coinneach knew not to challenge the blond-haired, blond-bearded man. He looked big enough and ferocious enough that he could be the chief's champion.

If the man took Coinneach down in a few minutes and he couldn't fight anyone else, how would that appear to others? That he couldn't fight well and join the men who worked for Hamish.

No one wanted to challenge the big man, and Coinneach straightened his shoulders and headed for him. The warrior flexed his massive muscles in a show of strength and intimidation. Coinneach wasn't backing down. He either did this or he didn't, but he had to try his best.

The man's blue eyes widened as Coinneach approached him.

Coinneach was not as muscled as this man, though when he was dressed for winter, he looked a lot bulkier, like the man before him. Yet he had worked hard all his life, and he thought he could make a good show of it.

"Are you sure you want to fight me?" the blond-haired man

asked, giving Coinneach the option of backing out. He wore his hair back in a tail, his muscles spectacular, and Coinneach knew the warrior would use them to his advantage.

"Aye."

He grinned. "I'm Aodhan. You have guts, I'll give you that." His eyes were as vivid a blue as the sea washing up near shore.

Coinneach was always ready for a challenge. "I'm Coinneach."

As soon as Aodhan swung his sword at Coinneach, he felt the wash of air sweep across his bare chest and leaped out of the way. If Aodhan's sword had connected with Coinneach's, he knew he would have been separated from it as much force as Aodhan had used to try and hit Coinneach's sword.

Coinneach quickly swung at Aodhan, connecting his sword with a clang.

"No' bad." Aodhan returned with a swing that could have cut a man in half.

Again, Coinneach dodged the blow, using the techniques Alasdair had taught him over the years to fight a heavier foe.

"You have wits," Aodhan said as Coinneach came in for a counterattack and easily swept Aodhan's sword to the side with a clank.

"You carry a Viking sword," Aodhan finally said, noticing the weapon Coinneach carried.

Coinneach did, though he hadn't had the honor of killing the Viking, and he didn't want to let on that he did. Since Aisling had sworn him to secrecy that she had killed the Viking as a wolf, he'd kept her secret, though he'd wanted to tell everyone of her bravery, that Aisling had killed the raider as a wolf.

"Mayhap you are better at sword fighting than I gave you credit for."

While Aodhan was wasting his breath in conversation, Coinneach was strategizing. Somehow, he had to take down the mountain of a man before Coinneach wore out.

He rushed forth, getting so close that he caught Aodhan off

guard. He grabbed Aodhan's massive arms, his sword still in hand, slid his leg behind Aodhan's right leg, and, kicking back, shoved him hard at the same time with all his might.

Despite or maybe because of Aodhan's massive bulk and size, the giant couldn't stop himself from falling and landed on his back on the ground.

Coinneach, relieved to the gods that the maneuver had worked on a man that size, a maneuver he had practiced with Tamhas until his brother could take Coinneach down, was worried now that Aodhan would be furious and take him to task.

Aodhan sat up and actually grinned at him. "You are all right."

Coinneach offered his hand to Aodhan to help him up as a gesture of friendship. Aodhan could have pulled him right down, but he took Coinneach's hand and helped himself up, mostly on his own. Then Coinneach realized that more than half the fighting men were watching them.

They all cheered to see that the bout had ended on friendly terms.

"You will sit beside me at the meal," Aodhan said. "Now go. Fight someone your own size."

Coinneach laughed. "You are a fearsome warrior to be reckoned with. If you'd hit my sword even once, I would have been done for."

"It would never have happened. Not with your fleetness of foot."

Coinneach inclined his head in thanks, then went off to fight someone else, but no one seemed to want to fight him after he had beaten Aodhan, even if it was in an unusual way.

Alasdair joined him and slapped him on the back. "I nearly died when I saw you take on Chief Hamish's champion. You did well, my friend. Come, fight me so you can get in some more practice."

Aodhan *was* Hamish's champion just like he'd suspected!

After Coinneach and Aodhan fought, both had sweat beading

their chests and faces. Both were flushed with exertion, their hearts beating wildly from their previous fights. Coinneach glanced around for Aisling.

Giving him a half smile, she looked relieved that he hadn't gotten himself killed. He was relieved he hadn't either.

"Let's do it." Coinneach had wanted to fight others to prove to himself that he could. But Alasdair had been trained well, and so any practice proved helpful.

They squared off and were about the same size, so Coinneach could still get a workout.

"You were holding out on me," Alasdair said.

"How's that?"

"You have to teach me that maneuver you used to take Aodhan down. Chief Hamish asked me who you are."

"Oh?" Coinneach struck Alasdair's sword and knocked him back a few paces.

To their surprise, another man stopped them and said to Coinneach, "I'll take you on."

Alasdair looked to see if Coinneach agreed.

Coinneach nodded. "More later, Alasdair."

"Aye, to be sure."

Coinneach was glad to fight someone else who might use some techniques different from what Alasdair had taught him and his brother.

This man was good, though, as he fought Coinneach, and he assumed that's why he challenged Coinneach. Maybe to prove to the rest of their men that Coinneach wasn't anyone to fear.

Coinneach put every ounce of his heart and muscles into the battle. He swung his sword with precision and a cool head, nearly knocking his opponent's sword from his grasp. In a real fight, Coinneach wouldn't have allowed him to recover.

"Who are you? One of Chief Alasdair's elite warriors?" the man asked, striking back at him, and Coinneach quickly deflected the blow.

He couldn't help but be pleased that the man, skilled in sword fighting, would think that a mere farmer was an elite warrior.

"I've never seen you before. I would have remembered you."

"Coinneach. I'm friends with Alasdair but work on a farm under Chief Hamish's rule."

"Coinneach," the man said, thrusting his sword at Coinneach. "I'm Drustan."

Again, Coinneach deflected it with a clash and thrust at the man, who had to parry and step back. "I'm in charge of our warriors. How did a farmer learn to fight so well?"

"Alasdair. He has been a good friend of mine for years."

"You carry a Viking sword."

Coinneach couldn't pretend to have killed the Viking. He hoped Drustan wouldn't tell anyone else, but felt he had to tell the man the truth. "Aye. My lass killed the Viking as a wolf, just so you know I didna kill him with a pitchfork."

Drustan laughed.

"I beg you no' to tell anyone else about this because she doesna want anyone to know."

"Who is she?"

If Coinneach didn't give a name, no one would still know. But something made him believe he could trust the man. "Aisling."

"One of Cook's assistants? She is as talented as you are when you took down Aodhan. No one has ever bested him. *Ever.* Do you have kinfolk who can help manage the farm?"

"My da and mother and my twin brother Tamhas."

"Then your brother, if he is capable, will take over the farm when your da can no longer manage. And you will work for me. What say you?"

Overwhelmed at the idea that it would truly come to pass, Coinneach stared at him in disbelief. In his wildest dreams, he had always hoped to do more with his life beyond farming. But he couldn't decide such a thing without talking to his family first to make sure they would be all right with it, even though he had spoken to them about this before.

Before now, he hadn't had a real plan. Though he knew his brother was much more suited to farming than he was.

"I would be honored, but I must speak with my family first."

"Aye, as it should be. I'll expect you to be here first thing in the morning, and you'll stay in the barracks with the other bachelors." Drustan sounded like he didn't take no for an answer. "You need a lot of training, but have the courage, wit, and strength to fight the other men. Mayhap you were a bit reckless in taking on Aodhan, but sometimes taking chances will mean the difference between life and death."

"I couldna conscientiously have left him without a sparring partner."

"And you didna know any better."

Coinneach smiled. He had known better. He just had to prove his worth in any way that he could.

After Coinneach spoke with Drustan, everyone headed to the great hall to eat.

Alasdair joined Coinneach and said, "What do you think of that?"

"I want my brother to have the farm one day, so I could find my own way in the world. I just hope my family is ready for it."

Alasdair nodded. "They will be proud of you."

Coinneach hoped they wouldn't be disappointed. But one day, Tamhas would have a wife and children, and Coinneach wouldn't be needed there. Being closer to Aisling was what Coinneach wanted more than anything. Somehow, he would convince her mother he was a good choice as a mate for Aisling.

5

——————

Aisling hurried to the kitchen, hoping she wouldn't be too late to arrive to do her duty after watching the sword play between the clans and annoy Cook. Cook was always on everyone's case when they didn't show up early to prepare the meals.

Her mother caught up with Aisling, but she didn't need the delay. "I'm late, Mother. I need to get to the kitchen."

"I will talk to you on the way there. I canna believe Coinneach is here."

"I dinna want to talk about it, " Aisling said, repeating her mother's often-repeated words. If her mother couldn't tell her what was bothering her about Coinneach, Aisling would continue to see him as she pleased. She adored him, and she knew he loved her. She reminded herself they would be mated in a fortnight, with or without her mother's consent.

"There are things you canna be privy to."

"You have told me that many times before." Aisling was tired of hearing it.

Her mother hurried after her. "I'm serious. It's dangerous for you, me, and Coinneach, too."

Aisling stopped. "Tell me why."

Tears filled her mother's eyes. "I...we'll have to talk about this privately, away from here."

"You'll tell me?"

"Aye, after the meal."

She hugged her mom. "That's good. I'll see you after the meal then. We can go to the meadow and speak."

"Aye."

Aisling was glad her mother would finally tell her what was bothering her. She just hoped it wasn't as dire as her mother thought it was.

She hurried into the kitchen, where everyone was busy cooking various dishes for the chief, the rest of the clan, and his guests.

Cook said to her, "That man of yours bested Aodhan. No one has ever done so, though he used some strange maneuver to do it."

Aisling was so surprised to hear admiration in the Cook's voice, not to mention she was shocked that she knew Aisling had been seeing Coinneach.

"Dinna be so surprised that everyone knows you are smitten with him."

Everyone?

"Och, everyone gossips whenever you have gone to the meadow."

"He is braw," Aisling admitted.

"Aye. Anyone choosing to fight Aodhan is either touched in the head or extremely brave. Because he won the battle, I believe he has the courage of an alpha wolf. Did you see that Viking sword he carries? Of course you have."

Aisling smiled, thinking back to when she'd saved Coinneach's life. But she never let on that he was anything but a great warrior and didn't want him to tell anyone she had killed the Viking to protect him.

Aisling stirred the pot of fish stew while Cook chastened others in the kitchen who were dawdling while listening to their conversation. Aisling felt her position had somewhat been elevated for the first time since she'd worked for Cook.

Of course, one mistake could change everything in an instant. But for now, Aisling was walking on the moon.

"All right, just this once, I'll let you serve the table where—what is his name?"

"Coinneach."

"Where Coinneach is sitting. For Aodhan to ask him to sit with him is a great honor. And serving him his meal is also so dinna spill or drop anything," Cook said.

"Aye, Cook." Aisling was beyond excited and hid her enthusiasm so she wouldn't make a fool of herself.

A redheaded woman, Gormelia, who usually served Aodhan's table, said, "But that's my table to serve." Her hair was often on display, but it wasn't half as showy as Cook's springy or Aisling's wavy curls, if she said so herself. Gormelia's hair was straight and fine, not as full and luxurious as Aisling's and Cook's.

And Gormelia's mouth was downturned more often than not, like she was always unhappy with something. Unless she were with her friends, and then she'd make a show of laughing and smiling, which all looked faked to high heaven. Her dark brown eyes were catlike and pretty but often narrowed with disdain, like she was trying to copy the chief's mate, Morag's demeanor.

"Aye, normally, and who is in charge here?" Cook asked, sounding annoyed that the woman would question her authority. "You will take care of the table Aisling normally serves."

Aisling should have known Gormelia would be irritated with her for taking over her table. Some of the lasses preferred serving the guards, hoping to find a mate. Aisling often served the women and was happy to do so.

She already had her man, but still wanted to convince her mother that he was the only one for her. She suspected Gormelia was interested in Aodhan, but he hadn't shown any interest back.

As soon as loaves of bread were brought up from the ovens below, the head table was served first, and then Aisling carried a tray to the table she was assigned while Gormelia bumped into her, nearly making her lose her tray. She could have bitten her; she was so mad.

When she saw Coinneach's smiling face, all her anger melted away. She smiled at him and hurried to serve Aodhan first. Before she could give him a slice of bread, Coinneach left his bench seat to assist her. He wasn't supposed to; he was an honored guest.

He also didn't know the rules here. She glanced at Aodhan to see if he would tell Coinneach it wasn't done, but he only grinned and winked at her. Which made her cheeks heat in embarrassment.

She knew everyone would be watching them, partly because Coinneach had bested the champion *and* befriended him in one fell swoop, and partly because of his actions now, which were gallant but not at all done. She hoped everyone wouldn't laugh at him as he helped her pass out the bread at his table.

"Two for me, love," Aodhan said with a smirk. He probably needed more for all his muscles.

She hurried to give him another slice of bread and whispered to Coinneach, "You're not supposed to help. You're a guest."

He only kissed her cheek. "I'll see you in the meadow following the meal, aye?"

She thought of her mother's comments, and now her mother had promised to tell her the truth about what bothered her so much about Coinneach being at the castle.

"Later." Aisling hurried off with her empty bread tray to deliver fish soup next.

"You had a helper, I'm told, which is why you returned so quickly," Cook said to Aisling, as she oversaw the rest of the meal.

"Uh, aye. He doesna know the rules."

"Well, serve the fish stew, but to the head table. They always get their food first."

"Aye, of course." Now this was even more stressful. She hoped Coinneach didn't try to help her serve the fish stew at the head table. And prayed she wouldn't spill any of it and make a mess of things.

As soon as she went to the head table, Alasdair smiled at her. She smiled back and then gave Chief Hamish his soup first, without spilling a drop. But when she came to Alasdair, she tripped on an uneven stone and spilled some on the table. Alasdair quickly reached out and steadied her hand.

She silently thanked him. Then she left the soup off for the rest of the people at the table and hurried off to the kitchen, perspiring like crazy. Venison was next, and she saw that Gormelia had rushed back to the kitchen so she could serve another table besides the women's. Maybe so she could serve the head table, which would suit Aisling fine. She wanted to see Coinneach instead.

Cook eyed the two of them. "All right. You can take the food to the head table, Gormelia. You work on the champion's table, Aisling."

"Thank you," Aisling said, even though it wasn't as prestigious as bringing the meals to the head table. But she didn't think it was as nerve-racking either. She just hoped Coinneach didn't come to assist her with the venison.

When she returned to the table, she told Coinneach, "Sit, and I will serve you."

"Aye, lass. I hope I didna get you into any trouble."

"Nay. I'm meeting my mother in the meadow. She's going to tell me the truth about what concerns her." She didn't say anything more than that, not wanting Aodhan or anyone else to be privy to their situation.

Coinneach nodded. "I will wait for you still, to learn what she has to say."

"Aye. But out of sight."

She glanced at Aodhan, who was already eating his venison, listening in, of course, to all that was being said.

Then she served Coinneach and hurried off to finish serving the rest of the clansmen at the table, even Drustan, in charge of the warriors.

"You fancy this Coinneach, aye?" Drustan asked.

Her cheeks heated in embarrassment. "Aye."

"Good. He will work for me."

She glanced back at Coinneach, worried about the danger her mother had alluded to.

"After he ensures his family can take care of the farm without him."

"Oh, aye." She was ecstatic about him living closer to her, but still worried about her mother's warnings of doom. She continued to serve the meal and then left with the empty tray to return to the kitchen. She couldn't believe it. Maybe that was what Coinneach had wanted to tell her about in the meadow.

She thought about her mother's haunting words again. She had to know what her mother would say, and she hoped it wouldn't upset the plan for Coinneach to work at the castle.

Coinneach was hopeful that Blair would tell Aisling what bothered her about him. And he hoped it wasn't any significant concern, just something she had worked up in her mind.

He was eager to tell Aisling he had the offer to work at the castle, but he still needed to ensure his family approved.

Once the meal was done, he wanted to see Aisling before he left. The chiefs of the two clans left the high table, signaling to everyone else that the meal had ended. Coinneach motioned to Alasdair that he was going to the kitchen and would return.

Alasdair nodded.

Then Coinneach headed into the kitchen, where Aisling and the others ate. "I'm leaving with Alasdair now. But I will see you in a bit, aye?"

"Aye."

He leaned over and kissed her. Everyone there was goggle-eyed. Even Cook.

Then he said, "See you soon." He hurried out of the kitchen, not wanting to keep Alasdair waiting. Even though they were good friends, Alasdair was a chief and needed to return to his people. And Coinneach wanted to give Aisling time to speak with her mother before she shared what was the matter.

AFTER THE MEAL, Aisling found her mother waiting for her at the castle's entrance, wringing her hands. They left the castle, hurried through the inner bailey, and then the outer one. Aisling was eager to learn what had been troubling her mother about Coinneach.

"We are no' related, are we?" Aisling blurted out before they were very far from the castle. She couldn't imagine that they would be.

"Gods no. 'Tis much more serious than that."

What could be more serious than that?

"I was forced to keep a secret when I was only sixteen summers. A terrible, dark secret that has eaten me up for years."

"Until you saw Coinneach?" Ailing ventured.

"Aye."

"He's no' a bad man." Aisling would never believe that about him.

"Nay. I...I did a terrible thing, but I had no choice."

Aisling's mother was a truly kind-hearted woman. She devoted herself to helping deliver babies and tending to the injuries and ailments of those in need. She never spoke ill of anyone. What could her mother have possibly done that was considered wrong?

"I was...was ordered to murder a healthy bairn." Her mother started to cry.

Aisling hugged her. "But you didna. If you had, you would have said you killed the bairn. What an evil thing to do. Who ordered you to kill a bairn?" She couldn't imagine anything more horrible than that.

Her mother took hold of her hands. "I canna tell you. I shouldna have told you this much. I canna believe Drustan wants Coinneach to work for him."

"The baby—was it Coinneach?" What would Coinneach have to do with any of this otherwise? He was probably the right age to have been a baby when her mother was sixteen.

"Aye, but you must tell no one."

"I dinna understand."

"His mother died in childbirth, and I was ordered to get rid of the baby."

"Who ordered such a thing?"

"I canna say."

"But you gave him to...no, you didna or you wouldna have been so shocked to see him. You didna know he lived."

"I was young and was threatened that I would die if I didna do it, but I couldna harm him. He was a beautiful baby. I checked on him the next day, but someone had taken him in. I knew by the footprints in the soil, but I didna know who had."

"You recognized the wolf on his shoulder."

"Aye. I was shocked to see that he had grown into a man, that the crofters had taken him in." Her mother wiped away tears.

"What about his da?"

"That I canna tell you."

"Magnus and Elspeth dinna know whose baby Coinneach is," Aisling said, astounded. She didn't know anyone who didn't cherish new wolf pups in the pack. How could the person who ordered the bairn to be murdered be so monstrous?

"Nay. They must have found him and taken him in as their own. You say that the boys are twins, Tamhas and Coinneach, but they are no'. I suspected Elspeth had just recently given birth to Tamhas, and they found the baby then. The men appear to be about the same age. Then she would have been able to nurse both."

"Mayhap they were afraid of mentioning to anyone that they found the bairn."

"And had they known, it would have been for good reason."

Aisling pondered the matter, then said, "So why is Coinneach in danger?" She understood her mother's concern because of the person who had threatened her with death. But how would anyone learn Coinneach wasn't the crofters' son? Then she thought of his birthmark.

"If anyone remembers what Hamish looked like at Coinneach's age and sees the resemblance?"

"And the wolf head on his shoulder."

"Only a few of us saw it."

"In the birthing room?" Now Aisling suspected the person who had ordered her mother to get rid of the child had been helping with the birth. A woman, not a man.

But it had to be someone older than her mother at the time, most likely someone in a position of authority.

"If the mother died and had a bairn, but then the bairn disappears, wouldna that have been suspicious?" Aisling couldn't understand how they could have deceived everyone.

"Another mother had twins and one didna live."

"Och, so you swapped out bairns!" Aisling couldn't help but be mortified at the idea. "But you didna give the healthy bairn to the one who had lost a twin."

"Nay. She knew it had died. There was no sense in taking the bairn to her and saying that he had miraculously lived."

No. There was more to it than that. The woman lost a bairn, and it would have been easy to swap out the deceased one for the live one instead of abandoning him to suffer what fate could have befallen him. He was just fortunate that Magnus and Elspeth had taken him in.

"The woman in charge of the birthing"—Aisling had no idea how that person could be so cruel so long ago—"must have ordered the bairn disposed of because she wouldn't allow him to remain in the castle. Am I right?"

Appearing morose, her mother bit her lip and nodded, looking out at the grasses surrounding them.

So, who was the da? Someone of importance? Or someone, the most likely person, the midwife wanted for her own. Once his mate was gone, she saw a way to ingratiate herself with him so that he would become her mate.

Aisling had seen that behavior between a woman and a man before, only no bairns had been involved. The woman would have had to be older than her mother, and the da would have had to be about Tamhas's dad's age.

"Who is Coinneach's real da?"

"I canna say. No' only would the woman who forced me to take him away—I left him by the river where I knew the crofters gathered to fish—but his own da would want my head. Dinna you see? I did a terrible thing."

"You were forced to." She didn't see her mother in a bad way.

"I've thought about it over the years, and maybe if I'd been stronger, less afraid of my own shadow, I could have spoken to his da. But important people surrounded him, and the woman who told me to get rid of the bairn was watching me. I couldna approach him."

Aisling wondered how she would have handled the situation at her mother's age. She thought she would have told the midwife that she would do it, but then taken the baby straight to the da and told him his son had survived.

But what if he didn't believe her? She could see her mother's dilemma.

"So you are saying the midwife would recognize Coinneach as his bairn if she saw his birthmark?"

"Aye. And he was shirtless when he was fighting in the inner bailey."

Aisling loved to see Coinneach shirtless, his beautiful, glistening muscles exposed. She loved his birthmark, distinguishing him from any other man she'd ever met.

"But"—Aisling suspected—"the woman in question wouldna have come out to watch the fighting?"

"Nay. She abhors seeing such a thing."

But it was all right to kill a newly born baby.

"His da wouldna know about it." Not if he hadn't seen the bairn, Aisling thought.

Now Aisling didn't know what to do. She'd been eager to learn the truth, but not half-truths. She wanted to tell Coinneach, but would it only hurt him? Would he be angry that Magnus and Elspeth hadn't told him the truth about how they had found him? Or want to take revenge against the midwife? And her mother?

"You see why I didna want to tell you about it? You canna mention this to Coinneach. His parents, though not his birth parents, have loved him like a mother and a da, and telling him the truth will only hurt him."

"Surely, the midwife no longer holds any power over you. You've been the midwife for years."

"Nay, love. She has great power."

"How? Does she have many friends and family who would do her bidding?" Aisling asked.

"Something like that."

Not much family and many friends. Aisling tried to think of who had that much power and blurted out, "Morag!"

"Shh, never say her name."

"Ohmigoddess, she married the Chief. Hamish is Coinneach's da."

Her mother wiped away tears. "I knew I could never keep the truth from you forever."

"No matter how much you wanted to keep the secret, you needed to tell someone."

"You canna tell Coinneach. He will make his way in the world on his own."

"Unlike Morag's son, Rupert. Morag spoils him rotten. But he's still the chief's son, if no' his first."

Her mother didn't respond, her eyes downcast.

"Dinna tell me, Rupert isna Hamish's son."

"I didna tell you that."

"But he isna, is he?"

Her mother shook her head.

"Whose then?"

"She had a roll in the hay with a stable hand, then she claimed Rupert was Hamish's. But I had witnessed her entering the barn, and, curious, I peeked in to see what they were doing. I caught them in the act, but they never saw me. They were too busy...well, you know. Hamish never realized the lie, though he'd been away at the time, battling another clan."

"Och, then Coinneach is the legitimate heir."

"Coinneach is a farm boy. Naught more. You dinna know the danger ahead for the three of us, maybe even Tamhas and his parents if...if Morag learns that Coinneach is Hamish's son and believes they know of it."

"Except for you, no one could prove he is Hamish's son," Aisling said morosely. Rupert had tried to kiss her repeatedly, and she'd fought off his advances. She'd gotten a black eye from him the last time for denying him. She would love to see Coinneach put him in his place.

"Morag has too much to lose if Hamish learns of it," her mother said. "She willna let that happen."

Aisling was glad her mother told her what it was all about, but she was torn about telling Coinneach. How would he feel if he learned Aisling had known the truth and hadn't shared it with him? Mates couldn't keep secrets from each other, not of that magnitude.

Morag should be found guilty of what she had done. Aisling just hoped her mother wouldn't have to pay for her part in the crime.

"What about Rupert? Does he know who his true da is? Wait, does Morag even love Hamish? Does she love Rupert's da?"

"If you look at Rupert and his dad, you can see the similarities. They both have finer features, red hair, the same long faces, and green eyes. I've never seen them together so I don't know if Rupert knows who his da is."

"Coinneach looks like Hamish," Aisling suddenly said.

"Aye, though unless anyone made the connection, they would think he was only a crofter. I've seen Morag speaking to Osmond. I'm sure others have seen them together. I dinna know if they are still lovers. But I dinna think she and Hamish love each other like he loved Orla."

Which made it even more terrible that Hamish hadn't had his son to raise after his mate had died.

"I canna force you no' to talk to Coinneach about any of this, but the more who know about it, the more dangerous it is for all of us. I know you plan to see Coinneach. Just take care of what you say. I must return to the castle." Then her mother hugged her.

Aisling lingered in her mother's arms, her grip tightening as if to shield Aisling from some unseen threat. When they finally broke apart, her mother hurried down the path through the meadow without a backward glance.

A knot formed in Aisling's stomach at the thought of meeting Coinneach—whose mere mention usually quickened her pulse.

As she approached the croft, she spotted him crossing the meadow with his familiar smile. Her chest tightened. She inhaled sharply, blinked back tears, and broke into a run toward him.

6

Coinneach couldn't wait to see Aisling. He hoped that her talk with her mother had resolved the issues of him mating Aisling. He wanted to be hopeful, but hope had always felt slippery to him, something best left to children and fools.

When he saw Aisling heading through the heather, her red hair flying behind her, making her appear like one of the fae folk, he rushed to join her. He caught her in the middle of the path, the two of them surrounded by a sea of bracken and blooming heather, pockets of purple and gold trembling under a skittish wind. He swept her up in his arms and kissed her mouth.

She gripped the back of his neck as if she meant to anchor herself to him forever. Her cheeks were flushed, her hair catching the fading, golden lights of day. She smelled of the earth, the woods, and the sweet fragrance of heather, the scent he loved on her.

He could see instantly that she'd been crying, but she met his gaze squarely, her lips parted in a way that spoke of wild, reckless longing.

He was desperate to ask her about her mother, desperate to

know if everything had changed or if everything was all right. At that moment, the only truth he could bear was the taste of her breath and the urgent, shuddering way she pressed herself against him. But when she pulled her soft mouth from his and licked her lips, he could see tears welling up in her eyes.

"What's wrong?" He just couldn't believe anything could be so bad.

She held onto him tight, resting her head against his chest, not letting go, not talking either.

"Do you want to visit the waterfall?"

She nodded, and he took hold of her hand, and they walked, arms tangled, to the mouth of the burn where the water ran fast and noisy, shielding them from the rest of the world. She perched on a flat stone, her skirts pulled tight around her knees, and he knelt before her, heart thundering. The silence between them was thick, textured by anticipation and dread.

Coinneach watched her, trying to read the future in the tilt of her chin, the tremble of her fingers. Behind her, the waterfall poured over the cliff in a deluge of water, as if waiting for the verdict. He didn't want to force her to tell him what she had learned. Maybe her mother hadn't even told her anything, just put her off like she had done so many times before.

Still, he couldn't quit thinking about it. "Is it really bad?"

Aisling nodded, which didn't reassure him. The birds were chirping in the trees, fluttering from one branch to another, a rabbit bounded off in the bracken, the forest alive.

He took hold of her hand and caressed it gently. "Whatever you say willna affect how I feel about you."

She looked up at him with woeful eyes, her shoulders bent as if she carried the weight of the world on them. "We're mating."

"Your mother agreed?" He was so surprised, he just stared at her. Then he smiled. "I'm so glad."

"Nay. 'Tis worse than you might imagine. But I love you and I want to be your mate. However, if I tell you what my mother told me, you may feel differently about me."

"Never."

"As mated wolves, we canna keep secrets from each other. But I dinna want to hurt you with the truth."

He couldn't imagine what she could reveal to him that would hurt him. "I agree about no' keeping secrets from one another. It could tear us apart."

Then she turned to face him and took both of his hands in hers. "You canna be angry with my mother."

He inclined his head. He still wanted to get her mother's approval.

"You...you are no' Magnus and Elspeth's son."

Coinneach just stared at her, his emotions flipping from disbelief to shock. "Nay. Whatever your mother believes isna true. Tamhas is my twin brother. Is he no' Magnus and Elspeth's son?"

"He is. You are no'." Aisling held onto his hands when he wanted to pull them away.

He wanted to pace, to get rid of some of the frustration building in his blood. "And your mother knows this, how?"

"She was only sixteen and helped with birthing the bairns of the clan. Your mother died while giving birth to you. The midwife at the time ordered my mother to get rid of you."

He parted his lips to speak, but no words came out. A jumble of thoughts was vying for his voice, but he didn't know what to say.

Aisling wiped her face with the heel of her palm and finally spoke. Her voice was rougher than he remembered, but so steady it made his chest ache. She told him what her mother had said, every word measured, she explained about the other woman giving birth and losing a twin that was swapped out for him.

Coinneach scrubbed his face. "Your mother gave me to Magnus and Elspeth?" Why hadn't his parents told him about it?

"My mother didna know what to do. She left you where crofters gathered and would find you. Magnus and Elspeth didna know who you belonged to. She must have just birthed Tamhas, and then she raised the two of you as twins."

He thought back to his earlier years growing up. "I...I couldna change into a wolf like Tamhas did when my mother shifted." Now, some of it was making sense.

They'd been so worried about it, but at the same time, reassuring. He knew that a mother had to shift for the baby to do so until they were older.

"Aye. I'm so sorry, Coinneach."

"My birth mother is dead then." Coinneach regretted that he had never met her, never had a chance to love her as he knew he would have. "What of my da?"

Aisling released his hands, turned away from him, and stared at the waterfall cascading down the rocky slope. "That is the dangerous part."

Coinneach listened, not daring to interrupt, his hands knotted together so tightly that they turned pale. Then he finally found his voice again. "Your mother is the midwife."

"No' back then."

He knew Aisling didn't want to tell him the whole truth. "I'm glad you've told me what you have. I thought there was something wrong with me that I couldn't shift when my brother did when I was younger."

"Nay, 'tis no' your fault. When a mother dies before her child is around five, they canna shift. 'Tis the natural order of things. My mother felt terrible about it. The midwife threatened to kill her if she revealed the truth."

"I dinna understand why a bairn would be any threat to anyone. Wait, how did your mother recognize I was the baby she had abandoned?" His parents had raised him, and he felt nothing but love for them. Though he planned to work at the castle, he would return home whenever he wasn't working to see how everyone was faring.

"Your birthmark."

Then it all made sense. He'd been working in the fields, shirtless, and Blair had seen the wolf's head on his shoulder. Her eyes had focused on it right before she fainted.

"So when I was born, the midwife had seen it also."

"Aye."

"Had anyone else? My da?"

"Nay. He never saw you. He only saw the deceased bairn. He was said to go off in the forest for hours and howl, so devastated he was from losing his mate and son. He dearly loved her."

Coinneach stared at the waterfall. Everything in his life had been a lie. Though he didn't fault his parents. Once he had been abandoned, he could have died, but they had saved his life. More than that, they had made him part of the family as if Elspeth had birthed him herself.

He ran his hands through his hair. "Who was the midwife?"

"If you're going to work at the castle—"

"I am. And I'll protect you and your mother."

Aisling's eyes widened, and her tense posture relaxed.

"I wouldna let anyone harm either of you."

"But you are at risk also."

"If I know what I'm up against, I can fight it."

"She's very powerful." Aisling was wringing her hands, looking fearful.

The only one he could think of that would be powerful enough to cause him trouble was the chief's wife. But he couldn't imagine she had been a midwife before that.

"No' Morag," he ventured.

"Aye." When Aisling's words finally faltered, she let out a breath that sounded like surrender. She looked at him, eyes shining, mouth trembling, and for a moment, he thought she might vanish —turn to mist, to memory, to myth. But then she reached for him, pulling his head into her lap, cradling him with a gentleness that undid him completely.

He waited, his face pressed to the warmth of her thigh, until she spoke again.

"I didna know about it."

He took hold of Aisling's cold hands, pulled them around him, and wrapped his arms around her. "This has naught to do with you. I dinna blame your mother for what she had done. I'm grateful that she didna kill me like Morag had ordered. You can tell her so."

"But dinna you see that Morag will want my mother dead, me too, if she suspects my mother told me about you, and she canna allow your da to know you are alive. But there is more. Rupert isna Hamish's son. Which is even more of a reason why Morag doesna want Hamish to learn you are his firstborn and only son."

"So Rupert isna my half brother."

"Nay. What will we do?"

Coinneach rubbed her back reassuringly, not wanting her to worry about it. "I willna discuss this with my parents. They are my mother and da as far as I'm concerned, and Tamhas is my twin brother."

"What about your birthmark?" Aisling ran her hand over it in a loving caress.

"I willna remove my shirt when I'm at the castle."

She still didn't look reassured.

"If only your mother, you, and I knew about it, it would be no problem."

"Did you talk to your parents about working for Drustan?"

"Nay, no' yet. I wanted to see what danger lay before us at the castle first." He smiled at her, trying to reassure her that he wasn't serious in the least. But he had wanted to meet with her first and learn what her mother had to say. "Come with me, and I'll tell them about working at the castle."

"Do you think it will be easier if I'm with you when you do it?"

No, but he wanted to spend more time with her, and if she was free, he wanted to take her with him. "Aye, of course."

"But you're no' going to mention that Hamish is your da?"

"Nay." Then Coinneach took her hand and walked back down the path through the woods and to the meadow.

"We have no' played as wolves in a while."

"Nay. We've both been busy. Maybe once I'm at the castle, we can do so."

"We will both be busy there."

He loved playing with her as a wolf, and he would make it his priority to find some time to take her to the forest and run as wolves.

When he saw his da helping Tamhas repair the roof, Coinneach felt bad that he had not been there to assist.

"I'll speak to my da on the roof, while you visit with my mother."

Aisling inclined her head and called into the house, "How now, Elspeth."

"Oh, my, 'tis always a pleasure to see you."

"How was the meal at the castle?" his da asked as Coinneach took his place and began adding the new thatched materials to the roof.

"I got to see Aisling."

His da smiled. "It appears you brought her home. Tell us what happened at the castle."

"I fought Chief Hamish's champion and unconventionally beat him."

His da and Tamhas laughed.

"Drustan, who is in charge of the guards, wants me to work for him." Coinneach wanted to tell his da right up front.

His da handed him some more thatch to add to the roof while Tamhas retrieved some more. "I knew the day would come that you would work for Chief Hamish."

"Tamhas needs to have his own family and run the croft when the time comes." Coinneach had told his family so many times.

"Aye. You are both good at farming, but Tamhas has his heart in it while you are aching to see the lass at the castle." His da sounded like he knew this would be the way it played out.

"I will be back to help out whenever I can."

"Aye. You are a good son."

But not his flesh and blood son. Coinneach had to shake loose of the grim thoughts he had about dealing with Morag. He wanted to expose her in the worst way—if only so that Blair and Aisling wouldn't be her targets for termination. He had to do so in a way that Blair wasn't harmed for her part in all this.

"I love being here, but you know me. I have always wanted to do something more." Coinneach helped overlap some of the thatch.

"Aye. Tamhas will be glad for it."

Tamhas returned to the house with another cartload of heather to rethatch the roof.

"Your brother is finally leaving the croft so that he can work at the castle," their da told Tamhas.

At first, Tamhas looked surprised, but then he smiled. "What are you going to do there?"

"I'll be a guard, a warrior." And Coinneach would protect Blair and her daughter at all costs.

"That suits you. Especially once you bested the chief's champion, I overheard." Tamhas looked thrilled. "When are you leaving?"

"So you can move a lass in to take over my palette?" Coinneach jested.

"Aye. You have your lass already. I was just waiting for us to have more room in the croft."

"I will start work on the morrow." Coinneach was glad his da and brother were all right with him moving out of the croft, but he still needed to tell his mother.

~

"LIFE IS SO UNCERTAIN," Elspeth said to Aisling as she helped her make bread.

"Aye." Aisling and Elspeth had heard everything Coinneach and Magnus had said on top of the roof.

His mother had only smiled. "To best the champion is something to behold."

"Aye. I've never seen anything like it, and what was so great was that he had Coinneach sit beside him in a place of honor at one of the tables." She hoped he wouldn't help her serve more of the meal, as he had before.

Elspeth glanced at her. "He will be well-liked among the other pack members, I'm sure. You and Coinneach need to mate, to be there for each other as humans and wolves."

"I agree."

"You dinna want to waste time—"

"Courting?" Aisling smiled at her.

Elspeth's cheeks reddened as she appeared flustered. "There is so much more to being mated wolves." She blushed anew.

"Aye. We look forward to it and we dinna intend to wait long."

"We will have a simple ceremony in the meadow?" Elspeth asked.

"Aye. We would be honored."

"Now that Coinneach will be working at the castle, he'll see more of you."

"I hope we willna be in trouble for it when we try to spend some time with each other."

"Some will understand young love." Elspeth took hold of Aisling's hands. "He is brave, kind, and caring. He will stand up for those who are downtrodden. But he...he sometimes believes someone is good of heart, when they are no'. He willna believe he needs to be looked after, but he does. That's why you will be good for him. Even when a Viking tries to shoot him with an arrow."

Aisling's mouth gaped. His mother had known about it?

"We couldna reach Coinneach in time to save him. We knew when you did, you had a bond that was meant to be. We kept your secret because you wanted it kept."

Aisling smiled. "He's a hero. I heard him howl to the castle guards and the other crofters about the trouble."

"Aye, he is a hero."

The men all came into the croft, and Aisling said, "I need to return to the castle."

"I'll escort you. Mother, I'll be..."

"Working as a castle guard. We heard you talking on the roof. I'm proud of you and know you'll do your duty wherever they put you." Elspeth hugged him. "We love you, son."

He hugged her back. "I'm returning."

"I'll have all your stuff packed before you get back." Tamhas laughed.

Smiling, Coinneach slapped him on the back. "I hate packing. I appreciate it."

He grasped Aisling's hand and led her out of the croft. Together, they made their way through the meadow toward the castle. As the moonlight shone over the heather, she hoped they would arrive before the gates were shut.

"I will see you in the morn. I'll probably have to break my fast there."

"You willna help me serve the meal."

He shared a flask of honeyed mead with her as they walked through the heather.

"Aye. I didna mean to embarrass you or get you in trouble."

"We served up the food so fast that I had to serve the head table after that."

He smiled. "I wondered why you were doing that and no' serving us further."

"Aye. And Gormelia was fit to be tied because she normally serves the champion's table."

"Who do you normally serve?"

"The women's table, which is fine with me."

They waved at the guards as they approached the gate. The guards inclined their heads toward them, a change from their previous behavior.

"It seems you now have some status among the guards for besting Aodhan."

"I probably wouldna be able to do it again."

7

Coinneach held Aisling's hand as they made their way through the inner bailey to the castle. "I will see you in the morning to break our fast."

"I canna wait to visit with you more often while you're working at the castle. What are you going to do about Morag?" Aisling sounded fearful that he would try to reveal the truth about what she had done.

"Naught. If she causes you and your mother trouble, I'll expose her for what she truly stands for."

"You will be her biggest target if she learns who you are. You have to be careful."

"I will be." But he worried more about Aisling and her mother and was glad he would be closer to them to help keep them safe.

When they reached the castle doors, tall and imposing, made of dark, weathered wood, they hugged and shared a kiss, their lips meeting in a soft and tender dance. The taste of each other's breath mingled with the sweetness of honeyed mead. Coinneach kissed her with an intensity that made his heart and hers race. She kissed him back with the same passion.

He ran his hands through her hair, flowing softly in the breeze, loving the feel of the soft, silky strands. Their bodies pressed against each other in a comforting warmth. He suspected that the guards posted on the wall walk were watching them, the most interesting thing that had happened while they were on duty this evening.

Drustan intervened, smiled at Aisling, and shook his head. "See you in the morning, Coinneach."

"Aye, see you then."

Following a final kiss goodbye with Aisling, Coinneach waved and made his way back to the croft. Nearly all his belongings were already packed in bags beside his pallet. As promised, Tamhas had taken care of packing Coinneach's items and was smiling at him from his own bed.

Coinneach laughed. "I knew you were serious."

"Aye. I will miss you though." Tamhas sounded sincere about it.

"I will miss you too, brother."

"You willna be a stranger," his mother said.

"Nay, you know me. I will be back."

"You will find what you are looking for," his da said, and then they retired to bed.

Coinneach pondered how he wanted to deal with Morag. Alternatively, his focus was on starting a new job, mastering as many combat skills as possible, and defending their clan from foes, provided Morag didn't harm Blair and Aisling.

That was the crux of the matter.

Being accepted as the chief's son wasn't a priority for him, as he doubted Blair's word would hold much weight after so long. He felt no particular connection to the chief, viewing him merely as a just and confident leader, not a father figure. To him, Magnus was his true father, the one who had imparted all his knowledge and taken care of him from the time he was born.

Coinneach was concerned that if Hamish believed Blair had abandoned him in the wilderness to endure any fate, the chief might decide to execute her or exile her from the pack. Coinneach didn't want that to happen.

He wished for Aisling's mother to understand that he held no grudges. However, if the chief were to banish Blair or do something worse, Aisling would be heartbroken, and Coinneach would have to consider other options.

As Aisling made her way to the women's quarters to settle in for the night, Gormelia, accompanied by two friends, confronted her, poking her finger at her chest. "You think you're so important now that you're seeing Coinneach because he defeated our champion."

"Not at all. Coinneach is the exceptional one. Don't worry, I'll be serving at the women's table tomorrow as usual. Cook only had me serve at the champion's table because Coinneach was a guest and we are courting." Aisling and Gormelia had never been on friendly terms.

Their animosity started when Gormelia belittled her mother's healing abilities. Aisling had dropped a heavy pot on her foot, though she had always sworn it had been an accident. Gormelia was a bully who always needed a couple of women by her side to boost her confidence. Alone, she wouldn't dare confront Aisling with her disparaging remarks.

Aisling suspected that Gormelia's hostility might also stem from Rupert ignoring Gormelia's attempts to catch his attention, when instead he continued to try to get Aisling's interest.

So instead, Gormelia had tried to gain the champion's attention, but he was more interested in fighting than courting lasses.

Aisling's mother approached, and Gormelia and her friends marched off to their pallets across the room.

"Trouble again with Gormelia?" Her mother was speaking low for Aisling's ears only.

"Aye. She was furious that I served the champion's table."

"I saw her try to upset your tray. I wanted to hit her for it. Most of the women at our table did too. And I saw Coinneach helping you serve the meal." Her mother took a deep breath. "What did you tell him?"

"Everything. But he doesna blame you for any of it. He still wants your favor so that we can mate. Elspeth wants the wedding to be in the meadow."

Her mother remained silent.

"Coinneach said he wouldna remove his shirt when he is at the castle."

Rubbing her eyes, her mother said, "What if anyone sees the resemblance between the chief and Coinneach? They're both tall, both have the same-colored hair and eyes. They have the same facial structure and when they smile..." Her mother shook her head. "'Tis so risky."

"You see these things because you know he's his son." Now Aisling saw the resemblance as well. She hoped no one else would.

"What about Magnus and Elspeth? Did Coinneach tell them the truth?"

"Nay, and he doesna plan to." However, if circumstances changed, Aisling suspected the truth would come out.

"He willna try to take revenge against"—her mother glanced around the room where everyone was settling down for the night, and they did too—"the person responsible?"

"Nay." However, Aisling knew things would change if Morag tried to harm them.

Her mother pulled her blanket over her shoulder and sighed. "I hope you have no' signed our death warrants."

∾

COINNEACH WAS UP EARLIER than anyone, chopping wood to add to the woodpile and gathering water for his mother to break their fast. Once he had awakened, he couldn't sleep, excited about his new position, but he didn't want to leave his family with all the chores before heading to the castle.

His mother peered out the door, rubbing the sleep from her eyes. "You are up early."

"I couldna sleep."

His mother came out and hugged him. "You be careful while you're working at the castle. We might live a simpler life, but we dinna have to deal with all the pack members' disputes within the clan. You willna be prepared for the backbiting between the wolves, vying for power."

Which made him think of Morag making a play for the chief when his wife died. "Aye, I will be careful."

He was glad that Aisling had told him the truth, or he wouldn't have known who to keep an eye on.

His da came out next. "Hey, son, you're no' going to do all the chores so Tamhas can sleep all day."

Coinneach knew Tamhas would have his work cut out for him when he was gone. "He packed my bags last night. I was returning the favor."

Stretching his arms above his head, Tamhas finally left the croft. "What's everybody doing up so early?" His eyes widened as he saw the woodpile. "You cut enough firewood to last us for months." Then he smiled. "Thanks."

"Well, they'll be expecting you at the castle," his da said. "They willna like it if you're late."

His mother hugged him again, as if he was going away for good.

"I'll be back." He hugged her, and then his da and his brother. "If you need me for anything, you come for me or howl." He was serious. If they needed help, he wouldn't hesitate to go to their aid.

∽

AISLING COULD BARELY SLEEP. She was so excited about seeing Coinneach at the champion's table, but then she realized she would be working the women's table again. Still, she hoped to see him after the meal.

When she arrived at the kitchen to prepare the meal, Cook said, "You will work the champion's table again."

Aisling couldn't help the smile that appeared. She was so thrilled. She glanced at Gormelia, who was scowling at her, but this time she didn't tell Cook that it was her table to work.

"What table will I serve then?" Gormelia asked.

"The women's table. And if you try to knock a tray from another server's hands out of spite again, you'll be dismissed from the kitchen and have to find a position to work elsewhere."

Aisling couldn't believe that Cook knew all about the incident. She was glad she had taken Gormelia to task. Gormelia gave Aisling a slicing glare as if she would get her back.

But Aisling hadn't been the one to start anything. Still, she would have to watch her back.

When she carried the bread to the champion's table, she smiled at Coinneach. Butterflies took flight in her stomach. She was so thrilled he was there.

He grinned at her, but didn't help her serve the bread this time, and she was relieved. She finished serving the table and saw Gormelia glowering at her as she delivered the last bread to the women's table.

They walked back to the kitchen, Gormelia leading the way. But then Gormelia turned around and scowled at Aisling. "One mistake and you willna get your way."

Aisling brushed past her. If anyone made a mistake, they paid for it; that was true. The same would apply to Gormelia, if she made a mistake while cooking or serving the pack members.

"Are you still practicing with that Viking bow?" Cook asked Aisling as they started to serve the porridge.

"Aye. Every chance I can get. If our enemies ever invade, I want to be able to fight them off."

"But you didna find that bow dropped in the woods."

Aisling didn't say anything. She wasn't giving up her secret.

"You killed a Viking for it." How did Cook even know that?

Everyone was watching them now, even Gormelia. Was Cook trying to tell Gormelia to lay off her? That she was a force to be reckoned with? That worked for Aisling.

"Aye," Aisling finally said, albeit reluctantly.

"Nay, you dinna." Gormelia waved a knife at her that she'd been using to cut up the cheese. "Coinneach has a Viking sword. He must have given you the dead man's bow, but *he* killed the Viking."

"Believe what you will." Aisling wasn't going to say that Coinneach hadn't killed the Viking. Besides, there could have been two Vikings that they had eliminated. Maybe Cook's words would make Gormelia back off with her threats before it escalated to something worse.

COINNEACH EYED the brown-haired Morag as she sat beside Chief Hamish at the long wooden head table with contempt. He couldn't feel any other way about her. Rupert wasn't to blame for his mother's actions, but if he was loyal to his mother, which Coinneach suspected, he needed to be watched also.

Morag's features were sharp and severe, carved as if from basalt, and her mouth was set in a sneer. Did she ever soften the look with a smile or by laughing? She had a hawkish nose, and her eyes were as dark brown as her hair.

Aodhan slapped Coinneach on the back. "Why do you look so serious this morn?"

Coinneach lost his frown and smiled. "I'm grateful to be here."

"And to have your lass serve you, aye?" Aodhan finished his bread.

"I'm glad to be able to see her, aye, certes."

Then the light of Coinneach's eyes swept into the great hall. Aisling served Aodhan first and then Coinneach, all smiles.

"I see you get to continue to serve our table," Aodhan said.

"Aye. Cook was very generous in allowing me to do so today." Then she smiled again at Coinneach and hurried off to deliver the rest of the porridge to the others at the table.

"She could brighten any man's day." Aodhan finished his porridge.

She certainly could.

Then she delivered the meat pies. She always gave Aodhan two of everything.

"Hamish's twin brother, Collum, wondered where you were from," Aodhan said as Aisling served the rest of the table.

"From the croft beyond the castle."

"Aye." Aodhan dug into the cheese and venison pie. "But you are bigger than Magnus and Tamhas. And you dinna look like them."

"I've been with them from birth." That was the truth, but it still chilled Coinneach to think that anyone but Blair and Aisling knew who he was.

Aodhan shoved in another mouthful of pie. "Aye. Collum asked Chief Alasdair how he had come to know you. He said Magnus had saved his uncle during a battle."

"Aye. I was proud of my da when I learned of it. He had never mentioned it before."

"Humble then."

"He is."

Then Aodhan changed the subject. "You are scheduled for

weapons training after we finish here." He ate the rest of his second pie.

Coinneach glanced back at the hall that led to the kitchen.

Aodhan chuckled. "I'm sure you can get a quick kiss in with the lass before you get sweaty with your workout."

That's all that Coinneach cared about. He eyed the high table, waiting for the chief to end the meal. When Hamish did, and those at the high table stood and started to leave, Coinneach sprinted for the kitchen, dodging other clansmen who were going to do their chores.

He heard Aodhan say loud enough for him to hear, "Aye, Drustan. The lad needs a kiss from Aisling to fortify himself for the workout."

The two men laughed.

Coinneach hurried into the kitchen, where Cook and her staff were now all eating.

They all turned to see him as he strode straight to the object of his affection and kissed her. "Good morning, lass. I'm off to prove my worth."

"Sword fighting?" She touched his shirt.

He placed his hand over hers. "Aye." He wanted to tell her he wouldn't remove his shirt, but he couldn't in front of the other women.

He kissed her again, but she stood and kissed him back. "Stay safe," she said.

Then he smiled at Cook and hurriedly left the kitchen before getting into trouble with Drustan. Coinneach had the fleeting thought that Drustan might pair him up with Aodhan, which could be a disaster.

8

J ust as Coinneach feared, he was pitted against Aodhan first. He couldn't use the same technique on Aodhan to take him down, not when the champion could be expecting it. Ready for the fight with Coinneach, Aodhan was grinning like a fool.

Coinneach's stomach twisted in knots; he sighed and drew his sword. Other men were gathered around, but they weren't fighting. They were watching to see what happened next between him and the champion. He had hoped no one would observe what was to come.

Aodhan had removed his shirt. Coinneach did not.

The two men took their stances. This time, Coinneach didn't hesitate to take the offensive and struck Aodhan's sword with such force that Aodhan faltered and nearly lost it.

Several of the men gasped in surprise. And then cheered.

Aodhan smiled, appearing pleased. His heart beating hard, Coinneach would not want to fight him in real combat. Aodhan swung at Coinneach, but he blocked his sword and leaped away to avoid the full brunt of the attack.

Coinneach jumped back into the fray and quickly thrust his

sword at Aodhan. The champion swung his sword to stop the thrust, but he didn't have the might that he would have had if he'd been more prepared.

Coinneach slashed at his sword again to keep him off guard, but striking the steel was like hitting a stone wall this time. Aodhan's muscular arms were massive. Again, Coinneach jumped out of the way to avoid another clash with Aodhan's sword.

And dove right in after Aodhan's swing missed him. Coinneach poked his sword at Aodhan's belly.

"I'll keep you on my side." Aodhan offered his hand.

Winded and sweating like crazy, Coinneach was glad the fight had ended. He shook Aodhan's hand in camaraderie. "I feel the same way about you."

"With you, I never know what to expect." Aodhan motioned to the other men. "Looks like some others want to try their chances with you."

Coinneach wondered if Aodhan had been holding back on him when fighting. He hated that he was second-guessing his ability to fight.

Then another man engaged Coinneach, and he gave it his all. Now that Coinneach wasn't fighting the champion, the others started to fight each other in practice. Aodhan was talking to a couple of maids who brought him ale, both smiling and fluttering their eyelashes at him.

The man Coinneach was fighting nearly knocked his sword from his hand, and he realized he had to concentrate!

Coinneach finally knocked his opponent's sword from his hand and was instantly besieged by a new sparring partner. He wasn't used to fighting this hard or long, and when he finally managed to knock the man off balance, he fell, and Coinneach was the victor.

Another man came to fight him, and Coinneach did his best to beat him. Farming worked different muscles, though swinging the ax to chop up so much firewood before he broke his fast this morning might have been one of the problems. He was ready to take a break.

This time, Coinneach was caught off guard. The man fighting him cut through his shirt and into his skin. Coinneach fell back. Blood stained the cloth.

Coinneach held up his hand to say he was done.

The other man shook his hand. "Are you all right?"

"Just a scratch."

Aisling rushed forth. "'Tis more than a scratch as much as you are bleeding. Come, we will see my mother and she'll take care of it."

Drustan came over to see how he fared. "Were you thinking of the lass when Tristan cut you?" Drustan smirked. "Remove your shirt so I can see how bad it is."

Her eyes wide, Aisling shook her head at Coinneach almost imperceptibly.

"'Tis naught," Coinneach said.

But Drustan insisted. "That's for me to decide since you work for me."

Coinneach didn't have a choice. He pulled off his shirt.

Aisling frowned. "I told you it was bad."

"So sorry, Coinneach," the man who had cut him said. Tristan was the same size as Coinneach, in terms of muscle and build.

"No problem." Coinneach would rather have lost his sword than been injured.

"Take him to see Blair." Drustan motioned to Aisling to take Coinneach with her.

"Aye." Aisling waited for Coinneach to put his shirt back on, took his hand, and pulled him toward the keep.

"'Tis no' that bad."

"If it gets infected, it will be bad." Aisling glanced at him. "I canna believe they pitted you against Aodhan again."

"Probably to see if I could best him in a swordfight this time. I dinna believe he used his full strength against me."

She scoffed. "He is the champion. He wouldna hold back."

Still, Coinneach had his doubts.

AISLING HAD BEEN HORRIFIED to see Coinneach pitted against Aodhan again. She was surprised when one of the men was ultimately able to cut Coinneach. She was glad Drustan had agreed with her that her mother needed to take care of Coinneach, but she wished he hadn't had him remove his shirt.

When they reached the castle doors, one of the men opened them, and they went inside. "I'll find my mother. You wait in the great hall."

He sighed. "Aye."

Aisling suspected he wished she hadn't made a fuss about his wound, but this could be serious. She ran up the stairs to the fourth floor and found her mother checking on Morag. Aisling didn't want to have to face her. Not that the woman paid her any attention, a lowly kitchen servant. But after learning what Morag had made her mother do, Aisling hated her.

"One of the men was wounded during the practice sword fight. He needs you to sew him up," Aisling said.

Her mother said, "Morag, you dinna have any issues with your health."

Morag waved her hand dismissively. "Go see to the man. Wait, who is it?"

Both women waited expectantly to hear who he was. Aisling didn't want to say in front of Morag, but she feared her silence would make her suspicious.

"Coinneach."

Morag gave a wicked smile. "Aodhan beat him this time."

"Nay, Tristan did."

"Tristan?" Morag's face turned into a scowl. "Coinneach was supposed to fight Aodhan."

"He did. And he beat him and three others. Then Tristan fought him and cut Coinneach." But Aisling couldn't believe that Morag knew that Coinneach was supposed to battle the champion. Had she set him up to take the fall?

"I must see to him," Aisling's mother said, and she and Aisling hurried off to the great hall.

They didn't speak for a while, but then her mother finally whispered, "Did he take off his shirt?"

"Nay, no' until Drustan wanted to see his wound. And then he put his shirt right back on."

"Och. And close up. Where is the wound?"

"Near his shoulder."

Her mother shook her head. "I tell you, this willna go well."

But Aisling was still thinking about Morag and how she had hoped Aodhan had hurt Coinneach. She was evil. She just hoped she didn't suspect who he was.

As soon as Aisling and her mother arrived at the great hall, they saw Gormelia giving Coinneach ale.

"You have no worries about him with her," Aisling's mother said.

Aisling knew she didn't have to worry that Coinneach would take an interest in Gormelia, but she still hated to see her try to stir up trouble between her and Coinneach.

"You can leave now, Gormelia," Aisling's mother said sternly.

"I was just keeping him company until you arrived." Gormelia smiled, but a glint of the devil marred her eyes. Then she sashayed off.

Aisling helped Coinneach remove his shirt. Her mother gasped.

"I told you he needed you."

"Aye. Tristan should be taken to task for injuring you so." Her mother cleaned the wound and then began to stitch it up.

"It was my folly." Coinneach winced when she poked the needle through his skin again.

"You can cry out if it makes you feel better." Aisling couldn't imagine suffering through the pain without making a sound, but all he did was grit his teeth, and her comment earned her a smile.

However, her mother was all business and continued to sew up the laceration. "You canna fight until this heals. You must change the dressing daily to avoid infection."

Once she had made twenty-one stitches, she applied an herbal poultice. Then she wrapped a bandage around his chest. When they heard someone else enter the great hall and saw it was Morag and a couple of her lady companions, Aisling's mother quickly wrapped the dressing around his shoulder to cover up his wolf birthmark and then tied it off.

Frowning, Morag drew close. "How bad is it?"

"He needed over twenty stitches," Aisling's mother said.

"Thank you, Blair. I must see where I'm needed now." Coinneach pulled on his shirt.

Before Aisling expected it, he kissed her on the mouth. Then he strode out of the great hall, maybe to avoid a confrontation with her mother for kissing her or Morag's continued interest in his wound. Then again, he probably just wanted to prove he could work on his first day on the job.

"Do you approve of their union?" Morag asked Aisling's mother.

Aisling held her breath to hear if her mother would say yes.

"You ken how it is with wolves when they meet the one who is the right one for them." Aisling's mother did not address the question.

"I suppose." Then Morag turned on her heel and left, her maids dutifully following her out of the great hall.

Once they were gone, Aisling's mother said, "You see how we can all be in danger?"

"WHAT DID Blair say about your working?" Drustan asked Coinneach when he sought him out.

"No fighting for a few days. You know, as wolves, we heal fast."

"All right. I'm putting you on wall duty. Aodhan, who no longer has to serve in that capacity, said he would show you how it's done. If you canna manage because of your wound, retire to the barracks."

"Aye." Coinneach had no intention of sleeping for now.

Aodhan joined them, and Drustan inclined his head to him and left.

"How bad is it?" Aodhan asked as he and Coinneach climbed the tower stairs to the wall walk.

"Nothing to worry about."

"If we are to work together and have each other's backs, we must be honest with each other. I need only to ask Blair, and she will tell me the truth."

"About twenty stitches."

"God's wounds. That's worse than any cut I've ever gotten. How did Tristan manage to slice you?"

"I lost focus. It willna happen again, though I would rather it be me that was injured than him."

"All right. We have this section of the wall to watch. Others are posted on the other wall walks. With our great wolf's night vision, we can see movement easily from way up here. Most of the time, our worst enemy is boredom and fighting sleep."

That didn't sound very appealing. Coinneach was thinking more of riding into battle and fighting their enemies.

"Because of your wound, if you feel as though you're succumbing to sleep—"

"I willna retire to the barracks." How would that look to everyone in the pack? Coinneach gets a little cut and has to sleep the day away?

"Nay. You can rest, and I'll keep watch. We will be relieved two hours after nightfall. Our meals will be served here. Mayhap your bonny lass will bring us our meals this time." Aodhan watched the meadow stretching out before them, the forest, and a couple of crofts closer to the castle.

Coinneach hoped so. His wound ached something fierce. He drank some of his ale. Then he took up a position about thirty feet from Aodhan.

When everyone working in the inner bailey went into the keep for the noon meal, Coinneach's stomach growled.

"After they have served the meal to everyone in the keep, some of the women will bring our food," Aodhan explained.

Coinneach wanted to watch the tower stairs, hoping Aisling would soon bring their meals, but his job was to watch for the enemy.

After what seemed like an eternity, they heard someone approaching the tower stairs.

Aisling appeared, carrying a wild boar and bread. She smiled brightly at them both, but then she frowned. "You make sure that Coinneach returns to the barracks if he grows fatigued."

Aodhan took the boar and bread from her, his eyes alight with mirth. "Aye, of course."

Then she handed the meal to Coinneach. Once he held it in his hands, she reached up and touched his forehead. "No fever, thank the goddesses."

Before he took a bite of his meat, he leaned over and kissed her. "Thank Cook for sending you to us."

"Gormelia wanted the task when she learned Aodhan was up

on the wall walk serving guard duty. She is even angrier with me than ever before. No matter. She canna get her way in all things." But Aisling knew the spiteful woman would cause more trouble for her.

"Is that why she brought me ale when I waited for your mother to stitch me up?" Coinneach raised his brows, appearing to realize the woman's motives suddenly.

Aisling hadn't wanted to tell him about her trouble with Gormelia, but she supposed it would come out eventually. "Aye. You need no' be concerned."

Both men frowned. Aodhan said, "I'm no' interested in the woman. She is a pest. Feel free to call upon me if you need my help in quelling her ire."

Coinneach said, "Why dinna you tell me this before?"

"She is a bully, naught more."

The dark look in his blue eyes meant he would deal with her in his own way.

Aisling patted his chest. "I know that look. I had already dropped a heavy iron pot on her foot when she spoke disparagingly about my mother. I can handle her."

But Coinneach disagreed, and she knew he planned to do something to discourage Gormelia from giving Aisling any further grief.

She quickly kissed him then. "I must hurry back to the castle, or I will miss my meal.

He set his food on top of the crenelated wall, pulled her into a hug, and kissed her. "Thank you for bringing the food to us. And take care, sweeting."

"Aye, you too." Then she quickly hurried off with a backward wave and disappeared into the tower.

~

"IF I WERE PURSUING a fierce lass like her, I would claim her as mine without delay," Aodhan declared.

Coinneach barely heard him, his thoughts lingering on that venomous Gormelia. The heavy meal and afternoon sun conspired against him, and sleep claimed him atop the wall walk against his will.

A gentle tugging at his garment roused him. He bolted upright, causing Blair to recoil in surprise.

"Aodhan mentioned you were...in need of rest." Worry flickered across her features.

"Just a moment's rest," Coinneach muttered. The crimson sunset told him otherwise—hours had passed. He wondered about Aodhan's failure to rouse him.

"Your injury needs tending," Blair insisted.

He was going to say it was fine, but Blair's expression, her set jaw, and her chin tilted up—now he knew where Aisling's stubbornness came from—he knew Aisling's mother would have her way. He pulled off his shirt, and she carefully removed his bandage.

She exhaled in relief. "It's starting to heal."

He felt pleased to hear it. At that moment, he understood she needed to witness it herself. Perhaps now she finally believed he would be a suitable partner for her daughter.

"You shouldna have served on guard duty. You should have been abed in the barracks."

"I'm well-rested now." He didn't want her to tell Drustan what had happened.

Blair scoffed as she covered up Coinneach's wound and his birthmark again, though there was no need to this time. "You will be no good to us if you are dead."

For the first time, she acknowledged that he could shield them, and he was humbled. "I will protect you and Aisling with my life."

Blair shook her head as he pulled his shirt back on and tucked it into his plaid. "Let's hope you willna have to." Then she hurried off.

When it came time for the last meal of the day, Aisling brought them bread, cheese, and pottage. "Mother said you were asleep on duty. I wanted to see you. She said if too many people did, the word would get out. Are you all right?"

"Aye. I feel much better. I barely just closed my eyes in truth."

From a distance, Aodhan contradicted him by holding up his right hand, indicating five hours had passed.

Aisling shook her head. "Och, Coinneach. We said there would be no secrets between us."

"How would I know how long I slept? Then Blair was here trying to undress me."

"Aodhan had to send a messenger to get my mother just to make sure you were all right."

"Your mother told you I was healing properly, aye?"

"And that you should have been sleeping in the barracks. She willna make the same mistake twice if you are ever wounded again. Next time, she will tell Druston what your restrictions are."

"Aye, but there will be no next time."

Aisling hugged him tightly. He wrapped his arms around her in a warm embrace, but then she kissed him quickly. "I've got to run and eat my meal."

"Thanks, Aisling."

Then she hurried off, waved, and disappeared into the tower.

"You got a proper scolding." Aodhan joined him, and they stood at the wall, observing the landscape, eating their food. "True sign of love."

Coinneach smiled. "Aye."

An hour before their relief arrived, Tamhas howled that danger was approaching the crofts.

Immediately, Coinneach bolted for the stairs.

"We still have guard duty," Aodhan reminded him, but he was right on his heels.

"Aye, but we're doing naught on guard duty, and that was my brother's warning of danger."

Drustan met them as they exited the tower stairs. "Where are you two going? You have another hour on watch duty."

"To save my family." Coinneach would never forgive himself if anything happened to his family because he wasn't there to protect them.

"I'm going with him so he doesna get himself killed," Aodhan said.

Drustan called out to two men to take their places on the wall walk.

Tristan joined them, wanting to go with them, but Coinneach said, "No. We'll be less easy to spot if it is just the two of us." He appreciated that Tristan offered, and that Aodhan volunteered to accompany him.

"I'm gathering reinforcements anyway," Drustan said.

"Aye," Aodhan said.

The two of them went to the gates where everyone was coming in for the night, and the gates would be shut. He and Aodhan raced across the meadow until they drew closer to Coinneach's family's croft.

There, they saw five Vikings, one holding up the short sword from the Viking Aisling had killed. All the Vikings held torches to see their way.

"I dinna see the other weapons my brother carried with him—neither his bow nor his sword. We will burn the croft," Holgar, the dead Viking's brother, said.

Coinneach recognized him from before. He couldn't allow them to burn down his family's home. He and Aodhan inched forward from where they were hiding in the tall grasses.

Aodhan whispered, "I'll take the three on the right, and you can take the two on the left."

Just as one of them was about to go into the croft again, an arrow whizzed past Coinneach's ear, only inches from behind him, and hit the man in the chest with a thud. Two more followed, and the raider fell to the ground, the torch landing on his chest and catching him on fire. But he was already dead.

Coinneach and Aodhan jerked around, figuring it was one of their archers, but it was Aisling, and she'd had her second Viking kill. He couldn't believe she'd followed them here to help them fight the Vikings. He was grateful to her, but also worried about her.

"The two on the left are mine, and the two on the right are yours," Aodhan whispered to Coinneach.

"Spread out," Holgar shouted. "Kill the archer!"

One of the men tried to toss his torch on the roof of the croft, and immediately an arrow struck his chest. Then another. He collapsed, his torch burning the grass around him.

"The one on the left is mine, and the two on the right are yours," Aodhan said to Coinneach. "And we'd better take them down before Aisling gets the rest."

Coinneach was on the move in a heartbeat, running low, hidden, a warrior unseen. Then he came upon one of the Vikings. They had to kill all the men, or word would get back to their people that they had to kill the crofters in this croft, burn them out, and seek revenge for Tamhas having Ivor's sword, and for killing two of their men.

The man's eyes widened in surprise as he saw Coinneach jump up from the tall grasses and strike at him. Coinneach felled him in one slash of his sword. But then Holgar came at him from the side, swinging an ax. Coinneach struck Holgar's ax as hard as he could, knocking it away from slicing his chest in two.

Aodhan was fighting the other man, their swords clashing,

metal clanging, the harsh reality of the ongoing battle ringing in the air.

Coinneach's earlier wound was hurting something fierce, streaks of pain shooting out of it, as Blair's words haunted him. "You canna fight for three days."

"You have my brother's sword," Holgar said, angrier than before.

Holgar came at him with a swing of the ax. Coinneach struck his ax again.

Holgar wasn't as massive as Aodhan, but he was heavily muscled, and every swing and thrust of his ax and, alternately, his short sword, if they had connected with Coinneach's flesh, would have killed him.

Holgar came in closer with his short sword and stabbed at Coinneach. He struck Holgar's sword so hard that he lost it in the tall grass.

Except for the torches and the fires they had ignited when they fell, the light was low. Holgar couldn't see half as well as Coinneach could in the dark.

Before Holgar could recover and swing his deadly ax again, Coinneach thrust his sword into the Viking's chest. He quickly yanked his sword out and readied it again, not trusting that he'd given Holgar a mortal wound. Holgar's eyes were wide with surprise.

Aodhan was watching from a few feet away.

Holgar fell forward, collapsing on the ground on his chest.

"We must put out the fires, but we dinna know if there are others who were with these men," Coinneach said. "And we must get rid of the bodies."

"Aye, I'm getting the water." Aisling was carrying two buckets filled with water.

Immediately, he wanted to carry the buckets for Aisling, but he knew that the three of them would be needed. He grabbed some more buckets for Aodhan and him, and they raced to the creek as Aisling poured water on one of the torchlit fires.

Aisling was headed for the creek again as they were returning with filled buckets when they heard horses galloping toward them from the direction of the castle.

"It looks like Drustan sent reinforcements to help us," Aodhan said.

"They're too late." Coinneach dumped his buckets on another fire, then rushed back to the creek.

"Nay, they will dispose of the bodies for us, finish putting the fires out, and we will retire to bed." Aodhan bypassed him and filled up his buckets with water.

Aisling joined them and filled hers.

"How long did you watch me fight Holgar?" Coinneach tried to keep up with Aodhan as Aisling followed them from a considerable distance behind.

"From the beginning. How did you know his name? I assume Tamhas didna kill his brother," Aodhan said.

"Nay, I did," Aisling called out from behind them.

"No' with a bow and arrow." Aodhan glanced back at her.

She smiled. "As a wolf."

Aodhan nodded. "She is a keeper."

"Aye. I know. She saved my life," Coinneach said. "You didna come to aid me against Holgar, Aodhan." Coinneach thought they were supposed to have each other's backs. And Coinneach was still dealing with a painful wound. He spoke the words not in condemnation but wishing to learn what Aodhan had been thinking.

"I told you. The two men on our right were yours to fight."

"But Aisling killed two of the men you said you would battle." Coinneach didn't see the logic in it as he poured more water on the fires, groaning in pain. He glanced down at his shirt and saw that it was covered in fresh blood.

"I was busy fighting when you killed the first man, and then you became engaged with Holgar. 'Tis a matter of honor. The man who sought revenge would have continued to come after your family once he learned you had his brother's weapons. Unless you couldna fight any longer, I had to let you prove you were the better fighter. And you showed you were."

The riders from the castle, including Tristan, soon joined them, dismounted, and began hauling water from the creek, and quickly put out the remaining fires.

A wave of dizziness crashed over Coinneach, and he grabbed Aodhan's arm before he fell headfirst into the grass.

Aodhan quickly held him up. "You're bleeding. Why didna you tell me? That would have been different. I would have killed Holgar for you."

Coinneach weakly laughed.

Aisling dropped her empty buckets and ran to Coinneach. She removed his shirt. "You were no' supposed to be fighting. What were you thinking? And you"—she gave Aodhan a stern look— "you knew he was wounded earlier. You should have taken care of Holgar. I would have, but Coinneach was in my line of sight and I couldna hit Holgar with one of my arrows."

"Aye, lass, just as I was saying. Coinneach fought so well, I didna remember him being wounded." Aodhan sounded truly repentant.

She wrapped the cloth from her head around Coinneach's bloody bandage. "Someone needs to give Coinneach a ride back to the castle. He needs to see my mother at once." She helped him on with his shirt.

Tristan offered his horse. "I'll help you to get him on the horse. Aisling, you can go with him to ensure he stays in the saddle. We'll take care of the dead men."

"Give Holgar's sword and the short sword to Tamhas," Coinneach said.

"Aye, it will be done." Tristan pointed at Holgar's weapons. "These?"

"Aye."

"You came late enough," Aodhan said to the gathered men who had finished putting the fires out and were now ready to take care of the bodies.

"Even though you said you didna need our help, we were gathering a force to come to your aid. Morag stopped us from helping you. She said you wouldna need anyone else's assistance. Then Chief Hamish learned about the two of you going to Coinneach's family's aid, that Aisling had slipped out to help you, and countermanded Morag's order. He wasna happy with her," Tristan said. "Nor was she with him."

Coinneach was glad for that. But Morag's actions made him wonder if she suspected who he was and hoped the Vikings would kill him, which would mean Blair was in more danger. And probably Aisling as well.

9

A isling's hands trembled with rage as she retrieved her bow and quiver from her pallet in the women's quarters. She'd heard every word of Morag's order for the soldiers to stand down, claiming that Aodhan and Coinneach would manage any trouble his family was having beyond the castle gates.

Once Morag had barked her command and the soldiers had fallen back like a tide retreating, Aisling stood dumbstruck in the dim corridor, her mouth agape, fists balled at her sides. Through the half-open door, she'd witnessed Morag's hard eyes, the clipped, private whisper in which she assured the captain that Aodhan and Coinneach could handle any threat the crofters could possibly be facing.

The words stank of conspiracy. Aisling's blood surged with a heat that lit her from scalp to toes, and she wanted nothing more than to throttle Morag right then and there, to scream her outrage until the castle's stones trembled and the banners shuddered from their poles.

But Morag's authority, for now, was absolute; the men would obey her, not some waifish girl with a wild streak and a bow. The guards outside the chamber door stood with their faces politely blank, but Aisling caught the glint of amusement in their eyes as she stormed past them, her braid lashing her back like a whip. She shouldered past a knot of servants cowering in the hallway and skidded on the rushes as she rounded the corner toward the gates.

Without wasting a moment, she'd waved to Niven, the lad who was their messenger boy, urgently telling him to warn Chief Hamish about the trouble at Coinneach's home.

She couldn't wait for Hamish to issue orders to send the men, if he even did. The gates had already been closed, and she had threatened the guards that if they did not open the gate, she would hold them accountable. Which had brought a smile to their lips as if they thought she was funny to think she could best any of them.

Her mind was a blizzard of curses. How dare Morag? How dare she? The crofters might not live at the castle, but they were still part of the wolf pack.

The gates themselves loomed massive, iron-bound, and shut fast. Two guards flanked the portal, one picking at his teeth with a twig, the other watching her. They straightened when they saw her, but neither moved to block her way; their orders, she guessed, were to keep the rabble outside, not to restrain a kitchen maid.

She didn't slow, didn't blink. "Open the gate," she ordered, already stringing her bow.

The first guard, young and pale, stammered, "We—Morag said—"

"Do you see she willna be stopped, Everett?" Ruadh and Everett pushed at the gates.

They creaked open a hand's breadth, then a full span. Aisling slipped through, into the half-wild meadow beyond the walls. The air outside was thick with the scent of bruised grass and distant heather.

She ran, bow in hand, every muscle in her body straining forward, as if she could outrun Morag's betrayal, outrun the years of being told to hold her tongue and know her place. The meadow grass whipped her shins; nettles stung her calves.

When she reached Aodhan and Coinneach, she couldn't believe Aodhan would lay out the tactics, and when she took out two of the men he planned to target, he only had one left. Coinneach had to fight two when he was wounded!

She was glad she had taken Aodhan to task and even gladder that Hamish was irritated with Morag for making such a decision and that Hamish had sent men to help. Morag had no business running warfare matters unless she was the only one left in charge at the castle to do so.

As Aisling hugged Coinneach while they rode to the castle, she didn't scold him for going into battle against an enemy intent on destroying his family's home, despite her mother telling him not to fight until his wound healed. She understood his need to protect his loved ones. She felt the same way about her mother and his family.

"You are much skilled with the bow," Coinneach said.

His comment pleased her. "I practice every chance I get in case I have to save you again and canna wear my wolf coat."

"You took down Aodhan's targets first." He sounded amused.

"They were about to torch your croft, so aye. I didna know he would continue to believe that the other two men were yours to handle."

"I'm glad Holgar didna know you had his brother's bow."

"He realized you had his sword though." She snuggled closer to Coinneach. "I canna lose you."

"Nor I you."

"Did Morag stop the soldiers from going to our aid because she suspects something about me?"

"I dinna know, but I sent a messenger to speak to the chief at once. I couldna wait for them to aid you. I must tell you that Cook asked me if I had killed the Viking who owned the bow, and I finally said I had. I believe Cook brought it up in front of the kitchen staff so Gormelia would know I wasna one to be trifled with."

"I'm glad Cook did."

"Gormelia said I couldna have done so, that you killed the Viking, took his sword and bow, and gave the bow to me."

"Well, now everyone will know you took down two Viking warriors with your bow. Only you, not Aodhan or me, were equipped with a bow."

"And you truly have taken down two Vikings on your own, though you shouldna have had to, wounded as you are." She was glad Coinneach wasn't killed during the encounter.

Some of the men who had come to their aid howled in their human form, telling the crofters the Vikings were gone, and they could safely return to their homes.

Once Coinneach and Aisling reached the castle, several pack members lingered to see that everyone was returning safe and sound. They would have to wait a bit longer for the others to return.

Blair also waited to see if anyone needed medical attention. Blair hurried forth when she observed only Coinneach and Aisling riding in together. She must have seen the fresh red stains on his shirt and smelled his blood.

Before Aisling could dismount, one man helped her off the horse. Two men aided Coinneach before he fell off the horse.

"Take him into the barracks," Blair ordered, sounding annoyed.

The men helped Coinneach into the barracks, despite his objections. "I'm fine. The stitches just broke loose."

"Because you were no' supposed to be fighting. Didna I say that?" Blair glanced at Aisling. "And what were you thinking? Going after Aodhan and Coinneach with just a bow and arrow?"

"She killed two of the five Vikings," Coinneach said. "Drustan will want to add you to his staff as well."

"Nay," Blair said.

"He is only jesting," Aisling said, scolding him. She helped him out of his shirt, and then her mother cleaned the wound again, repeatedly tsking.

Aisling retrieved fresh bandages and waited while her mother stitched the wound closed again. Then she helped her mother bandage him.

Drustan stalked into the barracks and shook his head. "Aodhan told me what the three of you had done." He smiled at Aisling. "I will have to have you join my archers."

Blair said, "Nay, you willna."

Drustan laughed.

Aodhan and the other men returned and joined them. "How bad is it?"

"It will heal." Coinneach was brusque with his response.

Aisling suspected he didn't like the warriors fussing over him.

"To bed with you," Blair said, with authority.

"Aye, do it," Drustan said, confirming that's where he needed to be. "I was sending a force to aid you, but learned afterward my order had been countermanded."

"We heard," Coinneach said.

Aodhan grabbed the bed next to him and removed his weapons and boots. "We both need sleep."

Aisling removed Coinneach's weapons and his boots. "Do you need anything? If Cook allows, I can go to the kitchen and get it for you."

"Nay, lass. All I need is sleep and you."

Aisling's cheeks grew hot. She wished he wouldn't say such a thing around her mother and others. To her privately, she welcomed his words.

"All right then." She leaned over and kissed him. "Sweet dreams, my hero."

He kissed her back. "Thanks for aiding us. I will see you in the morn."

Aisling and her mother left the barracks to return to the keep and retire to their beds. "Coinneach had to go to his family's aid," Aisling said.

"The other men should have gone in his place. And you shouldna have gone at all."

"He will be my mate." Aisling frowned at her mother. "We're serious about it and we'll mate with or without your approval before long."

"Aye, I know. It's inevitable."

"Then will you approve of our marriage?" Aisling hoped her mother was coming around.

"We are all tied together in this terrible mess. Aye, I give you my blessing."

Aisling hugged her mother. "I love you."

Her mother sighed. "We just have to be careful."

Aisling said, "Morag stopped the men from going to aid Coinneach and Aodhan."

"And you sent a messenger to inform Hamish."

Aisling had hoped no one would know she had done that. Morag would be angry with her if she were to learn of it.

"Niven only told me about what had happened."

The lad of nearly eleven was small for his age, but he held himself tall to make up for his small stature. Aisling had told him not to tell anyone who had sent him to see the Chief with the news. But Hamish might have asked him to verify the news's reliability.

From the far side of the bailey, Niven spotted Aisling with Blair, and his face split with a lopsided grin made for trouble. Niven was as much a fixture of the castle as the well-worn parapets or the echoing din of morning bells. His hair, dense and springing, seemed to have its own opinion about the wind that perpetually battered the keep.

He was ten, or nearly eleven—he asserted it was "ten and a third," but only when asked in front of others—and his brisk, self-important stride cut through the dirt floor of the inner bailey with the assurance of a grown man.

Aisling knew he was putting on a show in case anyone else was watching the lad. He was her best little spy, taking messages to whomever needed them with pride.

He darted past the blacksmith's stoop, past the pens where the pigs snuffled old straw, past two bickering maids who were fighting over who had done more washing than the other, and arrived at Blair's side. His breathing was quick as though he ran everywhere, and indeed, perhaps he did.

"I wish to tell you that I heard Morag questioning Hamish to learn who told him there was trouble at one of the crofts, Blair," Niven said.

Even though Aisling was the one who needed the news, she suspected Niven was trying to pretend he was speaking with Blair to ensure Morag or her friends wouldn't think anything of it if they saw them conversing.

"What did the chief say?" Aisling asked.

"He said he knows all that goes on in his pack, and didna say anything further."

Aisling sighed with relief.

"But there is other news," Niven continued, his brow furrowed. "I overheard Gormelia say she will get you back because Cook favored her by giving her the champion's table to serve."

"Even after she had to know Aisling used her bow on two Vikings?" Blair asked.

"Aye. Gormelia knows Aisling canna use them on her."

"What does she plan to do?" Aisling worried Gormelia would try something underhanded so that she wouldn't get into trouble for it.

"She stopped talking, and they headed to the keep. They didna see me."

"Good, thanks be to thee for telling us," Aisling said.

"Aye. She doesna like me. Morag told me to tell Gormelia she was the worst server she had ever seen, when Gormelia finally had a chance to serve the head table. I was happy to relay the information to Gormelia," Niven said.

Aisling smiled. "I know what you mean. I can imagine her vying for a bachelor's interest when she was serving the head table and ignoring Morag's commands.

Then Aisling and her mother headed for the keep, but once they bedded down for the night, Aisling couldn't quit worrying about Coinneach. What if he grew sicker in the night? Everyone would be sound asleep and wouldn't wake up in time to learn of it.

The more she thought of it, the more she couldn't sleep. Once her mother was fast asleep, Aisling slipped off her pallet, left the chamber, and headed for the doors that led to the inner bailey.

"Where are you off to?" one of the guards at the door asked.

"To check on Coinneach to ensure he has no fever."

The guard opened the door for her. "I thought that was your mother's duty."

"Aye, but she's tired and bade me to see him." A little lie. "Then I will return for her if she is needed." Aisling hurried out of the keep before the guard decided to check on her story.

Tristan approached her as she crossed the inner bailey to reach the barracks. Hopefully, he wouldn't stop her from her mission. "How now, lass. What are you doing out at this hour of the night?"

"I'm seeing Coinneach and making sure he doesna have a fever."

"Do you want me to check on him?"

"Nay, my mother bade me do it."

Looking like he suspected there was more to it, Tristan nodded. When Aisling entered the barracks, she was glad Coinneach slept on a bed near the entrance. Testosterone and snores filled the air.

She had to pass Aodhan's bed first, though. He was sound asleep. So was Coinneach, until she approached his bed. He must have smelled her, and he opened his eyes and smiled.

She was glad to see his smile, hoping it meant he wasn't in too much pain. She didn't speak, just leaned over to touch his forehead. He wasn't feverish, thank the gods. But before she could remove her hand from his forehead, he took hold of her wrist and pulled her onto his bed against his chest.

She stifled a squeal, not expecting his action. "You will reinjure yourself." She kissed his forehead.

"Stay with me and make sure I dinna become feverish."

"Aye. But I must leave before the other men wake."

"'Til then. I will heal better knowing you are safe with me."

She tried not to laugh. Anytime she lay with him, he became aroused. It was only a matter of time before they mated.

Then she snuggled against him, listening to his steady heart-beat, and didn't remember anything else until she heard a few male chuckles around the pallets behind them.

Och, she and Coinneach had slept through the night. She hadn't awakened early enough to leave before some men were dressing to break their fast before they started their workday. The naked and half-naked men were casting her small smiles.

Coinneach stirred.

"I must go." Aisling kissed Coinneach's cheek, but he tightened his hold on her when she tried to extricate herself from him.

She sighed. "My mother must no' find me with you."

Coinneach kissed her mouth. "Go then. I will see you in the great hall."

"Are you feeling better?"

"Aye, because you were keeping an eye on me."

She scoffed. "I was as sound asleep as you." Then she gave him one last hug and left the bed, not looking back to see if anyone else was watching her, though Aodhan gave her a wink as she hurried past him and out of the barracks.

Once she returned to the women's chamber, her mother plaited her hair and shook her head at Aisling.

"I went to check on Coinneach." Aisling figured that would be a good explanation.

"All night long?"

Aisling couldn't put anything past her mother. "He isna feverish and feels better this morn."

"But he hasna been up and about yet, so we will have to see how he does today."

"Will you tell Drustan that Coinneach canna serve on the wall walk?"

"I will see to Coinneach first. If he says he feels well enough, and he doesna fight with anyone for a few days, then he can serve his duty."

Aisling hugged her mother and hoped Coinneach would recover quickly. "I told him you were agreeable to our mating."

"No' agreeable but resigned to it. It has naught to do with Coinneach. He was brought up well. It has all to do with the other matters." Her mother glanced in the direction where Gormelia was getting up and speaking low to her friends. They all looked over at Aisling.

Aisling knew she'd have more trouble with Gormelia before long.

10

"You ken the lasses are no' allowed in the barracks, aye?" Aodhan asked.

Coinneach smiled. "After she protected a wounded soldier by killing two Vikings threatening my family's croft?"

Most of the men headed out of the barracks, shaking their heads. "He has all the luck." "You try to best Aodhan again." "I've tried. Three times!" "We all thought he was unbeatable."

"I am," Aodhan said. "Just try me."

"I am Fletcher. We are glad to have you in our ranks, Coinneach." The blond-haired and bearded Fletcher told Aodhan, "I'm sure that after he bested you, Coinneach will have special privileges."

"We heard that Aisling took down two of the Vikings herself." The man had flaming red hair and a beard to match. His sharp blue eyes connected with Coinneach's. Aodhan had told him Ruadh was trustworthy and a good fighter. "We could use her as one of our archers."

Coinneach wanted her safe from harm, not shooting arrows at their enemy from the wall walk or joining them in battle beyond the castle walls.

"You are mating her, aye?" Fletcher asked.

"Aye." Coinneach got up and dressed. "She was mine from the moment I saw her in the meadow with her mother."

"Watch out for Rupert. He has been plaguing Aisling for months now," Fletcher said.

"Rupert?" Why hadn't Aisling told Coinneach she'd been having trouble with him? Coinneach would put him in his place.

"Aye, but you know he's the chief's son, so be careful how you approach him," Fletcher said.

Aodhan pulled on his boots. "He would go whining to his mother, and she would tell Hamish how you intimidated her son."

"I didna see him in the practice battles." Coinneach wondered if he even knew how to fight.

"He has private lessons. Morag insisted on it."

So that no one could see how poorly he did against other men? It was essential to fight against others, to hone their skills, and to learn different techniques.

"Who has taught Rupert to fight?" Coinneach was curious if it was Aodhan.

"Drustan. But he says Rupert is lazy and doesna put any effort into it." Aodhan belted his plaid.

"Because his da is the chief." Coinneach couldn't believe Rupert wouldn't want to emulate his father.

"Because of his mother," Aodhan said. "If she didna have her hooks in him, he might have turned out to be of stronger character. As it is, he wants for nothing and helps nobody either."

"If anything happens to Hamish, goddess forbid, his son willna be able to fill his boots," Coinneach said.

If a chief's son were of the right age, as Rupert was, he would have stood a good chance of leading the pack if Hamish died. But only if Rupert had the pack behind him. Just because he was the chief's son, there was no guarantee the clan would allow him to take over. Even if Morag wanted it.

Though he wasn't even the chief's son.

Coinneach's wound was still sore when he and the other men walked to the great hall to break their fast. Even then, he knew he could work on the wall walk today. No one would dissuade him.

He couldn't believe Aisling had joined him in bed last night, but he hadn't wanted to let her go once she was with him. No matter that it wasn't allowed. He wanted everyone to know she was his, though he would have reluctantly let her leave if she had wanted to.

Now he looked forward to seeing her while she served the meal at his table.

When she came out with their bread, he smiled at her, letting her know he felt all right.

"I know you and you're going to pull guard duty today." She handed Aodhan two slices of bread. "If you weary, you let Aodhan know so you can lie down...in the barracks."

"Aye, I will."

"I dinna believe it." She handed Coinneach a slice of bread. "Aodhan, promise me if Coinneach becomes too fatigued, you'll send him to the barracks."

"Aye, lass."

Then she hurried off to serve the rest of the table and smiled at Coinneach as she passed him on her way to the kitchen.

"Are you feeling well enough to serve on guard duty today?" Aodhan asked Coinneach.

"I am." If he had been in the barracks asleep, he might not have heard Tamhas's wolf's cry of distress. Though with his wolf hearing, he might have.

Once they had finished their meal, the chief and his family left the high table, and as everyone was leaving the great hall, Coinneach told Aodhan that he would join him soon.

Drustan caught up with Coinneach. "Are you feeling well enough to work on the wall today?"

"Aye, I am."

"If you feel bad, let Aodhan know, and you'll retire to the barracks. I dinna want Blair to get after me for allowing you to work when you are injured."

"Thank you, Drustan."

"You, Aodhan, and Aisling did a good job."

Coinneach didn't want them to know he had been wounded just in practice fighting.

"Are you going to join Aodhan?" Drustan raised his brows.

Coinneach glanced at the kitchen.

"Aye, you have another mission first. Dinna make it a habit to sleep with Aisling in the barracks. The other men will want to bring other lasses into there," Drustan said.

"She was only seeing if I was all right."

"And stayed for the night."

Coinneach smiled.

Drustan slapped him on the back. "Join Aodhan soon."

"I will." Coinneach hurried to the kitchen to give Aisling a kiss. When he arrived there, Cook and her assistants were eating their meal.

Smiling, Aisling rose from the bench and kissed him. "Remember what I said."

"I will, lass." He kissed her back, then looked around for Gormelia and saw her glowering at them. He gave her his fiercest battle look that told her to take care.

Gormelia quickly looked away, and then Coinneach said, "I will see you, sweeting, when I can."

"At the next meal, if Cook will allow me to bring it to you."

"Aye, then." They kissed again, and then he left the kitchen, but gave Gormelia one last look that told her she would pay if she troubled Aisling further.

∾

"YOU WERE SO brave when you went to Coinneach's and Aodhan's aid," Nelly said, sitting next to Aisling. "I wouldna have been able to do what you did."

Nelly and Aisling could have passed for sisters: Aisling taller by a hand, with a sweep of copper that caught every trick of the sunlight, and Nelly the more pocket-sized, her hair a light-red blond that bleached nearly white in summer, always messy, always half pulled back.

They even swapped shawls so often they forgot whose shawl was whose. Even today, Aisling thought Nelly was wearing one of her shawls, but she couldn't quite remember.

They had known each other since they were barely walking, the kind of friendship that grew out of pack bonds, being the same age, living at the castle, and hungry curiosity, so that by the time they were fully employed in the kitchen, nobody could untangle the knots between their shared memories and their separate identities.

Aisling never said it out loud, but sometimes she watched the two of them reflected in the loch outside the castle walls—Aisling's long limbs draped over a monolithic stone, Nelly curled into the seat of it like a cat—and felt sure they'd been born from the same mold, only the kiln had set them differently.

Nelly, always the one with a joke half-cocked, had a voice that could cut through a crowd, a laugh that started as a hiccup and grew louder as it rolled. Aisling's voice was softer, deliberate; she spoke with the kind of carefulness that made people lean in to listen.

"If you love a man enough, you will do anything for him," another woman said, breaking into Aisling's thoughts.

Gormelia scoffed. "Too bad he had to have you fight his battles."

"I've seen you practicing with your Viking bow. Can you teach me how to shoot?" Nelly ate the rest of her bread.

"Aye, when we're free I can." Though Aisling wanted to see

Coinneach further. She suspected loitering on the wall walk wasn't acceptable. Like sleeping with him in the barracks wasn't either.

She was so glad Coinneach was better this morning and hoped he would continue to be all right. And she loved that he gave her a good morning kiss after they broke their fast. After they finished eating, she and the other assistant cooks began cleaning the pots for the next meal.

"You left the chamber last night," Gormelia said, splashing water on Aisling as she cleaned a pot.

Aisling wouldn't engage her. Instead, she finished her pot and moved off to clean up their table. Nelly came to assist her. She whispered, "Gormelia watches you all the time. She told everyone that you hadna slept on your pallet last eve."

"Doesna she have anything else to worry about?"

"Nay. She's angry that you are serving Aodhan's table." Nelly sighed. "So where were you? You couldna have slipped away to see Coinneach. He was in the...*barracks*." Her green eyes widened. "You were in the barracks with all the men?"

Aisling smiled. "Only with Coinneach, making sure he wasna feverish."

"Oh."

"If he had been, I would have run back to the keep to get my mother to check on him."

"Oh." Then Nelly smiled. "So what did the other men think when they saw you?"

"They were asleep. And thankfully no one said I couldna do it."

"He appeared to be just fine," Nelly said.

"Aye, I'm hoping he doesna engage in any more fighting before he is fully healed."

Gormelia left the kitchen with her friends, and Aisling was glad for it.

"Can you show me some archery skills now?" Nelly asked.

Cook shook her head. "If you and Aisling become expert archers, they'll want you to work for Drustan instead of me."

Aisling knew Cook was jesting. Drustan would never have the women fighting with the men.

"Nay, I will never be able to do what Aisling did, but I just want to learn," Nelly said.

"You're free to go," Cook said.

Aisling grabbed Nelly's hand, and they headed to the women's chamber. From there, Aisling retrieved her bow and quiver of arrows. Then the two women left the castle for where the targets were set up. They both glanced up to see where Coinneach was up on the wall walk and saw him and Aodhan several feet away. But the men were doing their duty and watching for danger.

"I sure wish I could catch someone like Coinneach for my own. He's so braw, but then you are too so you suit each other."

"You'll find just the wolf for you when the time comes."

Nelly was shy around the men, which gave Aisling an idea. Tamhas was such a nice man, but he didn't have many opportunities to meet women. But if Nelly and he really liked each other, would she be able to manage living on the farm? And Nelly was the only ally Aisling had in the kitchen.

"What do you think about farming?" Aisling readied an arrow and aimed it at the target. "See my stance?"

"Uh, yes. What about farming?"

"Would you like to live in a croft instead of the castle, cooking?" Aisling released the arrow, and it hit the target.

"I've never lived in a croft, so I dinna know anything about it."

Aisling helped her with her stance so that Nelly could shoot an arrow. It dropped at her feet. They both looked down at it and laughed. But Aisling was thinking that she could take Nelly with her to see Tamhas sometime, and then Nelly could see if that life might be preferable to the kitchen life at the castle.

Aisling helped Nelly again to prepare to shoot an arrow, and

this time it flew several feet. "That's great, Nelly. We'll keep practicing until you want to stop. Oh, and I...um, wanted to see Coinneach's family to see how they are faring after the fight last night."

"Oh, sure." Nelly kept trying and finally hit the edge of the
target. She whooped and hollered.

Aisling laughed. "Practice and you'll get so much better. You
should have seen me when I was starting out."

"Did you have anyone help you?"

"After struggling with it for a while, Drustan sent a man to help
me do it. Before we return to work, let's visit Coinneach's family to
see how they are."

"You want me to go with you?" Nelly's eyes were wide.

"Aye. I would love to have the company."

"Since you willna be seeing Coinneach." Nelly smiled. "Aye,
let's go."

They both headed through the outer bailey and waved at the
tiny figures atop the wall walk.

Coinneach cupped his mouth and hollered, "Where are you
off to?"

"To check on your family." Then Aisling waved, and she and
Nelly raced through the tall grasses.

"I have only been to the village once to get goods that Cook
needed and never even noticed the crofts. I mean, I saw them, but I
never paid attention to them. Will it be all right with them if I tag
along? They know you, but no' me." Nelly tucked a loose curl of
hair sweeping into her eyes behind her ear.

"They will welcome you because you are a good friend of
mine."

When they reached the family's croft, Tamhas and his da were
working in the field. They didn't see them, so Aisling and Nelly
went to the door of the croft and Aisling knocked. "'Tis me, Aisling,
and my friend Nelly."

The door was yanked open. "Aisling!" Coinneach's mother

threw her arms around her and hugged her. "Where is Coinneach?"

"Working as a guard on the wall walk. I told him we were coming to see you."

"Come and have some tea. And welcome, Nelly." Elspeth took both their hands and led them into the croft. "Sit and tell me what Coinneach has been up to." Then she turned her back on them to heat the water for the tea.

Aisling and Nelly shared looks. Aisling shook her head at Nelly, trying to tell her not to mention Coinneach had been injured in a practice fight.

"Well, he did some practice fighting, and then he worked on the wall walk. That's when he heard Tamhas's howl and came to the rescue," Aisling said.

"Aye, and—"

Aisling looked sharply at Nelly, but she only smiled.

"Aisling helped fight the Vikings, using a Viking bow. We're all so proud of her."

Not Gormelia, Aisling was thinking.

"We got word from one of the men who had come with the others to take the bodies away. He howled to let us know it was safe to return to our crofts, and he said Coinneach wanted one of the Viking's long swords to go to Tamhas. I canna believe you risked your life for just the croft. We could rebuild it. We couldna replace either of you." Elspeth sounded distraught, and when she turned to bring the tea to the table, her eyes were filled with tears.

Once Elspeth set the mugs on the table, Aisling hugged her. She knew she had to tell the whole story now.

"The one man was the brother of the one I had killed as a wolf. He was about to shoot Coinneach with an arrow. We took Ivor's weapons—the sword that Coinneach kept, the short sword that Coinneach gave Tamhas, and the bow and quiver of arrows that I claimed. His brother found the short sword that Coinneach had given to Tamhas in the croft. The brother vowed revenge."

"Och, we didna know that." Elspeth sat down at the table with them. "I'm glad you saved Coinneach's life as a wolf."

"Who couldn't have escaped in time. Once Holgar found the short sword in your croft, he would have killed all of you the first chance he got. It wasna just a case of him torching your croft." Aisling sipped some of her tea and saw Nelly was just staring at her.

That was what she'd been afraid of. Telling others that she had killed a Viking warrior when she had been in her wolf form. It just made her sound wilder, more unpredictable.

Elspeth sat back on her chair. "If Coinneach hadna already decided he wanted you for a mate, I would have insisted."

Aisling smiled. Nelly sat back on the chair and tapped her fingers on the table. "You didna tell me you saved Coinneach's life while wearing your wolf coat."

"I wouldna have left my hiding place otherwise," Aisling said.

"Aye, I mean, well, you didna have the bow before then so it was hard to imagine you killing a mighty Viking warrior with a *sgian dubh*. But in your wolf coat? So brave, Aisling. You are amazing." Nelly finished her tea, gathered the empty mugs, and took them into the kitchen.

Male voices approaching the croft made Elspeth and Aisling leave their chairs. They opened the door, and Tamhas smiled to see Aisling, giving her a hug. Magnus likewise hugged her.

"You are here, but where is Coinneach?" Magnus asked.

"He's guarding the castle. We, Nelly and I, came to see how you were doing after the fight."

"Due to your quick actions, we didna lose any of the crops or the croft from the fire from their torches." Magnus hugged her again.

"My mother agreed we could mate." Aisling hadn't meant to tell

Coinneach's family without him, but it just slipped out. She was so glad to be part of his family.

Tamhas glanced at Nelly.

"This is my good friend, Nelly." Aisling rushed over to bring her to where the family was standing.

"Are you staying for the noon meal?" Tamhas asked.

"Nay, we have to return to the castle to prepare it." Aisling decided she wasn't much of a matchmaker, as she couldn't think of anything to say to get Nelly to talk to Tamhas.

Tamhas likewise wasn't making the effort. Maybe they weren't meant to be together. Maybe Nelly wouldn't even like to live in a croft like this. Or work as a farmer's wife.

"I'm glad you are fine. I just wanted to make sure. We need to return to the castle before we are missed." Aisling had done her job in checking on the family.

"We're so glad you dropped by." Elspeth gave Aisling a hug and Nelly one too this time. She even gave her son a look that said he needed to do something.

"I'll escort you back to the castle," Tamhas said, as if recalling that's what Coinneach always did, and it sounded chivalrous.

"That would be great." Aisling hugged Magnus. "We'll see you again soon." We, meaning maybe Coinneach and Aisling, or Aisling and Nelly.

Then the three left the croft, saying their goodbyes. Still, Aisling saw the conspiratorial smiles that passed between Magnus and Elspeth, and she suspected they knew she was up to matchmaking Nelly and Tamhas and approved. Or just thought it was amusing.

Nelly was sticking by Aisling's side, not getting near Tamhas, and Aisling wanted to rectify the situation, but she didn't know how.

"Tamhas can fight like Coinneach, and he can ride a horse." Aisling figured she could tell Nelly some of his attributes while they made their way to the castle.

"I dinna fight as well as Coinneach," Tamhas said.

"He has had more training. I'm sure if you had more training, you could too," Nelly said.

Aisling was thrilled that Nelly finally spoke. Maybe her courage came from having Aisling between her and Tamhas.

Which gave Aisling an idea. Maybe Tamhas could come and train too at the castle on occasion when his da didn't need him, if Drustan approved of another crofter preparing for battle. If Tamhas was even interested.

"If you would like, I could ask Drustan if he would allow it. I'm sure since your brother works for him, he would put in a good word."

Tamhas scratched his head. "I dinna know. They were no' friendly toward Coinneach until Alasdair took him to the castle and Coinneach bested the champion in the practice fighting."

"Aye, and you are friends with Alasdair also. Coinneach would..." She started to say that he would protect him, but thought better of it. "He would spar with you for sure, and you can learn some of the new skills they've taught him."

"Aye." Tamhas brightened at the idea.

"And I will be cheering you on," Nelly said.

Tamhas smiled broadly at her.

So maybe Aisling had some matchmaking ability.

Before they arrived at the castle, they waved at Coinneach and Aodhan. Both men waved back.

When they reached the castle gates, Aisling took Tamhas's hand. "We'll see Drustan now." She figured since he was here, they might as well get this over with.

Then she saw Drustan and hauled Tamhas toward him, and Nelly running to keep up with them.

"Drustan, because of the assault on Tamhas's family's croft, he needs to learn more sword skills," Aisling said, taking charge of the situation.

Tamhas glanced at Nelly, and she nodded her head vigorously.

"Aye," Tamhas said. "Chief Alisdair taught Coinneach and me lots, but I need more experience."

"Your brother canna fight for three days because of the sword wound he received, but I welcome you to the practice fight we will have soon." Drustan glanced at the sword swinging from Tamhas's belt. "I see you have a Viking sword also."

"Aye. But it was Coinneach's kill," Tamhas said. "I'm willing to learn. My da approves."

"If more of the farmers were so armed and trained, the better for all of us." Drustan slapped him on the back. "You are welcome." He glanced up at the wall walk and saw Coinneach watching them. "Go. Tell your brother what you are up to. I'm sure he'll want to watch you fight."

Tamhas said to Aisling, "You didna tell us Coinneach was injured in the battle with the Vikings."

"He wasna. It was during sword practice. He didna want anyone to know." Now Aisling felt bad that she hadn't told the family the whole truth.

Tamhas glanced at Drustan. "It happens sometimes. Tristan apologized and was truly remorseful. Because we dinna know how well you can fight, we'll pair you with fighters who are more your skill level, and you can work up to what the skilled fighters can do."

"Aye." Tamhas straightened his shoulders. "I'll speak with Coinneach now."

Aisling waved at Coinneach and blew him a kiss. He smiled.

"Can we watch them fight?" Nelly asked.

Nelly had never wanted to watch a fight before, so Aisling thought she might be a wee bit interested in Tamhas.

"If Cook says you're free, then aye."

Nelly grabbed Aisling's hand and raced her to the keep.

11

W hen Coinneach had seen Aisling and the other woman leaving the castle grounds, he wanted to go with them. But when they returned with Tamhas, he didn't know what to think.

Aisling and her friend raced for the keep, but Tamhas appeared to be headed for the tower stairs. He hoped Drustan hadn't recruited him to be a soldier. Tamhas needed to run the farm. Or Coinneach would. One brother or the other.

Tamhas finally emerged from the tower and strode forth, his shoulders back, his expression serious until he drew closer as Coinneach walked to meet up with him.

"What are you doing here?" Coinneach hugged his brother, glad to see him.

"It is all Aisling's doing. She talked to Drustan, and I'm required to practice fighting with the others. You didna tell us you were wounded in a practice fight. How bad is it?"

"Just a cut, but I reopened the wound while battling the Vikings. It's getting better."

Tamhas cleared his throat. "Aisling also said her mother approved of your marriage to her. We're all thrilled."

"As am I."

"I think Aisling is playing matchmaker."

They both looked down at the inner bailey where Aisling and Nelly were just entering the castle.

"The lass with her?" Coinneach asked.

"Aye. Unless I'm mistaken. Nelly works on the kitchen staff with Aisling."

Coinneach laughed.

"What?"

"I never expected Aisling to try and find you a mate."

"Me either. Drustan said you couldna practice fight."

The men who were going to practice began gathering in the inner bailey.

"Aye. Blair said no to any fighting."

"I guess I've got to go." Tamhas looked like he was trying to put on a brave face.

Aodhan joined them. "Come on. A couple of men will relieve us while I fight, and you watch your brother work out."

Sure enough, two men came up to relieve them. "Are you going to fight Coinneach's brother now?" the one man asked.

"And risk getting thrown down again? Nay." Aodhan grinned.

The three of them began to go down the tower stairs. Coinneach was feeling better, and he thought that if he fought with one of the men, just one, and it was a practice fight rather than a battle to the death, he could manage.

Then he saw Drustan and Blair watching him, and he knew he wasn't going to be allowed to fight.

"You'll do fine, Tamhas. Remember everything that Alisdair taught us," Coinneach said to his brother.

"Aye."

Other spectators had gathered to watch the practice session. Coinneach realized that, because he couldn't join in the battle, he was able to stay with Aisling if she was allowed to watch the proceedings this time.

As soon as he saw her, she hurried toward him with Nelly in tow.

He hugged and kissed Aisling and then greeted Nelly. "Glad to meet you, lass."

"Aye, likewise. Where is Tamhas?" Nelly asked.

They looked to see who he was paired up with, and it was a man about his size. Then the fighting began. The man battling Tamhas struck his sword at Tamhas's new Viking sword, but Tamhas had learned from both Coinneach and Alisdair how to counter the attack.

He blocked the blow and knocked his opponent's sword downward, then quickly came up to thrust at the man's chest. He had won the match. They shook hands, but the man wanted to fight him again. They were more equally matched than Tamhas was against Alisdair and Coinneach, but again, Tamhas won the match.

Coinneach knew Tamhas needed a stronger opponent. One who would teach him more than he had already learned. But he could see that his brother was relieved that he hadn't been injured or lost the matches.

Drustan stepped in and had Tristan pair up with Tamhas. "Remember, Tristan, it's a practice match."

"Aye." Tristan glanced at Coinneach as if he knew Coinneach would give him grief if he cut his brother.

Then the match began. Tristan was a powerful fighter, and Coinneach would welcome him to watch his back. If Tamhas were careful and used the skills he had learned from Alisdair and Coinneach, he would do fine.

Even so, Coinneach realized he was tensing every time Tristan slashed at Tamhas. But Tamhas was holding his own and struck back at Tristan, forcing him several steps back. Tristan tried to recover, but Tamhas took advantage and continued to strike at him. Tristan couldn't do anything but parry and fall back.

Coinneach was proud of his brother, but when he heard Nelly gasp, he glanced at her and saw she was wringing her hands.

Aisling likewise was tense, and he ran his hand over her back. "I pray neither cuts the other," she whispered to him.

"I feel the same way." Coinneach hoped that Tamhas didn't know that Tristan had cut him during the last practice.

Then Tamhas knocked Tristan's sword from his hand, and Tristan smiled, inclining his head. "You are Coinneach's brother. I can tell how much the two of you have trained together. Both of you have an inner strength and physical prowess that we can use."

"I'm a crofter at heart. Coinneach is the warrior. Yet you bested him."

"Aye, a lass distracted him."

Tamhas laughed and looked back at Aisling and Coinneach.

"'Twas a good thing that no lass can distract you like that," Tristan continued.

"Aye." Then Tamhas saluted Nelly with his sword.

Coinneach chuckled. "I didna know you were into matchmaking, Aisling." He kissed her forehead.

"I didna know I was either. Nelly is my best friend at the castle, and she's so sweet, and so is Tamhas. Maybe the two of them will make a match if they are suited to each other."

"Aye. Only our wolf senses can tell. My parents are doing all right after the battle we had with the Viking raiders?"

"They are. They were glad to see me and asked about you. They were surprised to see me without you," Aisling said. "We come as a pair. I..." Aisling sighed. "I told your family that my mother approved of our marriage. They are thrilled, of course, but I should have waited for us to tell them together."

"Nay, I'm glad they know. I wouldna have been able to tell them until after duty tonight."

"Your brother did well against Tristan. Do you think he was easier on Tamhas because he was afraid to cut him and earn your wrath?"

Coinneach folded his arms. "Nay. Tamhas used many of the techniques Alasdair and I use, so he did just fine."

Drustan fought Tamhas next, worrying Coinneach. But Drustan took a teaching posture, showing Tamhas how to defend himself when attacked, and how to take the offensive.

Coinneach relaxed, feeling he could trust Drustan not to hurt his brother, and wrapped his arm around Aisling's waist. She snuggled closer to him. While he worked at the castle, he loved having intimate moments with her like this.

Once the practice fighting session ended, everyone cheered and returned to work.

Tamhas had proved he could fight well against an enemy. With more training, he would be even better. "Good job, brother," Coinneach said, slapping him on the back.

"Thanks. I think I learned a lot. And you were right. Fighting different opponents helps to improve skills."

"I would have thought you were already one of the soldiers at the keep after seeing you fight so well," Nelly said, encouraging him with praise.

Tamhas's ears reddened a wee bit at the unexpected compliment as he smiled at Nelly.

Aodhan joined them. "You have your brother's spirit, Tamhas. Come, sit with us at our table for the meal."

Coinneach frowned. "We are supposed to be on guard duty after watching the fight."

Aodhan asked Drustan, "Can we have a meal with Tamhas at the great hall and then return to duty?"

Drustan smiled. "Aye."

Then they all headed with the other men to wash up while Nelly and Aisling hurried to the keep. Drustan talked to Tamhas about sword fighting and farming while washing up at another water barrel across the inner bailey.

"What will Cook think if Tamhas steals Nelly from her duties?" Aodhan asked Coinneach as he used a wet cloth to wash his face and hands. Then he dried off.

Coinneach leaned against the rock wall, his arms folded across his chest. "That is the way of things. It doesna mean they will hit it off once they get to know each other better."

Aodhan cast him his signature smirk that said he didn't believe it.

Coinneach only knew how he felt about Aisling and how he had wanted her after seeing her. Did Tamhas feel that way about Nelly? The lass seemed sure to be intrigued by his brother. Working at the croft, they hadn't interacted with the lasses when they were off to the village to get supplies for the castle, since men had often accompanied them.

Which made Coinneach wonder why Blair and Aisling had been alone when he had first met them. He knew it had to have been a case of fate.

Then the men all headed into the castle to break their fast. Coinneach hoped he hadn't made an enemy of the two men who had to take their places on the wall walk. Tamhas stood tall and grand, and Coinneach was proud of him.

Drustan walked in with them, and Aodhan ushered Coinneach and Tamhas to his table. Coinneach was glad that Aodhan honored him by inviting him to dine with them.

However, the highlight for Coinneach was when Aisling served them. Instead, Nelly did. Coinneach frowned. Then he wondered if Aisling had asked Cook to allow Nelly to serve them instead so she could see more of Tamhas.

Nelly gave Tamhas two slices of bread instead of Aodhan, and Coinneach laughed. But Aodhan was of good humor and didn't tell

Nelly she had made a mistake when she didn't give the second portion of bread to Aodhan.

Then she finally hurried to serve the rest of the table, smiling at Tamhas on the way back to the kitchen.

"What say you about the lass?" Coinneach asked his brother.

"She is bonny. Thanks be to thee, Aodhan, for allowing me to eat with you today." Tamhas finished his second slice of bread, which should have been Aodhan's.

Coinneach was resigned to seeing Nelly bring the rest of their meal as he finally saw Aisling serving the women's table again. But he would meet up with Aisling after the meal before he returned to his duty on the wall walk.

When the meal was done, everyone got ready to leave the table.

Coinneach said to his brother. "I'm going to say goodbye to Aisling. Do you want to also?" He meant for his brother to say goodbye to Nelly, but he didn't want to embarrass his brother in front of Aodhan.

"I will see you at the wall walk," Aodhan said to Coinneach. "And thanks for joining us in the practice fight and for the meal."

"My pleasure," Tamhas said. "Aye, I'll join you, Coinneach."

He and Coinneach headed for the kitchen, where the women were preparing their meals to set on the table. Nelly immediately greeted them. "You did well at the practice fight."

The tips of Tamhas's ears reddened. "I learned a lot."

Aisling hurried over to hug Coinneach. "I was proud of you for no' joining the fight."

"Your mother might no' have stitched me up a third time if I hadna heeded her warning. And Drustan would be sure to give me grief if I had to spend more time sleeping in the barracks."

"Well, I'd best be getting back to the farm," Tamhas said to Nelly. "It was good seeing you again."

"I would like it if we could see each other again. Mayhap when I forage for nuts, berries, and mushrooms in the forest."

"Aye, I would like that."

Then Coinneach kissed Aisling, and they said their goodbyes so the lasses could eat their meal. "I'll bring your meal for later," Aisling said, giving Coinneach another kiss, and then she turned to help carry plates of food to the table.

Coinneach smiled. "I look forward to it." And another hug and kiss. If only she could sleep with him again tonight.

12

Aisling was still setting plates of food out on the table to help feed the cooking staff when Nelly grabbed her arm and whispered to her, "Change your plate with Gormelia's. I'll create a distraction."

Desperately wanting to know what was wrong, Aisling didn't hesitate to follow her friend's advice. While the others were getting ale, Aisling grabbed her plate, and Nelly slapped one of Gormelia's friends across the face. "I know you've been spreading rumors about me shirking my duties because I'm friends with Aisling."

The girl, Kenna, grabbed Nelly's hair, and everyone's attention was diverted to the ongoing fight. Kenna and Wilma, Gormelia's friends, both had unremarkable brown hair, and both were mousy in disposition, so neither stood out among the other pack members. Aisling was surprised when Kenna fought back.

"You think you're special because Coinneach's brother is paying attention to you now?" Kenna tried to scratch Nelly's face.

Nelly punched her in the stomach. Aisling switched the plates and then came to Nelly's rescue. Cook, as if suddenly aware of the fight in the kitchen, shouted, "If you want to eat, you will sit down now and eat. If you want to lose your position in the kitchen, then keep fighting."

Everyone quickly moved around the table to take their seats.

Nelly squeezed Aisling's hand under the table.

"'Tis accomplished," Aisling whispered to Nelly. "What had Gormelia done?"

"I saw her add something to the meal and then set it at your place on the table. She never serves you. I suspected foul play."

"Thank you, Nelly." Aisling wondered if Gormelia had put something in her food that was meant to sicken Aisling or kill her. If so, Gormelia would get a surprise.

"Aye, once she began threatening you, I've been watching her."

"I'm grateful to you for it. Did Kenna really disparage you to others?" Nelly had never told Aisling that she had, or she would have said something to her.

"Aye, she has. So it felt good to get her back for it and save you at the same time."

They began to eat their meal, but Aisling noticed Cook was watching Gormelia as she drank her ale before starting to eat. Had Cook caught sight of Aisling switching plates with Gormelia?

Gormelia wasn't observing Aisling, as if she were trying to pretend that if something bad happened to Aisling while she ate her meal, Gormelia hadn't had anything to do with it.

But Kenna and Gormelia's other friend, Wilma, both were watching Aisling, eating their food slowly, waiting for a reaction? Finally, Gormelia took a bite of her food, chewed it, swallowed it, and within minutes threw up all over the table, splattering her friends sitting on either side of her. They jumped back in horror, wiping the offending food off their kirtles.

Gormelia left the table and threw up on the floor several more times. Most of the women were aghast and stopped eating, but Cook, Aisling, and Nelly finished their meals.

"Eat up, ladies," Cook said. "You will be starving by the dinner meal if you dinna."

"Can we get new plates?" Kenna asked.

"Nay," Cook said. "Eat around the spit-up food on your plate. You'll live. The same goes for you, Wilma."

"What about Gormelia?" Wilma asked, her voice taut with concern.

"It appears she has become ill and willna be able to keep any food down. She can clean up the mess she has made and retire to the women's chambers. You can help her once you're done eating." Cook continued to eat her meal then.

The other women finished their meals and carried their plates from the table to wash. While Aisling, Nelly, and the others cleaned the pots and dishes, Kenna and Wilma brought their half-eaten meals to wash their plates.

"What could have made Gormelia sick?" Cook directly asked Kenna and Wilma.

They both looked back at Gormelia as she threw up some more on the stone floor.

Kenna and Wilma both shook their heads. Kenna grabbed Gormelia's plate and was going to dump the contents, but Cook stayed her hand. "Leave it on the table there."

Their eyes widened, and Aisling suspected Cook was planning to learn what had been added to the meal to make Gormelia so violently ill.

Cook motioned to Gormelia. "Aisling, can you get your mother to see to Gormelia? She appears too sick to clean up after herself so Kenna and Wilma will do the task."

"Aye, Cook." Aisling hurried off to fetch her mother. She hoped Gormelia didn't die, but if she did, it served her right because that would have been Aisling's fate instead. She ran through the great hall and up the stairs to where her mother was seeing to a new mother and her bairn.

As soon as she opened the door, the mother and Aisling's mother gasped. "Whatever is the matter?" Aisling's mother asked, and she had to know there was trouble that Blair had to see to as their pack's healer.

"Gormelia ate something that didna agree with her." Aisling didn't want to say what had happened in front of the new mother.

"I will return later," Aisling's mother said, patting the new mother's hand as she nursed her bairn.

"What is wrong?" her mother asked Aisling as they headed down the stairs. "I know you wouldna fetch me unless something was terribly wrong."

"Aye. I dinna know what Gormelia added to the food, but Nelly caught her doing it. Then Gormelia put the plate where I always sit. Nelly had to create a distraction, and I switched plates so Gormelia ended up with the tainted food. Cook wants you to see to her, and mayhap her food to determine what she added to it that made her so sick."

"Is Cook aware of this?"

"I believe so. I think she saw me switch plates while all the others watched Nelly and Kenna fight."

Her mother raised her brows.

"That was the distraction."

"I see. I hope that Cook will remove Gormelia from the kitchen then. She canna allow someone to try to poison anyone else out of spitefulness."

"I agree."

When they entered the kitchen, the other women had already cleared out, all except for Cook, Gormelia, her friends, and Nelly. The dishes, pots, table, and floor were clean. Gormelia was sitting at the table, looking pale and unwell.

Instead of checking on Gormelia to see how she fared, Aisling's mother examined the food. "Who would mistakenly put these mushrooms in the meal?" She looked at Gormelia as if she knew the truth.

"I will tell the chief what has happened here. She will be banished. If her friends, Kenna and Wilma, had anything to do with it, they will be banished as well," Cook said.

"You saw what had happened?" Aisling asked Cook.

"I saw Gormelia place that plate at your setting, and she has never done so before. I had thought maybe the two of you had reconciled and she was trying to be nice. But when Nelly started the fight and you switched plates with Gormelia's, I knew something was terribly wrong. For one thing, Nelly doesn't start fights."

"But you let Gormelia eat the poisonous mushrooms," Aisling's mother said.

Aisling was surprised at that also.

"Aye. I had to know if she had added something poisonous to the food. If she hadna, then it was as I thought at first. She was trying to make up to Aisling. But when she got sick from eating the food right away, I knew why Aisling had switched out the plates. How did you know Gormelia had poisoned your plate?" Cook asked Aisling.

"Nelly saw her add something to the food and then serve it to me." Aisling owed her life to her observant friend, and she would be forever grateful.

Cook nodded. "I'm sure Gormelia's friends were all in on it. They left after the morning meal to gather herbs and mushrooms from the forest. All three of them. They could easily have found the deadly mushrooms then and saved them for Aisling's food. Gormelia is lucky she didna eat too much of the food."

"She still may die," Aisling's mother said. "Someone doesna need to eat much of the mushrooms to kill them, but it can take a while to die a painful death from eating them. Have someone take her to her pallet to lie down. It's up to her whether she lives or dies. There's nothing I can do for her."

Cook left the kitchen and returned with a man who took hold of Gormelia's arm, but she could barely stand.

"Check her belongings for any hint of the deadly mushrooms or anything else that could have poisoned her," Cook said.

"Aye, Cook." He lifted Gormelia in his arms and carried her to the women's chamber.

"We need to tell the chief what has happened. The word will have already spread, but we must tell him all we know, or the stories will be so exaggerated, he willna know what to think," Aisling's mother said.

"Aye. I will have Kenna and Wilma go also so we can learn what they knew of the matter." Cook left the kitchen again.

"Nelly should be with us, too, since she saw what Gormelia had done."

"Aye, go find her." But before Aisling left the kitchen, her mother hugged her. "I canna believe Gormelia would go to such extremes to harm you."

"Neither can I. I was glad Nelly saw her do it." Aisling hurried off to find her friend. Nelly loved the herb gardens and would help the gardeners there when she wasn't cooking meals. Sure enough, as soon as Aisling reached the gardens, Nelly waved at her.

"What news? Is Gormelia going to be all right?"

"Mayhap no'. 'Tis her own fault for trying to poison me. But we need to see the chief about this." Aisling took her hand and led her out of the gardens.

"Just you and me?" Nelly's eyes were huge. She appeared to be afraid she would get into trouble with the chief for some reason.

"Nay, Cook and my mother also. And Kenna and Wilma."

Then they met up with Aisling's mother, Cook, with her jaw clamped so tight that her cheek twitched, and Kenna and Wilma, both ashen, both visibly shrinking from the weight of whatever they expected to happen next.

What had they thought? That if Aisling had died, no one would have suspected any of them of poisoning her? Gormelia had been the most antagonistic toward her, but Kenna and Wilma went right along with her mean behavior, companions in taunting Aisling.

But when they tried to see the chief, Morag intercepted them in the hall outside their chamber, her face a perpetual scowl, barring their way like a stone pillar. Her hair—so dark it looked blue in the right light—was rope-braided and looped over her shoulder.

Her dress was the color of oxblood, an omen if ever there was one, and her hands were folded in front of her with such stillness that for a brief moment, Aisling wondered how she could stand there, controlling her emotions when she had to have already heard what had happened.

"So," Morag said, the word dropping with the force of a hammer. "What is this all about?" She looked them over, eyes grazing Aisling's face and then immediately dismissing it, as if the very sight of her was a waste of time. "Is it true, then, that you tried to kill yourself?" The question caught in the air, heavy and raw. "What is this all about?"

Taken aback by the absurdity of the notion that Aisling had tried to kill herself, she was sure Morag had already heard the rumors of what had happened. And it had nothing to do with Aisling trying to kill herself!

"Come into my solar so we can talk privately," Morag said, softening her stance, as if she realized she might control the scenario better if she hid her anger from any clan members who might walk by.

Morag walked into her solar while the women followed her into the room. She sat high and straight on her embroidered chair, as if she were holding court, and gestured for the others to stand before her. The room smelled faintly of incense. For a moment, Morag said nothing. She allowed the silence to stretch, watched the discomfort flicker across the faces of her courtiers.

Morag was a scrawny woman despite all her bravado. But her rounded eyes could give anyone a chill.

Aisling didn't want to see her! She wanted to see the chief. She didn't expect justice at the hands of this woman.

Cook outlined the situation, and Aisling's mother verified that the mushrooms were indeed poisonous. Cook also shared that no one working for her would make a mistake in picking poisonous mushrooms, then preparing them for just one specific person. Nelly then recounted how she had orchestrated a distraction to ensure Gormelia consumed the food she had contaminated.

"Just because Kenna, Wilma, and Gormelia went to the forest to harvest mushrooms, doesna mean the *other* two women were involved," Morag said. "Further, Gormelia might no' have realized the mushrooms she had picked were poisonous."

"All of my assistants know which mushrooms are good and which are no'. They would no' have made the mistake," Cook reiterated. "The fact that Gormelia gave Aisling the plate with only the poisonous mushrooms indicates that she knew just what she was doing." Cook folded her arms.

The man who had taken Gormelia to her bed returned with one of her muslin herb bags. He held the bag at arm's length. Then passed the bag to her, his own hands trembling visibly, as if he'd half expected it to bite him. "Are these remnants of the poisonous mushrooms?"

Aisling's mother took the bundle with an expertise born of decades spent in the company of roots and rot. She pressed it between her fingers, then drew it close and gave it a deep, deliberate sniff.

She opened the cloth, her nails working deftly at the crude stitching, and spilled the contents into her palm: brittle threads of moss-green, a few shriveled caps of brownish fungus, what looked like the fibrous stems of something wild. Her face was an impassive mask while she sorted the contents into little piles in her hand, but her eyes flicked up to the man as if she were weighing him alongside the mushrooms.

"These are not from the market but from the forest." She pointed at a small clump of mushrooms with a kind of reverence and dread, then selected an individual and held it to the light. "These are deadly."

The man at her side exhaled, his jaw slackening with relief and apprehension in the same gesture.

"Aye, they are the same found in the dish meant for Aisling that Gormelia ate from," Blair said.

Morag defended them. "It still doesna mean that Kenna and Wilma were involved."

The door to the solar slammed back on its hinges with such force that all six women and the guard jumped as if the devil himself had burst into the room. Chief Hamish strode in, his stride clipped and heavy, the ceremonial iron clasp of his plaid catching the firelight.

His face was a mask, the kind highlanders wore at funerals, and his eyes swept the chamber once before settling, cold and merciless, on Morag.

"I'm handling it, Hamish," Morag said, her tone haughty. Morag drew herself up as only the chief's wife could do in front of an angry mate. "Rest assured, there's no need for male interference in the matter. It's a woman's matter."

"'Tis no' a 'woman's matter' when murder is attempted," Hamish shot back, his words crisp as the first frost. "Since when do my words constitute interference?"

Morag squirmed a little, seemingly torn between the urge to speak her mind, as she was used to doing with her courtiers, and the wisdom she'd earned by living with Hamish as his mate all these years.

Hamish gave Morag a steely-eyed glower. He planted himself squarely between the hearth and a small table, casting a long shadow over the ladies. "I have had word from Drustan," he said, in a voice that made the shutters tremble, "that there was an attempt to poison Aisling, and that the poisoner herself has now repented with her own suffering."

For a moment, Aisling felt a flicker of gratitude toward Hamish. He, at least, would not try to sweep her attempted poisoning under the rushes. She could believe he would mete out justice without regard to the ties of blood or clan since Morag seemed to be defending the ones who had tried to poison her. She was also sure Gormelia wouldn't have kept her misdeeds secret from her friends.

Morag was not one to yield ground on her turf despite knowing she was on treacherous grounds. Her eyes flared with a mixture of outrage and dread. "You presume too much, my laird. Women's feuds are the realm of women. Aisling has always been a trouble-maker, leading men astray and then casting them aside. It was likely a jest gone awry."

The laird's glare hardened. "Serving poisonous mushrooms to another pack member is no' a jest. If it pleases you, my lady"—he sounded facetious when he spoke the words—"we will have a full reckoning in the great hall. This is not the sort of justice that hides in the shadows. If poison has been used, I will see justice done, and the clan will know why."

Morag held his gaze steady, even as a violent crimson crept up her neck and cheeks. She was outmaneuvered, and she knew it. "Nay, if you wish to speak here, then we shall."

"Tell me what happened." Hamish folded his arms across his chest, looking indomitable.

Cook explained the situation, and Blair, Nelly, and Aisling shared their experiences.

Hamish looked at Kenna and Wilma, who had remained silent through the whole thing. "What say you?" His voice was hard.

Kenna meekly said, "We didna know that Gormelia had collected poisonous mushrooms."

"Yet you were with her. You talk to one another. You're loyal to her. I dinna believe that you wouldna have known what she planned to do." Hamish looked from one woman to the other with a searing glance.

"We didna know," Wilma said quietly. If they hadn't been wolves, they wouldn't have heard her words.

Hamish shook his head. "I dinna believe you."

"But there's no' proof that they were involved," Morag said, still defending them.

"I believe they were complicit. They will no longer work in the kitchen should they do what Gormelia did," Hamish said.

"They could take the place of a couple of the washer women, and they could come to work for me," Cook said.

"I was thinking more of them mucking the stalls out, but if a couple of the washer women can learn to cook for you and you're not short on servers, so be it. If the two of you women are involved in other matters like this, you'll be banished from the pack." He gave Morag a cutting glare. Then he stalked out of the solar.

"Get out. All of you," Morag screamed.

They all headed out of her solar. Aisling squeezed her mother's hand, glad Hamish had gotten involved and had irritated Morag over his decision.

Kenna and Wilma were crying. Aisling didn't feel bad for them. She was certain they knew what Gormelia had planned to do and had probably encouraged it. But when their plan didn't succeed, they were horrified, afraid they would be found responsible for it also.

The lad, Niven, hurried to speak with Aisling's mother. "You need to come to see Gormelia."

"Aye." Her mother hurried to the women's chamber.

"Do you want me to come with you?" Aisling asked.

"Nay. See Coinneach. I'm sure he has already learned of Gormelia's treachery and will be concerned for you."

"You two, come with me," Cook said to Kenna and Wilma. "And stop your blubbering. If I had been chief, you would have been thrown out of the pack and on your own."

Nelly asked Cook, "Can I do anything?"

"You can help me pick the two women who will replace Kenna and Wilma." Cook, Nelly, and the ostracized women headed down the tower stairs to the main floor.

Aisling followed them down to the inner bailey. She wanted to see who Cook chose to replace Kenna and Wilma, but she had to speak with Coinneach. As soon as she headed for the tower stairs to the wall walk, she saw Coinneach waving at her.

She rushed up the stairs and met him at the top. He pulled her into a hard embrace. "I heard that Nelly saved your life."

"Aye." She hugged him back, holding him tight. "I love you so much. I canna believe Gormelia would go to such lengths to get rid of me over some pettiness. Morag defended all of them." Aisling told him about the chief taking charge of the situation.

"Do you think Morag put Gormelia up to it?"

"The way she was defending her made me wonder. But the chief wasna happy with Morag for taking matters into her own hands without informing him."

"Good. He is an honorable man."

"We will have to train the new women to be cooks, so I need to check on that. But I just wanted to tell you that I'm fine and everything has been taken care of."

A couple of men pulled a cart to the castle doors, and another carried a body wrapped in a blanket out to the cart.

"Gormelia?" Coinneach asked.

"Most likely."

Coinneach hugged Aisling again as if he could have lost her and was so grateful that Gormelia had eaten the poisoned food instead.

Then they kissed, but Coinneach didn't want to let her go.

"I'll be fine. Kenna and Wilma willna dare try to harm me. Everyone will be watching them."

They looked out across the inner bailey where Kenna and Wilma were learning how to wash the clothes, dropping wet garments on the ground when they slipped out of their hands. Women were washing in two more barrels, chatting happily, giving Kenna and Wilma disparaging looks. No one wanted to be friends with someone who had been involved in attempting to murder Aisling.

Everyone already presumed they had as thick as they had been with Gormelia.

"If Cook will let me, I'll bring you dinner."

"Aye, I hope she will."

Then Aisling hurried off to the tower stairs and crossed the inner bailey at the bottom. She headed for the keep, but Rupert suddenly waylaid her. He grabbed her arm, and she tried to yank free of him, but he was too strong.

"Let go of me, Rupert!" she yelled out, hoping someone would hear her and come to her rescue. She would have broken his nose if she could have gotten away with it.

When she fetched eggs for a meal, he would sometimes catch her in the henhouse, and no one could protect her, but this time, they were out in the open, and someone would surely notice.

"You're naught more than a kitchen servant, yet you act like you're better than me." Rupert dragged her toward the stable, and she yanked as hard as she could to free herself.

"I think naught of the sort. You are the chief's son." But she wanted to tell him he wasn't.

Suddenly, Drustan grabbed Rupert's arm and jerked him aside. "The lass is betrothed to Coinneach. Everyone knows that. You would do well to leave her alone."

"I will tell my da that you dared put a hand on me."

Chief Hamish's brother, Collum, strode forth and joined them.

"Uncle, I want Drustan fired from his position," Rupert said.

"On what grounds?" Collum asked.

"Drustan dared to grab my arm and jerk me aside like I was some servant." Rupert was red-faced and furious, but she could smell that he was scared. Drustan was well-liked by Hamish, played a significant role in their security, and could get away with much more than she could concerning Rupert.

Collum folded his arms across his chest. "But it's all right for you to accost one of our lasses viciously."

"Aisling said I was the one who told Gormelia to poison her, so I wanted to speak to her about what she was saying and set her straight," Rupert said.

Collum raised his brows. "Did you?"

Rupert's face reddened. "Of course I didna."

"I didna accuse him of doing that either," Aisling said. "He just grabbed my arm and tried to force me into the stable. He has done so before." But now she wondered if he had been behind Gormelia's treachery. Why would he even say such a thing unless it was true?

She hadn't allowed him to kiss her, though he had manhandled her on numerous occasions, and maybe that was his way of getting even, especially since she was now marrying Coinneach.

Coinneach suddenly joined them. He looked in a fighting mood, ready to pummel Rupert. "You willna lay a hand on Aisling again, Rupert."

Collum placed his hand on Coinneach's chest to keep him away from Rupert.

Only in battle did Coinneach look so furious.

"Or you'll do what?" Rupert was an idiot if he thought to challenge Coinneach.

"You willna treat the lasses with disrespect, any of them, Rupert," Collum said. "Your mother should have taught you better."

But his mother treated most of the servants like they were dirt beneath her feet. So she certainly wasn't teaching her son to be respectful of the lasses in the clan.

"He isna allowed to touch me like he did." Rupert pointed to Drustan.

"Since you were hellbent on taking Aisling to the stable, he had to stop you. He was right in protecting the lass. I will speak to your da about this. Mayhap he can assign you some chores that will keep you out of mischief." Collum stalked off.

Rupert glowered at Aisling, as if she were the one at fault.

Coinneach took hold of her hand. "Where were you off to?"

"The kitchen gardens."

"I'll escort you there." Coinneach glared at Rupert, then led Aisling away.

Drustan left also, Rupert standing in the inner bailey, probably wondering if his da would give him some onerous task. Aisling hoped he would have to muck out the stables.

"Rupert accused me of saying that I believed he was behind Gormelia's attempt at poisoning me."

Coinneach frowned at her. "Why would he say such a thing?"

"Because it's true? I've thwarted his attempts to take advantage of me several times, and he becomes outraged that he can't have me the way he wants."

"The measly little bastard."

"Aye. Usually, the lasses he targets let him get away with it. Some are like me and fight him off. Gormelia wanted him to show her the same attention, but he wouldna. She probably thought he would become chief if Hamish died, and then she would mate him and be the lady of the castle."

"I've thought about the succession. Rupert willna be chief. Collum would take over. Hamish's brother is second in command, and everyone seems to like him."

"Except Rupert."

"His uncle holds him to a higher standard than his mother ever would. Are you feeling better now?" Coinneach asked, guiding Aisling through the stone archway into the gardens.

"I am. Thank you for not hitting Rupert."

Nelly knelt among the rosemary and thyme, a basket at her side. She straightened when she spotted them, the knife she used to cut the herbs glinting in the sunlight. "Were you no' meant to be patrolling the battlements this morning?"

Coinneach shook his head. "I needed to deal with the enemy within."

"Rupert," Aisling clarified for Nelly.

"Oh, you didna hit him, did you?" Nelly asked Coinneach, looking worried.

"Nay. Collum stopped me from laying a hand on the snake."

"Good, because Morag would go after you with a vengeance."

"Collum is talking to his da," Aisling said. "Hopefully, his da will give Rupert some disagreeable chores to do."

"I would love to see that. He thinks he's a prince among his slaves," Nelly said.

"I must return to work before Drustan fires me." Coinneach kissed Aisling.

"I'll watch over her," Nelly said.

"Let's run as wolves tonight." Aisling hadn't done that with Coinneach for a while, and she just wanted to leave the castle to spend time with him alone.

"May I go with you?" Nelly asked. "I mean, not to run as a wolf with you, but to stop by your family's home and visit with your family."

Coinneach finally smiled. "Aye. We'll make sure you get there safely and return to the castle."

Then he headed out of the gardens, and Aisling told Nelly what Rupert had said about Aisling saying he had been behind Gormelia's attempt to poison Aisling.

"Nay." Nelly cupped her face, her eyes wide. "But as many times as he has made advances toward you, you've rejected them, and now you're kissing Coinneach all the time, maybe he *was* involved. Or possibly the one who instigated it through Gormelia, promising her something like a mating or something."

"Aye. I have to consider the possibility. Luckily, Collum and Drustan heard Rupert's words. And Collum asked if Rupert had been behind the attempted murder. Which makes me think that he thought the same as us—that it was a possibility. Why else would Rupert say such a thing?"

"It's too awful to consider," Nelly said.

"Because he was afraid that I suspected he had something to do with it? I had never considered he might have been behind the attempt on my life." Aisling thought he should have kept his mouth shut.

"Me either." Nelly finished clipping herbs for the meal. "Then you could still be in danger. Not only from Rupert's wrath but also from his mother's."

Aisling thought about Coinneach being Hamish's son and the danger from that also. But what if she could prove that Rupert wasn't Hamish's son? Would Hamish banish Morag and Rupert from the pack? And that would end the problem with them?

"I have a secret to tell you." Aisling wouldn't tell Nelly about Coinneach's birthright, but she would need some help proving Rupert wasn't Hamish's son. Then again, what if Hamish knew and didn't care? Or he didn't want to admit that Morag had slept with another man when she'd been married to Hamish?

"Och, what else?" Nelly sounded serious because Aisling's voice was dark with warning.

"It's a dangerous thing to know, but my mother believes Osmond is Rupert's da."

"Nay, really?" Nelly looked around to make sure there was no one within hearing distance. "He does look like Osmond though."

"Aye. Both have the same facial features, high-bridged noses and no chin, the same red curly hair, the same slight body build. And they have the same kind of hair loss on their temples."

"I agree. Do you think Hamish knows and doesna want anyone else to learn the truth?"

"Perhaps." Aisling wanted to tell her the rest of the story. That having an illegitimate heir wasn't the half of it. Attempting to kill Hamish's true son was truly important.

"You want to expose him because of the trouble he still may cause you," Nelly said quietly.

"I want both of them gone, mother and son. But proving any of it could be impossible. And there's always the possibility that Hamish willna care since he has raised him as his own son. He may even vehemently deny that Rupert isna his son."

"How does your mother know?"

"She had seen Osmond and her together in the stables."

"Och." Then Nelly smiled. "We can share the rumors in a secretive way. Dinna you think Rupert favors Osmond? And then the rumors would spread. You know how that goes."

Nelly and Aisling walked through the garden to the keep. "We dinna want anyone to know we are the ones starting the rumors. When Morag learns of it, she will want us both dead."

"Aye." Nelly opened the door to the keep. "We will have to think about it."

When they arrived at the kitchen, Cook wanted Nelly and Aisling to teach the washer women how to prepare meals. The women looked a bit overwhelmed, but Aisling said, "We're so glad you are working with us. Working here, we get better food than most." Other than the more important members of the clan.

Ann and Marie smiled.

"It's hard work, but you've already done hard work with the washing, so you'll fit in fine." Aisling hoped the ladies would be friendly toward her and Nelly and not like Kenna and Wilma had been.

"Aye, we are eager to work on the kitchen staff," Ann said.

Marie nodded vigorously. "We didna think we would ever be anything but washer women, though we are sorry for the reason we gained the positions."

"Aye, so are we," Aisling said.

"We saw Rupert grab you before we moved inside the keep. He's a bully," Ann said. "And there are rumors he's no' even the chief's son."

Aisling's mouth gaped. She hadn't believed anyone else would think that. "What makes you believe that?"

"He looks just like Osmond, dinna you think? While cleaning laundry, we saw Morag and Osmond sneaking off to the stable often enough," Marie said.

"They looked disheveled when they left the stable," Ann said. "Morag had no reason to check out the stable, dinna you see?"

"Do others feel that way?" Nelly asked.

"All the washer women. We all saw the same and talked about it," Ann said.

13

Coinneach could have killed Rupert for accosting Aisling. By the time he'd heard her shouts, seen her being manhandled by Rupert, and raced down the tower stairs, Drustan had gone to her rescue. He was glad Collum had put Rupert in his place.

But that hadn't stopped Coinneach from letting Rupert know that he wouldn't tolerate his actions toward Aisling.

Aodhan immediately joined Coinneach on the wall walk as he came out of the tower stairs. "If he wasna the chief's son, I would have pummeled him myself. You showed great restraint, Coinneach."

"Collum stopped me from putting a hand on him."

"He was right to do so. He'll tell Hamish what had happened, which you know will be different from Rupert's version."

"Rupert said that the reason he was angry with Aisling was that she accused him of being behind Gormelia's attempted murder of her."

Aodhan stroked his bearded chin. "Is that what Aisling truly thinks?"

"Nay. Rupert was the one who brought it up, which makes us believe he was involved."

Aodhan looked out across the countryside. "If that is so, he is truly evil, the chief's son or no'."

"What if he isna the chief's son?" Perhaps that was the way to eliminate the threat in their midst. Reveal that part of the truth anyway.

Aodhan looked sharply at Coinneach.

"What if he is Osmond's son?" Coinneach hoped he wasn't making a mistake by bringing it up to Aodhan.

Aodhan laughed. "Because they are both redheaded? We have other redheads in the clan. Why no' any of them?"

"Because Morag doesna go to the stable with any other redheads?"

Aodhan frowned. "I canna believe he wouldna be Hamish's son."

"Mayhap Hamish knows it but chose to accept him as his son since he lost his firstborn."

Both of them looked out at the forests beyond the meadows.

Aodhan cleared his throat. "'Twas a shame that his first wife and baby son didna survive in childbirth. I was four years old then, so all I remember was Morag quickly taking Orla's place and becoming the chief's new wife."

"Did anyone question the fact that she took over Orla's position so suddenly?"

"I wouldna know. She was the midwife, our healer, and she comforted him in his time of grief. I dinna see any love between them, however, not like older pack members have said about Hamish and his first wife."

Coinneach didn't know if he could trust Aodhan to tell him the truth about Morag ordering Hamish's bairn to be murdered. Yet how else could Coinneach truly protect Aisling and her mother from the threats within? Unless he could get rid of Morag and Rupert.

"What if Hamish's firstborn son survived?" Coinneach leaned against the stone wall of the wall walk.

Aodhan glanced sharply at him. "Nay. They buried the baby with his mother."

"What if a child from another mother whose twin had passed away was buried in place of Hamish's true son?"

Aodhan furrowed his brow. "Where are you coming up with all of this? Is there some gossip going around the pack? I've never heard of it."

"What if Morag ordered Hamish's bairn to be murdered so she could mate him and no' have to raise his son, but have one of her own, only he isna Hamish's but Osmond's? Then her son would lead the pack instead of his firstborn."

Aodhan shook his head. "Preposterous."

"Aye. You are probably right." It did sound far-fetched, and even Coinneach had to agree he couldn't believe it when Aisling told him about it, either—at first.

Aodhan rested his arms on the top of the wall walk and glanced at Coinneach. "How do you know any of this?"

Coinneach didn't want to reveal Blair's role in this, should it go badly for her.

Aodhan let out his breath. "Where is the son then?"

"He would be full-grown, a year older than Rupert if he were born a year after the firstborn disappeared."

"But if Morag ordered the bairn killed—"

"And the person who took the bairn away couldna do it, then someone else raised him as their own. You see the problem with this? Morag would still want him dead if she learns he is alive. And she'd want the person dead who was supposed to carry out her orders. She couldna risk having this come back to haunt her."

Aodhan looked back out to the meadows. "It's too far-fetched.

Unless you're no' telling me something. Even if Hamish's son is out there, how could he prove he's his son? If Hamish never saw him, and he's fully grown, he wouldna know him now."

"The women in the birthing room saw the healthy bairn before Morag had him taken away and brought the other baby to rest with Orla."

Aodhan's eyes widened. "Blair had to have told you this. She was in training to be a midwife and healer when Morag became Hamish's wife. Why would she tell you this?" Aodhan glanced back at the inner bailey, where Collum and Hamish had a heated discussion with Rupert.

Rupert finally threw his hands up in response and headed for the stables.

Aodhan faced Coinneach. "You are no' Hamish's son."

"I didna say I was."

"You resemble Hamish and this twin brother, much more than Rupert does." Aodhan straightened. "Are you saying Magnus and Elspeth are no' your parents? That Tamhas isna your brother?"

"I'm saying naught of the sort."

Aodhan looked back out to the forests off in the distance. "So, how are we going to prove you're Hamish's son?"

NELLY AND AISLING showed their two new cooks how to serve the tables. Then Aisling served the champion's table, while Aodhan and Coinneach were still on the wall walk. She was so glad he hadn't hit Rupert and gotten banished from the pack.

Right after the meal was done, she hurried out to the wall walk with meals for Coinneach and Aodhan. They both thanked her.

Then she quickly kissed Coinneach. "I have to eat and then I'll meet you in the inner baily as a wolf?"

"Aye. Is Nelly still coming?"

"She has her heart set on it."

"I'll see you then."

Aisling hurried off, excited about running with Coinneach as a wolf, and she hoped Tamhas would be as thrilled to see Nelly as much as she was to see him.

She ended up in the kitchen with the others, everyone serving up meals, but this time Aisling served up her own. Nelly ate faster than Aisling had ever witnessed. "Slow down. The men are no' changing shifts for a while."

Nelly drank some more of her ale. "Do you think Tamhas likes me?"

"Aye, he does. But he's different from Coinneach. I can run up to Coinneach and hug him, whereas Tamhas is a bit more reserved. Still, as you get to know him, he may change."

Nelly sighed. "I will be cautious around him, no' wanting to scare him off."

"Be yourself, Nelly. If the two of you fall in love, you will know you're right for each other."

"Coinneach doesna have any other brothers, does he?" Ann asked.

"Nay." In truth, he didn't have *any* blood brothers.

As the head of the table, Cook cleared her throat. Everyone looked at her. "I've heard rumors for years that Rupert isna Hamish's son. But I wouldna want any of you to be in trouble for spreading these rumors should Morag, her son, or even the chief be angered about it."

So even Cook had heard the rumors. That was good news. How many more of the pack members felt the same way? And were afraid to mention it?

After they ate and cleaned up, Aisling told Cook, "Nelly and I are off to Coinneach's family's croft. Though Coinneach and I are running as wolves."

"Be safe and watch your surroundings." Cook had never said

that to Aisling before, and she wondered if she feared Rupert would try to retaliate against her.

"Thanks. We will be." Aisling and Nelly went to the women's chamber, and Aisling stripped off her clothes. "Take my bow with you. You've been practicing, and if we encounter any trouble, you can use it to take down the threat."

Nelly frowned and picked up the bow and quiver of arrows resting beside Aisling's pallet. "You think Cook is worried about us?"

"Aye. No telling what Rupert might do after getting in trouble with his uncle. And then having to muck out the stalls? He will be sure to want to get back at me." Aisling shifted.

The two of them headed out of the castle to the inner bailey, where Aodhan and Coinneach were coming down the tower stairs.

"I'll be out shortly," Coinneach said, smiling at Aisling. He went inside the barracks and soon emerged as a wolf, hurrying to join Nelly and Aisling.

"Howl if you get into trouble," Aodhan said, "and I will come with an army of men."

Aisling and Coinneach inclined their heads to him. They would have raced across the meadow if Nelly hadn't been with them. Instead, they walked beside her as her wolf companions.

"You might not have had a chance to tell Coinneach, Aisling," Nelly said, "but the washer women who have joined our kitchen staff said they believe that Rupert is Osmond's son. Even Cook said she'd heard the rumors for years. But she warned us no' to speak on the matter because we could be in trouble."

In real danger, Aisling wanted to say. She glanced at Coinneach to see how he viewed the news. He licked her face. She took that to mean he was glad others knew about it.

Aisling and Coinneach howled to let his family know they were coming.

They finally reached the croft where Magnus and Tamhas were

outside doing last-minute chores. As wolves, they could see well in the dark. Human crofters would have been abed by this time. His mother came out too.

Tamhas brightened to see them, but especially to see Nelly. She smiled brightly. But he seemed a bit tongue-tied. He needed some alone time with Nelly.

"They wanted to run as wolves. I came along to protect them." She showed them Aisling's bow. "Rupert accosted Aisling in the inner bailey and was punished by having to work in the stalls. So we worried he might retaliate."

"We're delighted you are here," his mother said.

"Come in," Magnus said, heartily. "Join us for some ale."

Aisling and Coinneach woofed at them and then raced through the meadow to the forest and to the trail to the waterfall, huffing and puffing. When they reached the spot, they sat watching the water spill down the rocks.

Coinneach shifted and sat on the stone they used for seating. "I told Aodhan what we suspect—that I could be Hamish's son."

Aisling shifted and sat on his lap. He wrapped his arms around her and kissed her cheek.

"Did he believe you?" She sounded worried.

"Finally, aye."

"You told him my mother took you away?" Real fear shown in Aisling's eyes.

"He assumed it."

"Can he be trusted?"

"I believe so. He wants to help me prove I'm the chief's son."

She let out her breath. "Which means my mother and other women in the birthing room that day would know you were healthy and very much alive. And that you were removed from the room."

"And replaced. Did they see my wolf mark?"

"My mother, aye. I dinna know about the others."

"Do you know the names of the women who were there when I was born?"

"I'll ask my mother. I should have done so before. What if Aodhan makes inquiries, and it spreads throughout the pack? Already, the rumors seem to be rampant that Rupert is Osmond's son. But hearing you are Hamish's son, that could be catastrophic."

"I love you, Aisling. I want no other mate for my wolf. I dinna care if it's proven that I'm the chief's son, but Morag's crime should be punished."

"I agree." She smiled at him. "You know I feel the same about you."

"Which is why I want to mate you now and no' delay the inevitable."

Her eyes widened. "Here? Now?"

"There's no other place for us to be alone. Your mother has consented to our marriage. When we are all free to do it, we'll have a simple marriage ceremony at the croft."

She got off his lap and seized his hand. "To the meadow where the grass is softer."

He swept her up in his arms and carried her along the path through the forest, but she shifted into her wolf and leaped from his arms. She woofed and raced off to the meadow.

He laughed, shifted, and ran after her, glad she was as eager to mate him as he was her.

He quickly caught up to her, but she was sitting in the tall grasses, her tail straight out, her ears twitching back and forth, her fur standing on end—and he knew she was wary of something she'd seen or heard.

He stood next to her, listening intently, watching for movement.

Then Coinneach saw two men armed with bows heading their way, but they were sneaking along, keeping low. He smelled their scent on the breeze and recognized they were stable hands who worked for Osmond.

Aisling shifted, crouching low. "They work for Osmond." Then she shifted back into her wolf.

Coinneach didn't know what the men were up to, maybe just hunting for Hamish, but he didn't think so. If the men followed Coinneach's and Aisling's trail, which they could do with their wolf senses, then Coinneach would be more assured that they were there to hunt them.

He shifted. "Aye. Follow my lead." Then he shifted and moved slowly away from the men while she trailed close behind him.

Once they were in the forest, he ran through the woods, leaping over fallen tree branches, driving through the branches, not taking any well-marked paths. It would make it more difficult for the men to follow them as humans.

As wolves, they would be way ahead of the men anyway, but Coinneach wanted to make it more difficult for them to follow if they were hunting them.

They finally reached the river, the fragrance of the water drawing him to it. He ran across the rocky beach to the river, and Aisling joined him. The water was flowing fast, but once they reached the other side, they could hide in the bracken at the foot of the trees and watch for the men to see if they were indeed following them.

Though in their human form, it would take the men time to reach the river.

Still, Coinneach had wanted to make sure that he and Aisling had enough time to swim across the river and conceal themselves.

He nuzzled her face, then walked into the water. She joined him, and the two began to swim across the swiftly flowing river. They struggled to reach the other side, bumping into each other, but staying together. Then they finally scrambled up the rocky shoulder on the other side, about a quarter of a mile from where they went in.

If the men were tracking them, they would most likely assume the currents pushed Coinneach and Aisling downstream. But he didn't want to chance that they would go downstream to search for them. He and Aisling shook the water off their fur, then raced through the woods to the approximate place where they'd gone into the water.

Once there, they waited for the men to reach the opposite river-bank. They hid in the bracken, lying down beside each other to rest. But then Coinneach shifted.

"I want to see if they truly were following us and aimed to hunt us down."

Aisling nodded.

Then he shifted back and cuddled with her, so much for mating her in the meadow. His first thought, if the men were sent to kill them, Rupert had everything to do with it. But what if Morag did? Or even Rupert's da, Osmond?

Their hearts were still beating hard after their swim and run. Coinneach licked Aisling's cheek, and she affectionately nuzzled him.

It seemed they waited forever when they finally heard the men coming through the trees on the other side of the river, except they were a bit north of Coinneach and Aisling's location. But at least they could still see the men. One was black-haired and bearded, and the other brown haired and bearded. Both were muscular, and Coinneach wondered if they'd ever been trained to fight with a sword.

They were huffing and puffing, still holding their bows, ready to shoot Coinneach and Aisling. They must have heard and smelled the river before they reached it, but maybe they believed they weren't as far behind them as they thought they were.

They stood staring at the forest on the opposite side of the river.

"What do we do now? We canna chase them as hunters. They'll run all over the forest and keep far away from us as wolves."

"We shift and kill them as wolves." Then the one man began stripping off his clothes and shifted.

The other followed his lead.

They entered the water, and the current carried them downstream. They didn't fight it, and Coinneach suspected they would go where they thought he and Aisling had left the water. As soon as they were around the bend in the river, Coinneach dashed upstream in the direction where the men's clothes and weapons were lying on the riverbank.

Aisling quickly followed him, and the two of them began to cross the river. This time, they were north of the location where the men's clothes were so the currents carried them to the bank where they were.

Coinneach shifted and carried one man's clothes into the deeper part of the water where they sank. After shifting, Aisling carried the men's bows and quivers of arrows to the river and dumped them. They returned to shore and rushed to where the men's remaining clothes and weapons were, then continued to submerge them in the river.

They swam quickly back to the shore as fast as they could, knowing the men would eventually reach the place where Aisling and he had left the river on the opposite bank, then follow their scent trail to the woods. They would realize that Aisling and Coinneach had been watching them when they shifted into their wolf forms to track down the couple.

Coinneach nudged Aisling to follow him. They raced toward his family's home.

He didn't think the men would be foolhardy enough to try to kill them there. But if they tried, they wouldn't be successful.

He would have howled a warning to his family, but he didn't want to alert the men. They were probably still crossing the river to reach their clothes and weapons. Coinneach would have loved to see the looks on their faces when they discovered they were missing.

When they were nearly to the farm, Coinneach and Aisling saw Tamhas and Nelly talking to each other in the meadow.

Coinneach headed straight for them to warn them of the trouble headed their way. Unless the men returned to the castle, giving up their quest.

Tamhas saw Coinneach and Aisling and furrowed his brow. He probably knew Coinneach and Aisling weren't racing each other to the croft in fun.

Coinneach barked at them to return to the croft.

Tamhas took hold of Nelly's hand and ran with her. Magnus was in the field and quickly glanced in their direction, realizing there was bound to be trouble.

Coinneach nudged Aisling ahead of them to the croft, while he protected Tamhas and Nelly. But Aisling stayed with them, and he knew she meant to fight the wolves if they reached them and attacked.

Coinneach looked back, thinking he'd seen something in the tall grasses. Sure enough, the two wolves were trying to reach them before they could seek shelter in the croft. Coinneach and his companions had been moving more slowly because his brother and Nelly were running as humans.

Tamhas made Nelly go inside the croft. Their da was armed with a pitchfork. Tamhas had his swords. But Nelly came out with Aisling's bow and arrows.

Aisling ran inside the croft and came out dressed in one of his mother's kirtles. Aisling took the bow and quiver of arrows from Nelly. "Go inside, now."

"What is happening?" Nelly asked.

"Someone has sent hunters to kill us," Aisling said.

Coinneach waited as a wolf, intending to kill at least one of the wolves in that way.

"Who?" their da asked.

"Two of the men who work in the stables. They're running as wolves now. We got rid of their clothes, bows, and other weapons in the river," Aisling said. She readied her bow and aimed for the movement in the tall grass. Then she released an arrow, and a wolf cried out.

Coinneach raced forward, intending to take down the other wolf. Tamhas and his da were right behind him, though they couldn't keep up as humans with his swift wolf speed.

Even Aisling was running behind them, trying to catch up to them. Coinneach knew she would stop and try to use her arrows on one of the two wolves, which was an excellent way for her to keep her distance and still take down a wolf or two.

Sure enough, before Coinneach clashed with the bigger of the two wolves, an arrow slid through the air and hit the wolf in the shoulder. Now, both wolves wore one of her arrows as Coinneach tackled the larger wolf—their mouths biting at each other, drawing blood.

The other wolf lunged at Coinneach, but Aisling shot him in the flank. Then Tamhas reached the smaller wolf and struck his shoulder with his sword. The wolf howled in pain. He whipped around to attack Tamhas, but his father plunged his pitchfork into the wolf's neck, and the wolf went down. The dead wolf shifted into his human form.

Aware that the other wolf was dead, Coinneach was still fighting the larger wolf. He tried to grab the wolf's neck, but the wolf leapt out of the way. Their da jabbed at the wolf, but Coinneach jumped at him, determined to keep him from attacking his da.

Aisling was closer now and readied an arrow, but as viciously as Coinneach attacked the wolf, Aisling couldn't get a clear shot.

Likewise, his da and brother couldn't attack him either.

Coinneach tore the wolf's skin at his shoulder. He attempted to bite Coinneach's neck. He darted out of the wolf's snapping canines and rounded on him again. This time, he managed to grab him by the back of the neck and held on for dear life as the wolf tried to shake him loose.

Then Coinneach bit hard, severing the wolf's spinal column, and the wolf collapsed, no longer a threat. Immediately, the dead wolf turned into his human form.

Coinneach ran into the nearby lake and cleaned off his bloody fur. Aisling hurried after him to see how he fared.

Tamhas and their da loaded the naked, bloody bodies into a cart. Their da asked, "Do we return them to the castle and explain what happened here?"

Coinneach shifted, and Aisling immediately hugged him. "Nay. If Rupert, Osmond, or Morag sent them, they will twist the story and say we killed them for whatever reason. Take them to the bog. They can wonder what happened to the men."

"Come, let me take care of your wounds," Aisling said. "How will you serve guard duty looking like this? How will you explain that you were in a fight and with whom?"

Coinneach smiled. "Come, sweeting. Take care of them, and we'll return to the castle to sleep. By morning, most of my wounds will be fading."

Once Aisling and his mother had bandaged Coinneach, he put on some of his spare clothes that Tamhas hadn't packed.

"I'll walk with you back to the castle," Tamhas said. "In case anyone attempts to ambush you again."

Coinneach inclined his head.

Nelly looked thrilled that Tamhas was going with them, even if it was just to protect them on the trip back to the castle. Perhaps it was because he wanted to spend more time with Nelly.

When they reached the castle gates, Nelly gave Tamhas a quick kiss, and he wrapped his arms around her, kissing her more soundly.

Beaming, she asked, "Do you want me to wait for you, Aisling?"

"Nay. Go to bed. I'll be there shortly."

Looking on top of the world, Tamhas bid them good night and headed off for home.

In the inner bailey, Aodhan quickly joined Aisling and Coinneach, eyeing him with concern. "What the hell happened to you?"

14

A isling should have known Aodhan would catch them when they arrived at the castle, and be concerned at once about Coinneach's wounds. Out of everyone's hearing, Coinneach explained to Aodhan what had happened.

"I would kill the son-of-a-two-headed beast, if we could prove Osmond sent his men to eliminate you and Aisling," Aodhan said.

But Aodhan would not terminate Rupert, whom the chief believed to be his son. Aisling suspected Aodhan wouldn't go that far.

Before changing topics, Aodhan let out his breath. "You are no' letting this keep you from a mating this eve, are you?"

Coinneach smiled. "Nay. I need to grab a couple of things from the barracks. Will you watch over Aisling in the meantime?"

"Aye, you know I will, with my life."

Aisling couldn't believe Coinneach would have brought up the mating to Aodhan, but she was glad Coinneach felt well enough to go through with it and not delay it.

Coinneach quickly left the barracks with blankets in hand, being obvious about what they were up to in case anyone noticed. Smiling, she shook her head.

"Do you want me to guard you and Aisling while you, uh, get on with business?" Aodhan asked.

"Nay. We'll be fine." Coinneach patted his sword.

Aisling realized that beneath the blankets, Coinneach was well armed, and she was glad for it.

"I will return."

"See you later then." Aodhan reached over to slap him on the back, then appearing to think better of it because he didn't know where all Coinneach's injuries were hidden under his shirt, he dropped his hand and smiled.

Coinneach hurried off with Aisling, neither wanting to alert the whole castle as to what they were up to. The pack members would know soon enough.

"The herb garden?" Some of the tall shrubs and herbs would provide sufficient shelter from prying eyes. The problem with wolves was that they could see in the dark, so they needed some privacy.

Coinneach led her to the castle doors. "What about the spicery pantry? I have no' been there, but you must have."

"Aye, perfect. No one will be in the kitchen or storage areas at this time of night." She led him inside and took him straight to the pantry. In the kitchen, a lantern was still burning, and she grabbed it.

No one was about, like she suspected, and they slipped into the pantry unnoticed. She pulled the door shut, wishing they could lock it from the inside. She put the lantern down, far enough away from where they set the blankets that they wouldn't knock it over in the throes of passionate lovemaking.

The faint light cast a majestic glow on the vaulted ceiling and shelves of spices—including ginger, cloves, peppercorns, dill, mustard, caraway, ginger, and even a large amount of saffron. All were in boxes to preserve them, scenting the air with a mixture of spicy aroma. Containers of cooking oils sat on the bottom shelves.

He laid the blankets on the floor, spreading them out to make a comfortable pallet for them. The notion of making love here was both arousing and daring.

Then he removed his sword and laid it down next to the makeshift bed, ready to protect them if someone came after them again. She knelt, nestling her bow and quiver of arrows at her side of the blankets—just as ready to protect them—and then turned to him.

The lantern's flame behind them flickered in the updraft, and the rising heat drew sweet, sharp scents from the air.

"Hmm, it smells heavenly in here," she whispered, her hands on his shoulders, her tongue licking his neck.

"The spices in here and the fragrance of heather collected on our clothes and hair, aye." He took hold of her shoulders and ran his hands over them in a loving caress and kissed her forehead.

"And us," she corrected, her voice growing huskier as she pressed her palm to the center of his chest, where his heart fluttered like a snared bird.

She took hold of his face and pulled him down, their mouths colliding, biting, joining as the need to speak was overtaken by the need to taste. He kissed her again, with the force of someone making a declaration that could not be unsaid or misunderstood.

They wanted this; they needed this—a mating, a joining of two wolves in love. She broke free first, breathless, laughing softly as she removed her kirtle, baring skin already dappled by the chill in the air.

He caught her hand, splaying her fingers wide, and bent to kiss each knuckle, the gesture oddly reverent. "You are the bravest person I have ever known," he murmured, words muffled as his lips traveled the length of her arm.

"You are too." She unfastened his belt and dropped it on the floor with a soft clatter.

He ran his hands over her breasts under the translucent shift.

Her nipples tingled with intense pleasure, and she moaned with delight. He kissed her breasts while she pulled off his plaid, wanting to mate before something else stopped them.

Once his plaid was on the floor in a puddle of fabric, she pulled up his shirt, the lower part tenting his desire for her.

Before she could lift his shirt all the way, he was pulling her shift over her head and tossing it on his plaid. She quickly pulled off his long shirt before he thwarted her again.

"Hmm." She nuzzled his chest with her mouth. "You smell of pine forest and the river."

"You smell of the same, the wilderness, and the tall meadow grasses filled with heather."

She ran her finger from his throat to the thatch of dark hair around his fully aroused manhood. He trembled, collected her hair in his hands, gently stroked it, and pressed his lips to hers. She licked his lips and plunged her tongue into his mouth. He quickly stroked her tongue with his as she ran her hands over his naked, muscled back.

Her body responded completely to his measured touches, her nipples hyperaware, the area between her thighs wet and eager for his penetration.

He swept her up in his arms and laid her reverently on the blanket, then joined her, his body pressed against hers. She opened her legs for him, allowing him to fall between them, warming them with their close contact.

He rubbed his erection between her legs, the friction of his manhood against her womanhood sending delicious chills up her body, the sensation both amazing and delightful.

She arched against him, wanting him inside of her now, but he wrapped her legs around his hips and continued to rub against her in such an unbelievable way, she felt she was going to burst into flames.

Their hearts were beating like crazy, their musky sex adding to the earthy tones they were already enveloped in. Their breaths came quickly as they relished the intimacy between them.

Then he was surging into her and filling her with his love. Suddenly, he pulled most of the way out and began to stroke her, where she nearly shattered at his touch. Goddess, she'd never experienced such a wonderment. She cried out and clapped her hand over her mouth. He chuckled, kissed her mouth, and thrust into her again.

He didn't stop this time until he came and she felt his seed in her, drenching her, making her wonder if he had produced a bairn in her.

"I love you, sweeting." He dragged the extra blanket over them. They merged then, limbs and intentions tangled, the world beyond the door unimportant. All that mattered was that they were mated wolves and she wanted desperately to share the news with the pack, but not here, not like this!

"I love you and think the world of you." She hoped her mother didn't worry about where she was this night, but suspected that Nelly would let her know that they were safe at the castle and would retire to bed when they were ready.

"Love you," Coinneach whispered against her ear, his hand caressing a breast.

"Love you back, Coinneach." She figured they would return to their pallets in their respective living areas, but she didn't want to leave him any more than he made a move to suggest they parted ways and went to their own beds.

Each time she tried to extract herself from his embrace with a halfhearted attempt, he tightened his grip and pressed his face into her neck or her hair, mumbling sweet sentiments until she relented.

Instead of leaving the spicery room, they made love again in the middle of the night. Again, she thought they would return to their beds, but they enjoyed this too much and continued to cuddle. She nestled herself against his side, her leg on top of his, and listened to his easy, contented breathing.

Until after sleeping a few hours more, she heard a soft, deliberate knock, so small it could have been a trick of the wind. But then it came again, more insistent, rapping three times at the spicery door, she realized the kitchen staff would soon be in the kitchen, preparing the morning meal.

She groaned. "Coinneach, we must get up. We've been caught. I need to get to work."

He smiled and folded his arms behind his head. She kissed his stomach. "Someone is at the door," she whispered.

He sighed. "Aye."

She got off him and hurried to dress. He watched her, smiling as he got up and dressed himself. She knew he was perfectly pleased that others would realize that they had mated.

She opened the door, expecting Cook and the whole kitchen staff to be watching them as they left the spicery room, but the kitchen was empty. "Come, hurry. We must leave at once. No one is here."

Had someone... Aisling smelled the most recent scent next to the door—Nelly. Had she come to warn them? She must have.

Aisling glanced back at Coinneach and shook her head as he carried his blankets out of the room, looking self-satisfied. Now he would return them to the men's barracks, and everyone would see him do it.

She gave him a quick kiss and a smile. "'Tis done."

"Aye. You can decide when to tell everyone."

"As if the word willna have already spread. No matter. I need to tell my mother though. I'll see you when we break our fast."

Then she rushed off to the women's quarters while he headed to the barracks.

Her mother was just getting dressed when Aisling hurried into the ladies' chamber. She set her bow and arrows down and changed her clothes. She would need to wash them and return them to Elspeth when she was free to do so.

"You mated Coinneach," her mom said, sounding resigned to the matter.

The other women were leaving to do their work until the meal was ready, casting glances at Aisling and smiling.

Nelly hurried into the lady's quarters. "Hurry. We're late."

"You wouldna have been except you wanted to save me," Aisling said. "Thanks."

Nelly smiled, then pulled at her arm. "Come, hurry."

Aisling realized then that Nelly wanted to know the details of what went on. She glanced at her mother.

"I'm good with it. Get to work before Cook scolds you girls for being late to the kitchen." Aisling's mother hugged her. "Congratulations." Then she hurried off to work.

Nelly raised her brows at Aisling, then hugged her. She whispered, "I guess your mother is finally all right with you mating Coinneach."

"Aye, 'tis good." Which was a good thing because it was done. Aisling wondered if she and Coinneach would be moved to a room set aside for married couples, where curtains would divide them from other couples. Though she and Coinneach weren't officially married yet, mating with another wolf made it a sure thing.

When she and Nelly arrived at the kitchen, Cook just shook her head at them. But then she smiled. "The spicery pantry?"

Nelly and Aisling laughed. They would have to find some other semi-private place to make love again.

AODHAN LAUGHED when Coinneach arrived at the barracks carrying the blankets. "So it's a done deed?"

"Aye. And we'll wed in the meadow by my family's croft when we can."

"You'll be leaving the barracks then."

"If they have room for us in the keep where other couples stay."

The other men congratulated Coinneach and headed out of the barracks.

"Drustan asked me where you were."

"And you told him?"

"Busy with your ladylove. He knew you would be mating each other sooner rather than later. Does Blair know?" Aodhan asked.

"Aye, she does. She had given us her approval. So we should be fine."

"If we can prove whose son you truly are, Hamish might have wanted to have a say in who you mated."

Coinneach slapped Aodhan on his shoulder. "No one would have decided that for us."

Aodhan nodded. "If anyone cared about who I mated, I would feel the same way."

Coinneach smiled. "No one would dare tell you what to do." He cleaned up in a water bucket, dried off, and dressed. "Let's go break our fast and then relieve the other men on duty."

"I'm still trying to figure out how to prove your da is our chief."

"It doesna really matter as long as Osmond, Rupert, or Morag dinna try to kill the ones I love."

"Or you either... At least no' on my watch."

15

This time, while Aisling served the champion's table their morning meal, Coinneach was thrilled she was now his mate. She gave him a big smile as she brought bread, two slices for Aodhan, and slipped another slice to Coinneach. He chuckled.

Then she hurried off to serve the rest of their table. Coinneach glanced at the table on the dais and noticed that Morag was glowering at him. He couldn't understand why she had so much animosity toward him. Or why she felt that way toward Aisling either.

Once he had issues with Rupert over accosting Aisling, he figured that's when Morag might be peeved with him. But before that? When she had pitted Aodhan against him? And when she tried to stop the men from coming to his and Aodhan's aid when the Vikings had planned to burn down his family's croft, Morag had no reason to side against him or Aodhan.

"It appears as though Morag is giving you the evil eye," Aodhan said low for Coinneach's ears only.

"Aye. I have no idea why. I mean, sure, after I had words with

Rupert, but before that? She was still against me. I didna even know about the issue of who I was at the time."

Aisling brought them porridge. "You both look so serious."

Coinneach realized he and Aodhan were frowning. Coinneach smiled at her. "We're just talking about why Morag would have had anything against me before I had the confrontation with Rupert over you."

"I dinna know." Then Aisling furrowed her brow. "Unless someone saw your wolf mark on your shoulder when you removed your shirt the first time and fought Aodhan and told Morag."

"What about the wolf mark?" Aodhan asked.

"He has a mark from birth of a wolf's head." Aisling glanced around. "I need to finish serving the meal." She hurried off.

"That's how Blair knew I had been the baby she was supposed to get rid of," Coinneach explained.

Aodhan rubbed his bearded chin, appearing deep in thought. "Then any of the women who saw you when you were born would have seen the mark."

"Aye. Unless Morag covered me up too fast with a swaddling cloth."

"Then it would only be Blair's word against Morag's, and the chief would be bound to believe his own mate."

"Aye."

Aisling returned with more ale for everyone at the table. "Rupert looks like he could kill you where you sit," she whispered to Coinneach.

"Aye. I wouldna put it past him to try and find someone else to do the job," Coinneach said. "Even if he had sent the hunters in the first place."

"Och, and Osmond is giving you the evil eye," Aisling said.

"If he's behind sending his thugs to hunt us down, I'm no' going to let that go," Coinneach said.

"Nor will I," Aodhan agreed. "The men worked for him. I canna imagine someone else could have convinced them to hunt you down."

Morag came to mind.

Aisling hurried off to serve ale to the others at the champion's table.

"So what do we do?" Aodhan asked.

"Talk to him?"

Aodhan drank some of his ale. "I'll do it. Osmond willna know what is coming. If you confront him, he will, if he is the one who arranged this."

But Coinneach wanted to be there when Aodhan questioned him. He really wanted to learn the truth for himself.

Once the meal was done, Coinneach walked off to speak to Aisling before he went up to the wall walk, but was surprised when Blair stopped him with a hand on his arm. "We need to speak. I've heard rumors that two of Osmond's men who work in the stables have...uh, vanished."

Coinneach looked around. Everyone had left the great hall. "Aye?"

"I wouldna think anything of it if some other men went missing. But when Niven told me the two men who work for Osmond left the outer bailey carrying bows and, as far as he knew, never came back, the rumors started. He said you and Aisling went running as wolves last night. Nelly carried Aisling's bow and was with you. The men didna have Hamish's permission to hunt, from what I learned."

"Certes, no', just any pack members. But they were trying to hunt down no' only me, but Aisling as well. Luckily, Nelly was at the croft and safe."

Blair's eyes filled with tears. "What are we going to do about it?"

"We have to expose that Rupert isna Hamish's son."

"And that you are?"

"Nay. No' at the moment. We need to prove Rupert is no'

Hamish's legitimate son and mayhap Hamish will force Osmond, Morag, and Rupert out of the pack." At least that's what Coinneach hoped for. "Then they will no longer be a threat. I'm going to see Aisling and then go to work." But he decided he couldn't let Aodhan be the only one to speak with Osmond.

"Let me know what you plan to do."

"Aye. I need to know who else was in the birthing room with you when I was born."

"Senga and Isla."

"All right. Thanks." He didn't know the women, but he was sure Blair or Aisling could point them out to him. He hurried off to the kitchen and found Aisling helping to clean up after they had eaten their meal. Then he kissed her and said he had to hurry to work.

She eyed him with suspicion.

He smiled. "Aodhan will no' be happy with me if I dinna join him on the wall walk and he has to do all the guarding." He kissed her again. "I will see you at the meal?"

"Aye. Dinna get yourself into trouble before then."

"No' me." Then he gave her a bear hug of an embrace and hurried out of the kitchen. It didn't take him long to leave the castle and head straight for the stables.

Aodhan was talking to Hamish's brother, Collum.

What was *that* all about?

As soon as they saw Coinneach coming, Collum said, "I want a word with you, Coinneach."

"Aye." Coinneach figured he was in trouble.

"What happened last night?"

Coinneach hadn't planned to tell anyone, but he couldn't lie to the chief's brother. "Two of the stable hands tried to hunt Aisling and me down when we were running as wolves last night."

Collum's brows raised. So did Aodhan's.

Och, maybe that wasn't what Collum had come to talk to him about. "Aisling and I went running as wolves. We decided to mate in the meadow in privacy, and the next thing we knew, two men, the two stable hands who had worked for Osmond, were coming after us with bows, intent on hunting us. Still, we gave them the benefit of the doubt. We took extra measures to stay out of their sight."

"But?"

"They continued to track us to the river. We crossed to the other side and waited for them to follow us. Once they did, we returned to the opposite side of the river and got rid of their clothes and weapons. Then we returned to my family's croft. We had given them every chance to leave us alone, but they came after us as wolves. We had no choice but to take them down."

"Why would they go after you?" Collum asked.

"Mayhap because I confronted Rupert about being aggressive toward Aisling."

"Rupert? Why would he have solicited two of the stable hands to kill you?"

"Maybe because he was humiliated when he was forced to work in the stables, mucking out the stalls. I dinna know for sure if he was the one to send them after us. Unless his da did it."

"His laird wouldna have done so." Collum folded his arms and looked furiously at Coinneach.

Gods' wounds, Coinneach hadn't meant to let that slip. Coinneach rubbed his beard. "I misspoke. I meant that Osmond might have sent the men after us."

Collum eyed him with suspicion. "What would *his* motive be?"

That Osmond was Rupert's da, but Coinneach didn't want to make mention of that again. "Maybe he didna like that Rupert had to clean out the stables. I dinna know."

"I've heard the rumors. My brother has too. That Osmond is Rupert's da. Is that why you think Osmond might have sent his men after you? Because he felt he had to protect his son? We dinna believe that Rupert isna the chief's son, by the way. 'Tis just a malicious gossip started by wagging tongues."

"Aye, well, I have no idea."

Collum considered Coinneach's expression and then said, "I came to tell you I heard you and Aisling had mated and wanted you to know you and she can stay in the couple's quarters. I'd heard whispers that a couple of our pack members left the castle and hadna returned, but I didna think much of it because no one raised the alarm. If you killed them, where are their bodies and why didna you report it?"

"Their bodies are in the bog. We didna report it because we didna know who was behind it. We thought if we didna say anything about it, someone would slip up and say something or would send someone else after us again." Which was the truth.

"Come with me. You need to tell the chief about this." Collum waved at Niven, who raced to join them. "Tell Aisling to join us." Then he asked Coinneach, "Who else had seen what happened?"

"Aisling, Nelly, Tamhas, and my parents." Coinneach didn't want to involve his family, but they had been witnesses, and they could help corroborate their story. But since they were family, the chief might think they were saying what they did to protect them.

"All right. Niven, go get Nelly and Aisling and bring them here." Collum said to Aodhan, "What were you doing in the stables? You and Coinneach are supposed to be on guard duty."

Niven dashed off to the castle to get Nelly and Aisling.

"Well?" Collum asked Aodhan.

"I asked if Osmond sent the men to kill Coinneach and Aisling since they worked for him. He said he didna. All that he knew was that they hadna returned to sleep here last night and they hadna come to work this morning. He wanted to know what I knew about it. I didna tell him what had happened because I hadna witnessed it," Aodhan said.

"But you believe Coinneach," Collum said.

"Aye."

"Do you also believe Rupert is Osmond's son?" Collum asked.

"I didna, but now I believe so."

Collum frowned at him. "Go get Tamhas and his parents and have them meet us at Chief Hamish's solar to discuss the fight between Coinneach, Aisling, and the two men."

"Aye, Collum." Aodhan stalked off toward the castle gates.

Niven walked out to Collum and Coinneach, with Nelly and Aisling following behind him. To Coinneach's surprise, Blair ran to catch up with them.

"Did you witness the fight between Coinneach and Aisling and the two men from the stable?" Collum asked Blair.

"I have witnessed much more," Blair said.

Coinneach wondered if she planned to reveal what she had seen between Osmond and Morag. Or if she was ready to divulge the truth about him. But Coinneach didn't want her to, fearing for her safety.

"We're just going to discuss the fight between the stable hands and us," Coinneach, trying to persuade Blair not to go with them.

"I'm going with you," Blair said, her arms folded across her waist, her chin tilted up, determined.

"Tell Chief Hamish we need to speak with him in his solar," Collum said to Niven.

"Aye." Niven raced off to find the chief.

Coinneach didn't feel Blair needed to be in on the discussion. She hadn't been there, and he was afraid she might say something that would get her into trouble.

AISLING TOLD HER MOTHER, "You didna see the fight. You dinna need to be there." She was afraid of what her mother might say in front of Chief Hamish.

"I'm going. Nothing you will say will convince me to stay away," her mother said.

Collum nodded. "Aye, you can come. You can tell His Lordship what happened, and your parents and your brother can give their accounts afterwards.

Niven dashed out of the castle to join them, nearly out of breath, huffing and puffing. "He...Chief Hamish...wants to know what it is about."

Collum shook his head. "Let's go."

"Lady Morag said Chief Hamish said that," Niven said, trying to keep up with the adults' longer strides. "I should say."

Aisling felt the mood shift for everyone. When they were going to talk to Hamish, she thought he would listen to reason. Not so with Morag.

When they arrived at the chief's solar, Morag was there. "What is this concerning? Niven was supposed to report back with the answer to my question, no' bother the chief with unimportant issues."

"Did you speak with the chief?" Collum asked Niven. At once, Collum sounded like he believed Morag had stopped Niven from getting word to Hamish.

"Nay. Lady Morag stopped me and asked me to find out what the discussion was about. She says she speaks for Lord Hamish. So I ran back to see you and ask."

"Go find my brother, Niven," Collum said, sounding irritated that Morag would interfere with his business with the chief.

"Aye." Niven rushed off, looking like he was in trouble for giving the message to Morag, not to Hamish.

He was only ten and three-quarters, and Morag *was* intimidating, so Aisling didn't blame the lad. As before, she didn't want to speak in front of Morag, knowing she would take the stable hands' side and not hers and Coinneach's.

It seemed to take forever for Hamish to arrive at the solar with a red-faced Niven; by the time even Tamhas and his parents came, accompanied by Aodhan. Everyone was breathing hard, and their faces were flushed with exertion.

"All right, what's this all about?" Hamish asked, taking a seat, and Morag did too.

Then everyone who had witnessed the attempted murder told their versions of what they had seen, how the stable hands had tried to kill Aisling and Coinneach, even at the crofters' home. The stable hands had had a mission, and they'd been determined to carry it out.

"What motivated them to do such a thing?" Hamish asked.

Coinneach glanced at Collum, as if waiting for him to offer an answer that didn't have to do with accusing Morag of being Rupert's mother while his father was Osmond, not Hamish.

"No one knows why they would do such a thing," Collum said. "I haven't spoken with Osmond yet, but I will. I just wanted you to know what was going on with the men's disappearance and what they'd been up to."

"See that you do." Hamish looked at Blair, the only one who hadn't said anything.

Blair shook her head. "I only came in case I was needed, for my daughter's sake. I only learned what had happened late this day."

Hamish inclined his head.

"You're no' going to have them all held accountable for two of our pack members' deaths?" Morag asked, sounding furious.

Hamish sighed. "From the sounds of it, they were defending themselves as any pack member has the right to do."

"You will take the word of their family? Canna you see they are sticking up for each other? Spinning a tale that would absolve them of any crime?" Morag raged at Hamish.

"What would their motive be? They had planned to mate in the meadow, not kill a couple of stable hands who had no business out hunting for anything. I hadna approved it," Hamish said, sounding irritated with her tone of voice. He motioned to the gathered group in his solar. "Leave us."

Everyone showed their respect and then left the solar while Hamish said to Morag, "Why would you defend the stable hands who were obviously at fault in the whole matter?"

They didn't hear her response, though Aisling was dying to eavesdrop and learn what Morag said to that.

16

"We're going to speak to Osmond," Collum said, surprising Aisling as they left the chief's solar. She thought Collum would interrogate Osmond, but not have the rest of them go with him.

Collum turned to Aodhan, Blair, Nelly, and Coinneach's family. "None of you need to come with me, just Aisling and Coinneach."

"Aye," Nelly and Blair said, and hurried off to the castle.

Aodhan said to Coinneach, "I'll see you on the wall walk."

"Soon," Coinneach said.

Aodhan stalked off to the north tower stairs.

"If you need our help further, feel free to ask for it," Coinneach's father said to Collum.

"I will," Collum said.

Aisling and Coinneach both hugged his family, then they left.

"Why did Blair join us when she had nothing to offer when we spoke to Chief Hamish?" Collum asked.

Aisling wasn't surprised that Collum still wanted to know why her mother wanted to be in on the discussion. "You would have to ask her."

"But I think you know as close as you are to your mother," Collum said.

They walked into the stable and saw the red-haired Osmond speaking to one of his men. He was of such small stature that it was hard to imagine he could do any job and succeed. "Collum." Osmond sounded surprised to see Collum entering the stable.

"We have a matter to discuss—actually, a couple of matters. Two of the men in your employ hunted down Aisling and Coinneach last eve while they were running as wolves in the meadow. I need to know your role in all of it."

"My ro...role?" Osmond said, his hand on his chest as if he were shocked to hear that anyone would think ill of him.

"Aye. They were your men."

"Were?" Osmond glanced at Coinneach, as if he knew Coinneach was the one to dispatch his men.

"We've heard the rumors about you and Morag," Aisling said.

"What? What rumors?" Osmond asked, his eyes wide, but she didn't think he looked surprised in the least bit.

"That you are Rupert's da," Collum said. "After the trouble Rupert caused with Aisling, and then Coinneach took him to task, it would be easy to believe that you would set the men on them to eliminate them."

"Nay, I would never have done that."

Aisling noted that Osmond didn't object to the rumors that he was Rupert's da. Was he proud of it? Despite how Hamish might react toward Morag and Osmond's relationship, and that Rupert was their son. He had to be delusional if he thought anyone in the pact would accept it.

Or maybe he was ready to give up the farce and wanted to claim his son and Morag as his own, forget that Hamish would most likely have them banished. Maybe even worse.

"You're Rupert's da," Collum said again, trying to get confirmation.

What about Morag? Aisling couldn't imagine her wanting to give up her position as the chief's mate, where she could give orders to pack members at will. Only Hamish could override her commands. After all that she'd done to get that position, Aisling couldn't imagine she'd want to admit she had been Osmond's lover for years.

Osmond shrugged. "You know how often there is some truth to rumors."

Did he also know how Morag had gotten rid of Hamish's real son?

Aisling glanced at Collum to get his take on it.

"So you are admitting that you and Morag conceived Rupert?" Collum asked.

Osmond smirked. "Dinna you see the similarities between me and my son? No' to mention he doesna wear the mark of the wolf on his body."

Aisling and Coinneach quickly exchanged glances. She didn't understand. Had he seen Coinneach's birthmark? Did Osmond know he was Hamish's son? Did Morag?

But she hadn't attempted to kill Blair, who would have been a witness to what had happened, or possibly the other women there at the time of the birthing.

"You will tell Hamish this?" Collum asked.

"Aye."

"Come with me then." Collum escorted Osmond to the castle, telling Aisling and Coinneach that they were dismissed.

Coinneach hugged Aisling. "Does Osmond know about me then?"

"I dinna know. I would think Morag would have silenced my mother and the two other women who had been in the chamber when Hamish's mate gave birth," Aisling said.

"I agree with you."

"I've got to go to work, and so do you. I'm sure we'll hear about what Hamish wants to do about Osmond soon enough."

"I would love to have heard what was said." He kissed her mouth. "Mayhap Hamish will ban Osmond and Morag from the pack. Rupert, too, so he can be with his parents. And then we will be done with all this."

"I agree."

"We'll stay together in the couple's quarters."

"Oh, my, 'tis the best of news." Aisling just hoped that Osmond's telling the truth about Rupert being his son truly would be the end of all this, as long as Hamish believed Osmond. "I'll see you for the meal."

They hugged again, and Coinneach hurried off to the tower stairs. Aisling went to look for her mother to warn her about what had happened, just in case Morag learned of it and went after her, fearing her mother would also tell the chief about the baby she had ordered murdered?

"Where is my mother?" Aisling asked one of the washer women.

"She's delivering twins in the women's chamber," one of the women said.

"Thank you," Aisling said and hurried off to the women's chamber. No one but her mother, the woman having the babies, and two other women were there. Everyone else was working at their various stations.

Her mother glanced in her direction, must have seen the panic in Aisling's expression, and told the other women that the expectant mother needed to shift and have her babies as pups. Then she joined Aisling and took hold of her arms.

"What is wrong?"

"Osmond is with Collum. He's going to reveal to Chief Hamish that he's Rupert's da. I just didna want Morag to come after you, should she think you will tell the laird about Coinneach."

"Are you sure Osmond will do that? Hamish could kill him for his traitorous actions," her mother said, sounding and smelling anxious.

Aisling glanced at the mother in labor, now birthing her twins as wolf pups. "I dinna know. See to the mother and her pups, and I'll watch for Morag or anybody who might show up who shouldn't be here."

"Aye. The other lasses are here who attended Orla's mother when she birthed her bairn."

Aisling inclined her head, then went to her palette and retrieved her bow and arrows. Then she stood near the entrance to the ladies' chamber, watching for trouble. At least she didn't need to be in the kitchen just now.

"Do you have your *sgian dubh*?" her mother asked.

"Aye. Always." Then Aisling peeked out of the chamber and kept guard.

ON THE WALL WALK, Coinneach told Aodhan about what Osmond had told them, and that Collum was taking him to see Hamish.

"Osmond must be crazy to want to do so," Aodhan said.

"Aye, but what will Morag do? Agree with him? Tell Hamish that Osmond has lied so she can keep her position as the chief's mate? But here's the thing. Osmond said Rupert doesna have the mark of the wolf on him, as if that proves he isna Hamish's son." Coinneach glanced down at the inner bailey, waiting to hear some commotion that would indicate Hamish was ready to kill Osmond.

Aodhan frowned. "But you wear the wolf's mark."

"Aye. Is it inherited then?" Coinneach asked.

"Mayhap."

"Have you ever seen a wolf mark on Hamish or Collum? If a child of Hamish's should bear the mark, it would have to come from Hamish's line, wouldna you think?" Coinneach asked as he gazed out at the forest beyond the meadow.

"Unless it came from your mother."

"Oh, aye, I hadna considered that." Coinneach felt bad that he had discounted his mother. He wished he had known her.

"I wish I could hear what is being said between Hamish and Osmond." Aodhan leaned against the outer wall.

"Me also." Coinneach glanced back at the castle. "I wonder if Hamish will put Osmond in the dungeon, kill him outright, or banish him."

"And Morag and Rupert. Unless Morag denies it's true or Osmond gets scared and doesna tell the chief the truth."

"That's a possibility. He doesna appear to be a strong man. He was sneaky and underhanded. I was shocked to learn he planned to tell Hamish that Rupert was his son."

Then they heard a commotion in the inner bailey and both of them turned their attention there.

Two of the guards were dragging Osmond out of the castle. He was bruised and bleeding and shouting for all to hear, "Rupert is my son! Morag has been my mistress for years!"

Humans did such a thing, but wolves mated for life, unless the one they mated had died. And even then, they might never take another mate. But have an affair on the side? Rarely. In Morag's position, it was unbelievable. Sometimes, though, people in power thought they could get away with anything. Often, they did. For many years, she had.

Dunstan and two guards, including Tristan, forced Osmond out of the inner bailey, through the outer bailey, and beyond the gates. He was lucky he hadn't been killed outright for his transgressions.

"Banishment, it appears," Aodhan said.

"But what about Morag and Rupert?" Coinneach couldn't believe she would get away with what she'd pulled.

"How much do you want to bet she convinced Hamish that Osmond was out of his mind, and she had no idea what he was talking about?"

Coinneach considered what she'd already done that he knew of. What else had she been up to over the years? "Aye. She convinced the chief to mate her. And threatened Blair to get rid of me. She could be capable of deceiving anyone about anything."

"I agree."

They watched as Osmond headed across the meadow, Drustan, Tristan, and the other guards watching him leave.

Drustan glanced up at the wall walk and studied Coinneach and Aodhan observing him. Then he and the other men went through the gates, and Tristan ran up the tower stairs to join Coinneach and Aodhan.

"Was Osmond banished from the pack?" Coinneach asked Tristan.

"Aye. Gods' wounds, Drustan said that he was sure you would know something about it. He told me to come up and make sure you watch for Osmond in the event he returns. So what do you know about it?" Tristan was wide-eyed, looking like he couldn't believe Coinneach would know about it since he had been working on the wall walk.

"He and Morag had a longstanding affair, and Rupert was the result of it," Coinneach said.

"Nay." Tristan's eyes sparkled with intrigue.

"Aye," Aodhan said.

"He told Collum in front of Aisling and me," Coinneach confirmed.

"So why isna Morag going with him? And Rupert also?" Tristan asked.

"She convinced the chief that she is innocent of the charges. That Osmond made up the whole story. That Osmond had made overtures toward her, but she had rebuffed them." Coinneach glanced back at the meadow where Osmond continued to walk toward the forest.

"I'm off to sleep before I have duty tonight. Oh,"—Tristan turned before he left them alone on the wall walk—"is it true that you killed two of Osmond's stable hands who attempted to hunt you and Aisling down last night?"

"With the help of Aisling and my family." Coinneach was so proud of her.

"Osmond said Rupert didna have a wolf mark on him when he was born. But"—Tristan glanced at Aodhan as if worried that he shouldn't make any further comment—"uh, but you have one."

Aodhan's eyes widened. "Och, you are right, Tristan."

"It means naught, I'm sure." Tristan glanced at Coinneach as if waiting for confirmation.

"What difference does it make?" Coinneach asked, not sure what to make of it.

"Both Collum and Hamish have a wolf mark on their bodies 'Tis said their da and his da also had wolf marks. They were different shapes in different places, but when Hamish learned Rupert didn't have one, I've heard tell he was more than surprised."

"Surely, others have such a mark who dinna share the same lineage," Coinneach said.

"No' that I know of. But you appear to be about the same age as Rupert, mayhap a wee bit older." Tristan scrubbed his bearded chin. "Then again you would have been raised by Hamish if you were his son. Not by Elspeth and Magnus. And Tamhas is your twin brother."

Could Coinneach trust Tristan with the truth? Coinneach didn't want Blair to get into trouble over it. If Morag had convinced Hamish she hadn't been with him in a carnal way, it would be even easier to convince him how ridiculous it sounded that Coinneach had been raised by the crofters when he was Hamish's son.

As to the business of his wolf mark, if Morag learned of it, she would attempt to have him, Blair, and the other ladies who had helped with his mother's delivery murdered. Aisling too, he was certain.

Tristan cleared his throat. "Elspeth, Magnus, and Tamhas are your family, are they no'?"

"Aye."

But Tristan didn't seem to believe it.

What if Hamish thought his parents had something to do with stealing Coinneach from the castle? He certainly didn't want his family to be in trouble over all this!

"Oh, and Hamish wants our fighters to practice fighting after the nooning meal," Tristan said.

"We're serving on guard duty," Coinneach reminded him.

"He specifically said he wants you and Aodhan to be there."

"The others who have to take our place will become annoyed that we always get to leave the wall walk during duty," Coinneach said.

"You leave even when you are no' supposed to," Tristan said, referring to when Coinneach had left the castle to save his family and the croft. "Off to sleep for a while."

"Are you going to join us in the practice fighting?" Coinneach asked him.

"Aye. I wouldn't miss it for the world." Then Tristan took off for the tower stairs.

"Usually, Hamish schedules the fight in the morning before we break our fast." Aodhan looked back at the forest.

"Do you believe he's angry about Osmond, and this is a way for him to release his anger? I have no' seen him fight before though."

"Aye. I believe he has said we must join the fight so he can"—Aodhan smiled—"battle you, just to see how good one of his newest guards is since you bested me. I would recommend you remove your shirt again this time, unlike last time."

"And if Morag happens to see the wolf on my shoulder?"

"She never comes to see the men fighting."

Coinneach wondered if Morag would this time, to appease Hamish, if he wasn't sure if she'd had the affair with Osmond or not, to pretend she was interested in watching Hamish fight.

17

Blair entered the kitchen and pulled Aisling aside from cooking a boar. It normally wasn't done when Aisling was helping to prepare a meal, but she figured something was wrong the way her mother looked so pale.

Cook might have had words with Aisling over it if it hadn't been that Blair took care of all injuries and illnesses, and no one wanted to get on her bad side.

Besides, it seemed that Aisling and Blair were in the know about a lot of things concerning what was going on with Osmond and Morag, which was piquing everyone's interest.

"What is wrong?" Aisling asked her mother.

"The chief has ordered that all able-bodied men practice fighting after the meal. Specifically, he wants Aodhan and Coinneach to fight."

"Each other again?"

"Nay, well, I dinna know. He just wants them to relinquish their duties on the wall walk and focus on practicing fighting. It is rumored that Hamish will be fighting this time as well. They want me to watch the practice session in case anyone gets hurt."

"Which makes sense since Tristan hurt Coinneach the one time."

"Aye, but Morag is attending for the first time in forever also."

"Morag?" Aisling's voice rose a little too high, and she lowered her voice. "Why?"

Blair took hold of Aisling's hands and tightened her hold on them. "Something is up. Tell Coinneach no' to remove his shirt during the fight. Morag canna see the mark on his shoulder no matter what."

"If I arrive after you do, then you can tell him." Aisling still wasn't sure her mother was happy she had mated him.

"If Morag sees me talking to him—"

"If she sees you talking to him, she has to know he is part of our family now, and that is the reason."

"And that he has a wolf mark?"

"Whoever gets there first, talks to him," Aisling said, feeling anxious now.

"If you must go, go, Aisling," Cook said, winding one of her unruly red curls around her finger, then poking it back into her plaited hair. "I'm sure many of us will be watching Chief Hamish to see him fight. It's been a long time since he battled with his men."

"Aye, thank you," Aisling said, glancing back at Nelly, who had taken her place to turn the boar along with some of the other women.

She cast a worried frown at Aisling.

Aisling left the kitchen, her mother hurrying after her.

"I think there are hints of a rumor floating around the pack that Coinneach is Hamish's son," Aisling's mother said.

"Who has started such rumors?"

"Mayhap Aodhan. I've heard it said he wants to learn the truth."

"Och. Has Hamish or Collum learned of this?" Aisling asked, heading out of the castle.

"I wouldna know. But Morag has spies all over the castle. So if one of them hears of it, they'll be sure to tell her."

"Who?"

"The women who wanted you dead, for one."

"That's why Morag stood up for them."

"Aye. Rupert and Osmond also, though now Osmond is banished from the castle and the pack."

"Two fewer spies then." Before Aisling could go to the tower stairs, she saw Magnus, Elspeth, and Tamhas coming into the inner bailey. Was Tamhas going to fight too?

But why call on their parents to be here, who looked glum about the whole thing?

Aisling took her mother's hand and walked her toward them, wanting to learn what was going on.

Now that she got closer to them, she saw Elspeth had tears streaking down her face, and her eyes were red. "What is wrong?" Aisling hugged her.

"Osmond said he was excommunicated from the pack, but he knows far worse things about Morag. He said she denied she had ever been with him, but we all know they've been seen together in the stables. What business would she have in them when she never rides?" Elspeth said. "We knew of this before the boys were born."

"What worse things does he know about Morag?" Aisling asked.

Magnus, Elspeth, and Tamhas shared glances, then looked at Blair.

Aisling had the sinking feeling they knew then about the baby Blair had left by the river, and where it had come from.

"Does Coinneach know about this?" Elspeth asked.

"Aye," Aisling said.

Magnus wrapped his arm around Elspeth's waist as if he were afraid she was going to faint.

"And Blair," Magnus said, sounding a little harsh then.

Blair took a steadying breath and told them what had happened.

"Morag is the devil," Elspeth said.

"Aye, we all think so," Aisling said. "But you see the problem? If we tell Hamish what Blair had done at Morag's command, he might want to terminate her. Blair, I mean."

Elspeth took hold of Magnus's hand and squeezed. "We could say that Blair brought the babe to us, knowing I had just lost a twin and would take care of both of them. She said the mother had died and she had no one else to care for her."

"Then my mother would be a liar."

"It would be worse for her if Hamish learned she had abandoned the baby by the river, hoping a crofter would find him."

"All right. I'll tell Coinneach and Aodhan, since they are the other two who know about it," Aisling said. She raced off before she didn't have a chance to warn him.

Niven intercepted her. "Morag wants to see you."

"Why?" Aisling's heart was beating triple time already.

"Morag wouldna say, and I dinna trust her. She was smiling like a cat that had just caught a mouse."

Aisling glanced back at the tower stairs. If she didn't obey Morag's command, she could get a lashing. Then she saw Hamish greeting his men. She did what she normally wouldn't have done and changed direction to speak with Hamish. He glanced at her with disdain. She wasn't one of the men he might challenge to a fight. She was nothing but a lowly cook. What could be so important that he would speak with her?

"My laird, Lady Morag has requested my presence, but I must discuss a very urgent matter with Coinneach first." Aisling was certain Hamish regarded her as if she were out of her mind.

"What is this about?" Hamish eventually asked, now seeming to believe it could be significant and that she should not be dismissed so readily.

But then she blurted out, "I was going to tell Coinneach not to remove his shirt while fighting the others."

Hamish raised his brows.

"Because he has a wolf mark on his shoulder and some would want him and others dead if they knew he was...he was...well, if he were kin to you." She couldn't say his son. Mayhap Collum had dallied with a lass and had a child by her; she had died, and the child was given to another family to raise. She hadn't considered that before.

Though none of that had aligned with anything her mother had told her.

Hamish motioned to his brother, and Collum quickly joined him, glancing at Aisling as if knowing she was the reason the fight was being held up. "Come with me, brother."

Aisling wrung her hands. She had done it now. As soon as the brothers headed for the tower stairs, Blair joined Aisling.

"What was said?" Blair asked.

"Oh, Momma, Morag wanted to see me. I was afraid she would stop me from telling Coinneach to wear his shirt. And then I had the brilliant, but no'-so-brilliant, plan to tell Hamish I was to see Morag, but I had important business with Coinneach. Then I blurted it all out. Well, just about Coinneach wearing a wolf mark, and he might be kin to Hamish."

"That's why they're going up to the tower stairs?"

"Aye."

Everyone was talking and laughing. A few of the men ready to fight glanced in the direction of the wall walk.

Hamish was talking to Coinneach, and then Coinneach removed his shirt.

Tears filled Aisling's eyes. She hadn't had time to tell him the new story that his mother had made up.

Then Coinneach put on his shirt, and he and Aodhan followed Hamish and Collum down the stairs.

Morag and two of her lady friends approached Aisling and Blair. "I told you to come see me, Aisling. I wished to have you serve me as one of my ladies-in-waiting. I would have done that with Blair, but she's indispensable as our healer. Beth and Jane will take you up to my solar and explain what you will do as your assigned duties."

Morag glanced at Blair. "You come too so you know what your darling daughter will be doing."

Aisling knew this wasn't good. She said, "Aye." Then she hurried off to the women's quarters.

"Where are you going?" Morag asked.

"To get something from my quarters."

Morag eyed her with distrust but finally relinquished. "Jane and Beth will meet you up in my solar. My mate wishes me here."

"And Blair also," Aisling said. If Morag had someone on her solar who wished Aisling harm, she didn't want her mother to get hurt also.

"Aye, she can return to the inner bailey if anyone gets hurt."

Blair left with Aisling, and she said, "I dinna believe she wants you on her staff."

"Nay, she wants to get rid of both of us so you canna tell Hamish the truth."

"But others know about it," Blair reasoned.

"The crofter family? Morag willna think for a moment that Hamish would believe what they have to say is the truth. You see how the chief did nothing to her even after Osmond accused her of being his lover for all those years. And he probably confessed that he is Rupert's da."

The men began fighting, and Aisling paused to see who Coinneach was fighting. Hamish, but Coinneach was at least wearing his shirt. Did Hamish not believe Coinneach was his kin?

"What do you have to get from your quarters?" Blair suddenly asked.

"My bow and quiver of arrows. I suspect someone else is waiting for us in Morag's solar, no' her ladies. You see? They are still standing with her while they watch the men battle it out." Aisling really wished she could watch the fight. But she had another plan in mind.

"And then what?"

"We go to the crofters' farm, but we'll go through the back gate." Aisling motioned to Niven, and he raced to meet up with her. "Tell Coinneach's family to leave out the back gate and go to their farm. I'll follow."

"I will too," Blair said.

"But dinna tell Morag any of this."

"Aye, Aisling," Niven ran to speak to Magnus, who gathered his mate and son to escort them to the back gate.

"I would like to see what they planned to do with us, but I think that would be a foolhardy quest," Blair said.

"Aye, especially if we had to kill the men to protect ourselves. And who would believe us?"

"*If* we managed to kill them and they didn't kill us first," Blair said.

COINNEACH AND AODHAN were about to go down the tower stairs when he saw Aisling heading his way, then thwarted by Morag. He didn't trust the chief's mate in the least.

But then Aisling had spoken to Hamish, and he called his brother over, and the next thing he knew, Hamish and Collum were joining them up at the wall walk. Though Coinneach barely heard Hamish's gruff words, "Take off your shirt," because he was watching what Aisling was doing—running to the castle, pausing, then waving Niven over to speak to her. Then Niven went to see Coinneach's parents.

What was going on?

When Aodhan slapped him on the back to remind Coinneach what Hamish had commanded of him and said, "Remove your shirt as his lairdship says." The command his lord had given finally filled Coinneach's thoughts.

Had Aisling given him up because it was too dangerous not to? He pulled off his shirt, and both Hamish and Collum looked closer to see the wolf head. Both men were frowning, looking at Coinneach, then at the wolf mark again.

Hamish touched it as if it would disappear if he rubbed it off. Collum did the same after him. But it was not ink or dirt that could be rubbed off.

"You've had this since you were born?" Hamish asked.

"Aye, my laird."

"Your parents are no' your parents?"

"I always believed they were so, and I will always cherish them as my parents who raised me. Tamhas likewise is my twin."

Hamish frowned. "Does he also have the mark of the wolf?"

"No, my laird. We didna think there was any significance to it."

"If the mother of your blood died and you were given to the crofter family, when did you first shift?" Hamish asked.

"When I was five years old."

Hamish glanced at Collum. Collum said, "If his mother had died, he couldn't shift into the wolf until he was old enough to handle shifting in front of others."

"Aye." Hamish looked over the wall walk to see his men gathered to fight, Morag standing off to the side, watching him. "You are saying that Morag had someone take you away to live with someone else so that she could have her own son with me?"

Coinneach didn't say anything, afraid to get Blair in trouble.

"You knew you were...uh, kin to me, and that's why you wanted to work here," Hamish said.

"No, only that...that someone didna want me to work here for fear you might realize I was uh, related to you."

"Who?"

"Morag."

"And? I will learn the truth, you do ken?"

"Aye." Then Coinneach told him everything he knew—even about Blair's part in it. "Blair was young and scared. Morag threatened to kill her. She didna know what to do."

"I remember seeing Blair take a swaddled baby in a basket and hurry out of the castle, and through the gates at the same time you were getting the news that Orla and the baby had died. I wondered at the time about it since I knew Blair didna have a child," Collum said.

"God's wounds, what else has that woman been up to, Morag, I mean?" Hamish ran his hands through his hair. "Come, we will speak to Blair and the other women who were there that day, and Morag last."

As soon as he reached the inner courtyard, Hamish glanced around, then spied Blair and saw her heading for the back gates. Aisling and Coinneach's family were also headed out. Coinneach didn't see any sign of Morag, though she was supposed to be watching the fight. And Rupert, who always managed to get out of fighting, was nowhere to be seen.

Coinneach didn't like seeing that his family was leaving when he suspected they had been asked to be there. Immediately, he went after them.

But Hamish and Collum did also.

Coinneach thought it might be some trouble with Morag, and they decided to go home, where they would be safer.

18

As soon as Aisling saw two men guarding the gates at the back of the castle, she drew alarmed. They pulled their swords out of their sheaths and motioned to the castle. One of them said, "Morag wants an audience with you. Didna you get her message?"

"Go," Aisling said to Coinneach's family. "They came about a bairn in trouble at one of the crofters' homes when they were on their way here, and my mother is going to help them. I also wished to ask if I could offer some assistance."

"Nay, Lady Morag said that both of you are to meet her in her solar."

"But she is no' in her solar. She is there to watch the men practice fighting. By the time she returns, I will be there." She heard footfalls crunching on stones underfoot and turned, figuring more guards were coming for them, but was surprised to see Coinneach, Aodhan, Collum, and Hamish all abreast of each other, now wielding their own swords.

"Drop your weapons," Hamish commanded. His voice was deep and commanding.

"My laird, Lady Morag wanted to see Aisling and Blair in her chambers," the guard insisted as if Morag's wishes were more critical than Hamish's.

Hamish took another step toward them, the other men with him following his lead. "What did I tell you?"

Then the men sheathed their swords.

"I told you to drop them."

The men looked startled, afraid of what their laird intended to do to them. They slowly pulled out their swords and dropped them on the rocky ground. Then Collum and Coinneach retrieved the men's swords.

"Why would you threaten the women in such a manner?" Hamish asked, his voice booming in the archway over the big, burly gates.

"We were supposed to take any force necessary to detain them," the one guard said, the other nodding emphatically. "Look, Aisling is armed with her bow even."

"And she could have shot you how at this short distance before you knocked it away from her with your sword?" To Aodhan and Collum, Hamish said, "Take them to the dungeon until I can determine what's going on here."

Aisling wondered if he feared there was about to be a coup at the castle. "Armed guards might be at Morag's chamber also."

"I'll check it out," Coinneach said.

But she didn't want him to go alone if two men were waiting for her and her mother to show up at Morag's solar.

"I will go with you," Hamish said.

The two of them strode off to Morag's quarters.

Hamish asked Coinneach, "Do you believe Morag had something to do with attempting to poison Aisling?"

"Aye, I do. Morag could have wanted Aisling dead for any number of reasons. To keep Blair from telling the truth about me. To punish Aisling for getting her son in trouble. Or Rupert could have been behind it. Gormelia was interested in Rupert and was angry that he was only intrigued with Aisling, especially when I became part of her life."

They finally reached Morag's chamber and found the two guards waiting there. They appeared shocked that Hamish and Coinneach would arrive and not Aisling and her mother.

"Why do you guard Morag's room?" Hamish asked, his voice hushed.

Coinneach suspected Morag had left the inner bailey and was waiting for her victims to arrive.

"My laird, Lady Morag wanted us to wait for Blair and her daughter to turn up," the gray-bearded man said.

The younger man didn't say a word, but he looked like he wanted to be anywhere but here right then.

"Who are you loyal to?" Hamish asked.

"Well to you and the lady, my laird," the man said.

"Why did Morag want the ladies to come here?"

"We dinna know." This time, the older man's voice cracked with concern.

"If I tell you to return to your posts—"

"We will go."

The younger man nodded vigorously.

"If I tell you to arrest Morag..."

The men exchanged glances.

"Open the door."

The older man started to knock.

"Nay dinna knock, just open the door."

"Aye, my laird." Appearing nervous about earning Morag's wrath, he still did as he was told and yanked the door open.

"Were you born in a wheat field? You never barge in on me without getting permission," Morag screeched.

"It was at my behest," Hamish said and pushed the guards aside. "What did you want with Aisling and her mother?"

"I wished to congratulate them on Aisling's mating with Coinneach."

"Come with me." Hamish waited a moment for her to comply, but when she didn't, he told the guards, "Bring her. We have some business to attend to."

"What...what business?" She didn't appear as waspish now, more afraid she wouldn't be able to get out of whatever trouble she had gotten herself into.

The guards hesitated to escort her out of her chamber.

"You are either with me or with her. Choose now. Choose wisely."

To help the chief make his point, Coinneach drew his sword. Hamish had his hand on the hilt of his.

The two men quickly grabbed Morag and pulled her out of the chamber.

When they reached the bottom of the stairs, Hamish said, "We go to the inner bailey."

In the inner bailey, Hamish said in his booming voice, "We have news, as disturbing as it is."

Everyone gathered there was quiet.

"Morag is guilty of trying to murder my son."

Aisling and her mother joined Coinneach, and he hugged them both in a heartfelt embrace.

Rupert instantly defended his mother. "I dinna know where you got that idea, but 'tis no' true."

"I mean my real and only son, Coinneach."

Morag fainted as an accumulated gasp went over the pack members.

"I have come to learn that Rupert is Osmond's son."

"Mother, how could you?" Rupert said, sounding indignant.

She recovered. "I told you that years ago."

So Rupert was well aware of the deception. But did he know that she had tried to kill Orla's baby?

"I could sentence you to death for this horrific plan of yours," Hamish said.

"My laird," Blair said. "I know you are deeply offended, but I believe she will feel the regret of her actions more if she and Rupert are banished from the pack. By his own words, he had Gormelia attempt to murder Aisling. So he is no' an innocent in these matters."

"Does anyone want to join them?" Hamish asked, making a pointed look at the guards who had been at Morag's chamber door.

Nobody said a word.

"Aodhan, Tristan, bring the other guards up from the dungeon."

"Aye, my laird." Tristan hurried off, and Aodhan quickly joined him.

Hamish said to Morag and Rupert, "Leave the castle grounds at once."

"I must pack," Morag said.

"You leave with all that you have on your back. You deserve no more."

She headed for the stable.

"Halt! You willna take one of my fine horses."

"You gave them to Rupert and me."

"And I take them away. Dinna you see, woman, that you are getting off easy? If I had my way, you both would be dead for your murderous plots. It doesna matter that they were unsuccessful."

"One was successful," she muttered under her breath.

"What's that you say?" Hamish asked.

"Naught, my laird. We're going now." Morag stomped off.

Rupert looked back at the castle as if wishing he could stay here and not be stuck living out in the world.

"Go with your mother, Rupert. I dinna want to see you a second longer."

Then the guards who had been put in the dungeon joined the

chief and repledged their loyalty. So did the ones who had been staying at Morag's chamber.

All his men, including Coinneach pledged their undying loyalty. Aisling smiled at him.

Aodhan said, "Come fight me, Coinneach."

"Not before he fights me," Hamish said.

Well, gods' wounds. Coinneach didn't want to fight his chief da. What if he hurt him badly?

"After the chief, then," Aodhan said, good-naturedly.

"But first, remove your shirt," Hamish said. "This is how we know Coinneach is my son."

Coinneach pulled off his shirt and winked at Aisling and her mother. Her mother's cheeks reddened in embarrassment.

"The mark of the wolf. Only my offspring or my brother's will have this symbol at birth."

Several gasped. Hamish pulled off his shirt and showed his wolf on his chest, partly obscured by his chest hair. He motioned to Collum to show off his wolf, and Collum, who had already removed his shirt to fight with the other men, pulled his kilt down low on his hip to show off his mark.

All were different, but they all belonged to the same family line.

"Rupert had no wolf's mark," Hamish said. "I thought it meant our line would no longer share that special mark, but it turned out that Rupert wasna my son. So let the battle begin."

Hamish drew his sword, and Coinneach hurried to draw his. Then they began to fight, but no one else did. Of all the combinations of fighters, this was the most important.

Thankfully, Coinneach managed to use his footing to keep an edge in the fight. But he could see that his da had a lot more years of fighting in him.

After fighting for what seemed like forever and neither man outplaying the other, Hamish called it a draw, which seemed to please him mightily. Then Coinneach fought Drustan, not Aodhan, like Coinneach thought he might. Before Aodhan could challenge Coinneach, Collum approached him. "See if you can best your uncle."

Neither man had been in the previous fights, so like with Hamish, Coinneach had no idea how Collum would fare. But like his brother, he was powerful and used his footwork to the maximum to fight his foe. Still, like Hamish, Collum finally called it a draw.

Coinneach wondered if they didn't want to show off to the others how much they could defeat him. He had to quit thinking thoughts like that. He was as good a fighter now as they were.

Then Aodhan challenged him. Wasn't anyone going to fight anyone else other than those who had battled him and Hamish, who fought against Drustan? And to fight the monster of a warrior again.

Coinneach was already getting tired, and when he readied his sword, Aodhan swept his sword away, but he didn't use his sword on a vulnerable spot; instead, he used the same maneuver on him as Coinneach had used on Aodhan. Before he knew it, Aodhan swept his leg behind Coinneach and grabbed his arms, pushing him back until Coinneach landed on his back.

Then Aodhan laughed. "I've been privately practicing the maneuver ever since you did that to me."

Coinneach laughed. "Well done." He grabbed Aodhan's proffered arm and pulled himself to his feet.

Then everyone else paired up with partners and began to practice fight.

The guards on top were watching the inner bailey, not the surrounding land, as they were supposed to.

Swords were clanging in the inner bailey, shouts of camaraderie, taunting jabs in good humor, while Aisling took the moment to cuddle next to Coinneach. If anyone asked him to fight now, he would say he had more important matters to attend to.

Suddenly, one of the men on top of the wall walk shouted, "Fire! Coinneach! Your family's croft is on fire."

Coinneach and Aisling headed for the gates, but Hamish said, "Nay, we take the horses."

They broke into a dead sprint for the stables, feet pounding the earth, shouting over one another in a frantic litany of orders, each intent to be the first to mount. Inside, the tang of sweat and hay and horseflesh was sharp as vinegar.

Coinneach's hands shook as he fumbled for the bridle, his fingers failing him once, twice, before he managed to cinch the buckle. Someone else was already leading his mare out, and he vaulted onto her back, pulling Aisling onto his lap. The rest of the men mounted in similar haste. There were only the beat of hooves and the hot, desperate animal breath of the pursuit as they tore across the field.

The croft was half a mile off, across the hollow and up the rise, and as they neared, the orange glow intensified, seething at the edge of the afternoon sky. Coinneach felt the dread like a stone in his throat. Every stride closer confirmed what he'd feared: the roof was fully ablaze, the thatch curling back in tongues, hurling sparks.

He could not hear his own screams. He could only hear the hissing collapse of the roof timbers, the shrill keening of his mother, and above it all, the thunder of the fire itself.

When he reached the yard, he flung himself from the horse, landing hard enough to jar his bones, and dashed for the nearest window. The shutters over the windows were blocked, but he could see shadows, bodies pressing up to the other side, shrieking for release. He grabbed a rock and smashed it through the shutters.

Smoke billowed out. He tried to climb in, but the opening was too small, and he could do nothing but shove his arm inside, shouting for them to back away, to cover their faces, to make themselves as small as possible and crawl toward his voice.

From somewhere behind, Aisling's voice, hoarse and trembling, "They've blocked the door from the outside—look!"

The men, overcome by horror, turned their attention to the thick, spiked beam hammered across the front of the house, the heads of the nails glinting in the firelight. Someone had done this knowing full well it would kill everyone inside. Coinneach understood then that this was not an accident, but calculated, and the taste of bile filled his mouth.

The whole world shrank to the task: yank away the carts and other items meant to keep his family in the smoke-filled croft. He had to save them before the roof completely caved in. The men set to the barricade with axes, stones, and bare hands, bellowing with the effort.

Each blow sent splinters flying and rattled the frame, but the fire was quicker than they were, and the smoke burned their eyes and lungs. He felt the hours of his childhood, his father's hands, his mother's gentle admonishments, burning away with every moment of delay.

His mother screamed inside, high and desperate. For a heartbeat, everything stopped; even the fire seemed to hold its breath. Coinneach dropped his shoulder and rammed the door with all his weight. The first time, nothing.

The second, a groan of splintering wood. The third, the barricade shifted, and the men surged forward in a tangle of limbs, finally toppling the beam. The door swung open, spewing fire and choking blackness.

Coinneach plunged in first, the heat singeing his eyebrows and beard. He groped for anything living, found his mother's wrist, and yanked her toward the threshold. The others followed, dragging his father and his brother out of the building.

He heard, distantly, the voices of the men calling out to each other, and then the cool, sweet relief of the afternoon air as he fell backwards onto the grass, clutching his mother to his chest, and saw the rest emerge, coughing and weeping, alive.

Aisling saw Coinneach and ran to him, kneeling beside him. "You did it," she gasped. "You got them out."

Coinneach could only nod, his throat raw and useless. But as he looked up at the blazing ruin of his family's home, he knew this was not the end. It was the beginning of a reckoning.

Then he saw Morag, her dress on fire as she tried to extinguish it. She screamed at Rupert to help her, but he saw Hamish and the others coming, and Rupert took off to leave her to her dilemma. Then they saw Osmond.

He had his hands on his head, staring at Morag as the flames took over. He finally realized Hamish and his men were coming, and he looked around, saw Rupert, and ran in a different direction. It appeared he was keen to save his own worthless hide.

Aisling immediately began to take care of Coinneach's mother while Hamish and Aodhan saw to Magnus and Tamhas.

At the same time, Blair arrived, seated behind Tristan, looking a little green from the wild ride. She began helping Aisling with the care of the victims while the men put out the flames.

Hamish glanced at Morag, who had died. "She deserved what she got."

"What about Osmond and Rupert?" Coinneach asked.

"We take them down. They get no more chances."

Coinneach kissed his mother, put his hand on his da's shoulder, and said to his brother, "Tamhas, didna you die on us."

"I have...cough...no intention...cough, cough, of doing so. Where is Nelly?"

About that time, Nelly came riding behind Ruadh on his horse. She slipped off the horse and ran to Tamhas.

He would be in good hands.

Ruadh, Aodhan, and Tristan went with Coinneach to track

down Osmond. As far as he was concerned, he was the biggest threat. Rupert was just spineless.

Hamish, Collum, and Fletcher chased down Rupert.

On horseback, Coinneach and his team had the advantage until they were deeper in the woods. Then Coinneach left his horse with Tristan, removed his clothes, and shifted. He could find Osmond more quickly as a wolf.

They were deeper in the woods. Roots and brambles tripped even the most sure-footed of their party, but Coinneach, with his keen sense of scent and direction, pressed on ahead. The chase had become a hunt, and the human mind in him yielded by degrees to the primal urge that simmered beneath.

The world brightened as his senses recalibrated. Smells billowed toward him—sap, rot, musk. The track was clear: this was not just a manhunt. This was a pursuit through every evolutionary shortcut his body had ever known.

He moved through the underbrush with all the fluidity of memory. The ground was damp, the air thick, and every sound was an invitation; every rustle a warning or a lure. Osmond's scent was easy to follow. Fear-sweat laced with wolf, a hybrid trail of desperation and cunning. Coinneach found him at last, huddled inside a shallow depression beneath a tangle of bracken and broken branches.

Osmond's eyes, wide and shining, reflected every glint of sunlight that managed to sift through the canopy. He was trembling, but even before Coinneach could close the distance, Osmond pulled away from his hiding place and began to undress.

Omond's movements were less the flailings of a desperate man than the precise, almost reverent gestures of someone who had repeated this act many times, each time expecting it might save him. He dropped his sword and *sgian dubh*, ditched his tunic, shirt, breeches, and boots. He stood naked for only a second before the transformation overtook him.

His wolf form was smaller than Coinneach's, leaner, with a ruff of fur around the neck and an angular, almost foxlike head. His jaws were already agape, tongue lolling in anticipation. Coinneach had never seen him fight as a wolf. Had he ever fought wolves before? Like with any venture, they needed to practice to succeed.

Osmond looked more ill at ease than ever. Not waiting another second, Coinneach lunged first. He landed on Osmond's back, snapping at the scruff, dragging him through wet leaves and upended loam. Osmond bucked, twisting his head to clamp down on Coinneach's foreleg, but Coinneach barely felt the puncture; adrenaline overrode all but the deepest pain.

They tumbled together in a blur of fur and teeth, every bite and claw a message written in the oldest language of all. Osmond's technique was extraordinary—he fought dirty, going for the soft underside of the throat, for the eyes, for the places that a wolf would usually never dare to attack. The rules of wolf etiquette did not bind him.

He was a man who had lost the right to be a man, and so he fought with the desperation of an animal that had been caged too long.

The others caught up quickly. They approached on horseback, swords drawn, but dismounted at the edge of the clearing, their faces taut with the realization that they were witnessing something ancient and ungovernable.

Tristan and the others tethered their horses, forming a loose ring around the combatants, but none interfered. This was between Coinneach and Osmond. It was an honor, yes, but also a necessity: these attempted murders had to count for something, even if it was only the settling of a private balance.

The fight escalated. Coinneach felt a jagged pain in his left flank where Osmond had ripped a patch of skin away, but he retaliated with a bite to the ear, tearing it nearly in half. They broke apart, circled, and came together again. Blood spattered the leaves and pooled in the hollows of the earth; the smell of it drove both wolves into a frenzy.

They moved so fast that for a moment it seemed the very trees were closing in, the world shrinking to the size of this single, brutal contest. Osmond feinted left, then darted right, catching Coinneach off-guard and sinking his teeth into Coinneach's haunch. Coinneach roared, shaking him off, and then drove him backward, step by step, toward the waiting semicircle of men.

Osmond must have realized, at some point, that he could not win. His attacks grew more erratic, the space between them lengthening. He tried to dart past Coinneach, aiming for an escape into the deeper woods, but Coinneach anticipated the move and cut him off, forcing him into the open. Osmond faltered, limping now, one forepaw dragging uselessly.

He looked up at Coinneach with a strange, almost human expression—regret, or perhaps resignation, as if he knew exactly what he had become and what he deserved.

The others waited, silent, at the edge of the clearing. Their swords drooped, forgotten at their sides. They would not interfere now, would not rob Coinneach of this grim rite. It was a reckoning, not just between two wolves, but between two ways of life: one that survived by rules, and one that survived by breaking them.

Coinneach drew a deep breath, filled his lungs with the humid air, and advanced. Osmond bared his teeth, but the snarl was feeble, more a memory of defiance than the real thing. They crashed together, fur and blood and muscle and bone, and this time Coinneach did not hold back.

He clamped onto Osmond's throat, felt the pulse fluttering beneath his jaws, and squeezed. Osmond thrashed, but Coinneach held fast, feeling the life ebb from his enemy with each passing second. When at last Osmond went limp, Coinneach released him, panting, and stood over the body, the taste of iron thick in his mouth.

Coinneach straightened, licking blood from his muzzle, and looked at the ring of men. Their faces were wary, a mix of awe and apprehension. It was not easy, watching a man become a wolf and then take a life as one. It stripped away the easy comforts of civilization, reminding them all of what they were beneath the armor and swords.

Coinneach shifted back. He stood, naked and trembling, covered in blood and grime, and waited for someone to speak. Though he at once thought of getting another scolding from Blair once she saw his wounds.

The gathering was silent for a long time, the only sound the slow drip of blood onto leaves. Then Tristan stepped forward, his voice low and steady. "It's done."

But it wasn't done. Not until Coinneach learned of Rupert's fate. They wouldn't be safe until he was dead too.

19

When Coinneach and the others arrived back at the croft, Hamish said, "Rupert was so scared he got too close to the edge of the cliffs overlooking the sea and perished. I would have had a more satisfactory ending if I had managed to fight the man. What about Osmond? From your bite marks, I venture to say you fought him as a wolf."

"You would be right." He looked around for his family. Morag's body was already gone.

"We've taken Magnus, Elspeth, and Tamhas to the castle to rest up and eat with us on the morrow. They will stay there as long as they like. Do you know why they would never take part in the celebrations with the clan?" Hamish asked.

"They were afraid someone would realize I belonged at the castle?"

"Aye. Your uh, mother told me that. Not only that, but Rupert's last remarks were, his da killed Aisling's da when they were in a battle fighting our enemy," Hamish said. "All these years, we thought her da was killed in battle. He was, but from the enemy within. It's up to you to share the information with Aisling and Blair if you wish."

"Aisling and I dinna keep secrets from each other." Yet Coinneach wondered if this one secret should be an exception.

"I know your mind is on your family, your other family, but I wanted to say that you will have a private chamber of your own now. And we've got men who will rebuild your family's croft in the meantime."

"I appreciate it—"

"Da. You can say it whenever it pleases you."

Coinneach smiled. "Da." But when his family was nearby, Magnus would always be his da.

Then they rode back to the castle as the others got busy rebuilding the roof and pulling any of the furniture out of the croft to clean and rebuild where necessary.

Nelly, Aisling, and Blair had gone back to the castle with Coinneach's family.

He still figured Blair would have a fit when she saw him all torn up after fighting Osmond.

When they finally arrived at the castle, he saw his parents and brother in the chamber where they were staying, but they looked horrified to see him all chewed up.

"It only hurts a little bit. How are you doing?"

"Better than you, son," Magnus said.

Blair came rushing into the chamber and said, "Oh, goddess, no. Come. Lie down, and I'll take care of your wounds. No more guard duty for you for a while."

Hamish said, "He'll have a more important role to play."

Aisling kissed Coinneach and helped her mother care for his wounds.

"The chief said we will have a chamber to ourselves."

Aisling blushed to high heaven.

"Aye," Hamish said. "I have other duties to tend to. If you need me, Blair, just send Niven."

Niven moved out of the shadows as if he knew he shouldn't

have been eavesdropping. His eyes were wide when he saw all the injuries that Coinneach had sustained.

"We'll move you to your chamber once I've tended to your wounds. Aisling can look after you. Niven can wait outside your chamber door, and Aisling will send him to come for me if Coinneach becomes feverish during the night," Blair said.

"Aye," Niven said.

Aodhan appeared in the doorway, solid as an oak, and after a moment's hesitation—perhaps weighing the wisdom of touching so battered a man—stooped to wrap one arm gingerly around Coinneach's waist and the other under his uninjured shoulder. He smelled of leather and the wind off the loch.

Together, with Coinneach limping and cursing in a half-hearted, exhausted way, they made a slow, shuffling journey past the main hall, up the narrow, spiraling stairs, past the laughing shadows of the torch sconces and the lingering, acrid scent of burning pitch.

The corridors emptied as they passed, news of Coinneach's wounds perhaps preceding them, or perhaps it was merely respect for the sanctity of his pain.

Aodhan guided him to a thick wooden door at the outer bend of the tower. He opened it with a flourish and stood aside. "Hamish thought you would like your own place for the night," he said. "No more sleeping in the barracks for you or the couples' quarters that you had been destined for."

The room was large and opulent, but mostly it was private—a courtesy Coinneach had not expected. The walls, built of massive stones quarried from the same hill the tower stood upon, were mortared so tightly that not even the breath of winter could pry its way inside. The single window was narrow and arrow-slit high, but it let in a shaft of silver light and the distant tang of rain. The bed— he wondered if Hamish himself had arranged for it—was newly made up with woolen blankets and furs folded neatly at the foot.

On the bedside table, someone on the staff had left a shallow basin of steaming water, a rag, and a single flagon of ale.

He sat at the edge of the bed, easing his battered body down with a hiss. His wounds were bandaged tightly—Blair's and Aisling's doing. The pain in Coinneach's side and thigh throbbed in time with his pulse, but it was a pain he could wear, like any other piece of clothing.

He took an experimental sip from the flagon. It was a local brew, sour and pungent, with the aftertaste of thistle and peat. His mind drifted, as minds are wont to do in the aftermath of violence, to the question of whether Aisling would come to him tonight or whether she would keep to herself, seeing to his family instead. He would not blame her if she did because she loved them as much as he did.

He lay back, staring at the ceiling, listening to his own breath and the faint drip of rain from the windowsill. He thought of his mother's croft and the stories she'd told of Highland ghosts that haunted the hours between dusk and dawn, and he wondered, not for the first time, which of the many dead he might find waiting for him if he drifted off now and did not wake again.

The handle turned, and Aisling stepped into the room, her red hair braided tightly, and her face scrubbed clean—paler than he remembered, but just as beautiful. He smiled and held his hand out to her, ready to sleep with her, glad she had come to him.

"If you need anything, just call me," Aodhan said. Then he left them alone and shut the door.

Aisling sat beside him on the bed and put her head against his uninjured shoulder. "You couldna let Aodhan take Osmond on as a wolf, could you?"

"It was my task."

She nodded and kissed his shoulder.

"You know we've talked about no' keeping secrets from each other."

"Aye." She looked up at him, waiting expectantly to hear the news.

"Rupert, before he died, said that his da killed your da while they were in battle against a common enemy. He did it to ensure that Blair never gave up Morag's secret. But your mother never knew?"

"Nay. She thought he had died in battle honorably. I dinna want to share the news with her."

"We willna. I just thought you should know."

"I'm glad you did, and I'm even gladder that my da's murderer is dead."

"I agree." Then he began to caress her breast and kiss her mouth.

"You canna think of making love. You're injured."

"No' where it counts, and of course I want to make love to my lovely mate. The first night in our new quarters? No one to bother us? No Nelly to warn us the kitchen staff is coming?"

Aisling laughed. Then she started to undress him, removing his plaid and boots. His shirt was already off because Blair had to bandage his wounds.

Then Aisling quickly removed her clothes, no' wanting him to have to waste the energy. She kissed around his bandaged areas, but before she thought he would be ready, he had her flat on her back on the bed and was pressed in between her legs.

His manhood was poised to enter her, but he did as before, coaxed her into the most delicious feeling she'd ever felt. Then he was centering himself and thrusting into her as if he was in pain, and he wanted to make love to her as quickly as possible.

She didn't mind. She wanted to make love to him as fast as possible, just to feel his shaft deep inside her before he finally came. She held his face and kissed him. Then they came together, her being careful not to press against his wounds. He pulled the blankets and furs over them.

Next time will be longer, I promise," he said, stroking her back.

"Quick or long, I love being with you like this." She had no regrets as long as he didn't.

Then they dozed off to sleep until she heard a little whispered voice next to the bed.

"Coinneach, my lady, wake up. Trouble is brewing beyond yonder door."

"Niven?" Aisling asked, still half asleep.

"Aye, the guards loyal to Morag are here. The two who were in the dungeon briefly, and the two who were waiting for you at the door."

She sat up. Coinneach was dead asleep. "Coinneach, wake up. Guards loyal to Morag are outside our chamber door."

Coinneach scrambled to get out of bed. Aisling shifted into her wolf. Then she howled, the best and fastest way for her to let others know they were in trouble. Coinneach also howled, but as a human. He hastened to bolt the door, but Niven had already done it. He hadn't thought they would have any more trouble, so he hadn't done so last night.

Niven helped him to dress.

"Where did you come from?" Coinneach asked Niven.

"Through that little trapdoor. I heard the men coming and then slipped into the room next door and came in through there."

"Aisling, I want you and Niven to go through the door."

She shook her head.

"You can attack them while I try to go after them from here. Others should be here shortly. To help us."

She didn't want to leave him, and if there were four men, she would be cut down in short order.

When she went through the door meant for a wolf or a small lad, she found she was in the chamber where Magnus, Elspeth, and Tamhas had been sleeping. Tamhas was already getting dressed. Magnus was following suit. Elspeth was in her wolf form.

Niven came into the room after that and explained the trouble.

"I have my sword, but, da, you do no'," Tamhas said.

"I'll get Aisling's *sgian dubh*." Then Niven stole into her room before she could stop him.

She slipped out of the chamber and saw the four traitorous guards conversing in whispers, trying her chamber door and finding it locked. All four had their swords out. There was no doubt in her mind what they planned to do. Avenge Morag's death with her and Coinneach's deaths, even though Morag caused her own death by setting the croft and herself ablaze.

Aisling waited for reinforcements, but one of the men suddenly saw her. That was not good. He rushed at her with his sword. She tore off, not about to face down his sword with her wolf's teeth. She ran down the stairs to the next landing, where Hamish and Collum were coming up. Several men who were staying in the couple's quarters were also following behind them in various stages of undress, but all armed.

She quickly shifted and said, "The four guards who were supportive of Morag are at our chamber door with the intent to kill us. Coinneach is in the chamber, armed with his sword." Then she changed back into her wolf and followed after them.

Hamish was the first to reach the stone corridor, his sword raised, catching the glint of torchlight as he intercepted the gray-bearded man. The two met at the threshold of Coinneach and Aisling's chamber, steel grinding against steel with a shriek that echoed down the ancient hall.

The gray-bearded man aimed each blow to incapacitate, while Hamish fought with a deep sense of duty that gave an edge to every parry. For a moment, it was as if the rest of the world had fallen away, leaving only the clang and rasp of their duel, the two men determined not to yield.

But the assault had come in pairs, and Tamhas, never one to cower in the shadow of his older brother's renown, took on the second invader—a younger, broad-shouldered man in a patched leather tunic.

Tamhas felt the thud of adrenaline as his training took over, the lessons between him and his brother and their friend Chief Alasdair, and the workouts at Hamish's castle. He moved low, forcing the attacker off-balance, using the close walls to his advantage.

Fury and fear mingled in Tamhas's chest; with each blow he blocked or landed, a well-wielded attack.

Even as Tamhas drove the younger man back, he saw out of the corner of his eye the gray-bearded leader feign a fall back, then smash the guard of Hamish aside with a vicious upward strike. Hamish grunted, staggered, then countered with the blunt hilt of his sword to the man's temple.

The gray-bearded man reeled, grabbing Hamish's wrist and twisting, sending the blade clattering against the flagstones. For a heartbeat, Hamish and his foe were locked in a bare-knuckled struggle, years of grudges compressed into the press of bone and sinew.

Aisling's bark, sharp and raw, cut through the din. Tamhas's mind snapped back to her as he realized the younger attacker had stopped feinting and was now trying to bull his way past him, desperate to reach Coinneach's chamber door.

Tamhas planted his feet and lunged, slicing a shallow gash across his opponent's thigh. Blood welled, and the man fell to one knee, cursing as he swung his sword in a wild arc. Tamhas ducked it, then brought the pommel of his weapon down on the man's collarbone, the sickening crunch followed by a spasm of pain that left the attacker howling and clutching at his own arm.

The passage narrowed, the fighting tightening into a series of short, brutal exchanges. The gray-bearded man, sensing his comrade's distress, disengaged from Hamish with a shoving kick and turned his attention to Tamhas. Tamhas found himself backing up, forced into a defensive crouch as both men now advanced on him.

It was then that the door to Coinneach and Aisling's room shuddered, and Tamhas realized with a cold certainty that the only thing between the intruders and his brother was the thickness of the wood and his own resolve.

He gritted his teeth and dug in his heels, refusing to give up even an inch of ground. Boldly and decisively, Tamhas thrust his sword at the second man's chest. Unprepared for the sudden onslaught, the man took the brunt of the sword straight through his heart. He collapsed on the stone floor in a muddled heap.

The third man, Collum's target, was a burly, freckled brute, hair the color of wet straw plastered to his brow with sweat and blood— a man who had taken the oath with Hamish earlier that day, and now, had drawn steel on his erstwhile liege.

Collum's loyalty to his family was a blind spot, a place in his mind that glowed like a hot coal, and to see it betrayed made him savage. He sliced at the man's chest, knocking his opponent back against a wall where he bounced and sprawled, wheezing, dropping his own sword.

Then the man went after Collum with the knife he kept hidden in his boot, the blade trembling in his big, white-knuckled fist.

The man fought back, dirty and desperate, stabbing at Collum's belly, but Collum was relentless. He leapt out of the way and sliced him with his sword, but it was not fatal. When the man tried to scream for quarter, Collum shoved his forearm into the man's mouth and drove the sword into his lower belly, twisting until the man stopped struggling.

A sob of air left the traitor, and he slumped against the stone wall. Collum straightened and looked for another foe, his face whiter than ever, his mouth a thin, trembling line.

Meanwhile, Magnus tried to reach the fourth man—another

traitor, another oathbreaker—but he was hemmed in behind a press of bodies, limbs, and torsos writhing in the glow of the torches, too many arms swinging swords, too many feet tripping him up. Every time he tried to break free, someone else crashed into his path.

He must have bitten his cheek or tongue and spat blood and cursed, swinging Aisling's *sgian dubh*, trying to reach the unengaged fourth man, who seemed to be considering his options. But always the fourth man slipped away, always just out of reach, as if the fight itself conspired to keep Magnus from settling the score.

Aisling hadn't wanted Magnus to fight against the men who were warrior-trained. He wasn't trained in the art of fighting. Just as a farmer, handy with a pitchfork.

Above the din in the narrow rocky hallway, Coinneach was at the door, looking intent on joining the fight, hoping to strike at the first man Hamish was fighting. She barked at Coinneach, voice sharp as a thrown axe, telling him to stay out of it, to get back, that he was still healing, and did he want to die for nothing? The other men could handle this. He had nothing to prove.

Coinneach ignored her, his face twisted with the kind of stubbornness that looked like pain, and that was part of why she loved him; he could never be controlled. Even as she watched, wishing she could reach him, Coinneach managed to strike the brigand in the side with his well-honed Viking sword, then tried to stagger toward the traitor again.

As all this unfolded, Hamish continued to battle the first man. Their fight was a blur of glinting metal and ragged breathing. They were evenly matched, both quick and both skilled, the clatter of their blades ringing out.

Hamish had already scored several shallow cuts on the man's arms and chest, and blood was running in bright rivulets down the traitor's side. But Hamish was not untouched. He had taken a cut to his cheek—a lucky, grazing swipe that had opened a red mouth from his ear to the corner of his lips. Blood seeped down his jaw and onto his chest, but he didn't notice or didn't care.

The traitor, emboldened by the sight of Hamish's blood, pressed the attack, hacking at Hamish with a two-handed grip, trying to break the lord's guard. But Hamish was too clever; he sidestepped, parried, and closed in, slapping the man's blade away and driving his own sword into the hollow just below the ribs. The traitor gasped, his eyes widening, and Hamish stepped back, letting him fall.

Hamish said to Coinneach, "Return to your chamber. We've got this."

The fourth man was fully engaged by several of the married men. He didn't stand a chance.

They drove the fourth man, the traitor, up against the far wall. Several of Hamish's men stabbed him in the abdomen while he cried out, fell to the floor, and died.

"Dress and get rid of them," Hamish said, since some of the men were barely wearing anything.

"Aye, my laird." Still, they dragged the men out of the way, down the stairs to where the couples' chambers were, and left them at the entrance, before they dressed and dragged them the rest of the way down the stairs.

Niven dashed past them to inform Blair to take care of anyone who was hurt.

Thankfully, almost everyone who had fought the men had minor sword cuts. Hamish needed stitches, but with their healing genetics, the scar would heal up and be gone in a few days. Magnus grumbled about not getting a chance to fight the vermin. Elspeth had shifted, dressed, and came out of the chamber that they were staying in, courtesy of Hamish, and took Magnus's hand and led him back to bed.

Tamhas likewise retired to the chamber.

Blair checked out Hamish's cuts and tended to them. "They should be well healed in a few days."

That was the thing about wolves. They healed so well in half the time that humans did and never wore scars.

She checked on the other men and then, lastly, saw to Coinneach. Aisling was glad he hadn't sustained any further injuries or pulled any stitches loose.

To Aisling's surprise and annoyance, he lifted Blair off her feet and swung her around, then set her on her feet. "I'm so lucky to have a woman who is such a great healer take care of me night and day." He kissed her cheek, and her mother's cheeks blossomed with color.

"You're bound to tear your stitches loose, doing such a thing."

"It was well worth it." He smiled at Blair as if he truly loved her.

She finally gave him just a wee bit of a smile, then shook her head. "Off to bed with ye."

Hamish said, "No more murder attempts on your life."

Aisling and Coinneach agreed. Then everyone slowly left the area, and she and her mate returned to bed. Niven settled down outside their door to alert Blair if Coinneach became feverish again.

"I wasna expecting that," Coinneach said to Aisling as they wrapped each other up together.

"Nay, me either. Niven is a clever lad."

"Aye, that he is, though at first, I was angry that he had slipped into our chamber."

"My mother was glad that you hugged her."

"I was afraid to before this, but I wanted to show how much I care about her. She is as much family to me as you and my own are."

"Well, she was thrilled. But she already knew how much you care about her."

They settled in bed, hoping the rest of the night would be uneventful, as he wrapped his arms around Aisling in a loving embrace.

EPILOGUE

Coinneach still planned to have the wedding ceremony with Aisling in the meadow to honor his parents, who had raised them all those years. But Hamish wouldn't hear of it. He told Cook to make the most lavish meal for the feast, and they would celebrate for days.

Aisling wore the most beautiful kirtle of pale blue that set off her red hair. Elspeth and Blair both wore green gowns, as the women who sewed clothes at the castle honored them with kirtles as well. Even Nelly, who was so much like a sister, wore one too.

Then the procession got on the way, with Coinneach wedding Aisling in the inner bailey. They promised to run as wolves after the feast in the meadows. Once they were wed, though the mating had made it official, he kissed her like there was no tomorrow. She was just as exuberantly kissing him back, and everyone laughed and cheered at the union of Hamish's true son and Aisling.

This time, Blair, Tamhas, Magnus, Elspeth, and Nelly sat at the head table along with Aisling and Coinneach. He thought about how much his life had changed with Aisling in it as several pack members toasted to the happy couple. She made him complete.

Hamish leaned over and said to Aisling, "Here, I planned to add you to my company of archers. But Coinneach wouldn't hear of it."

She smiled at Hamish. "If we are in a battle, I can help your archers fight the enemy."

Coinneach reached over and took Aisling's hand in his. "Unless you are with child."

Hamish laughed. "You better work on that faster."

Coinneach looked at Aisling and said, "Do you have anything to share?"

"I was going to wait until after the wedding." She sighed, sounding exasperated with him.

"Your mother said..."

"Aye, she said we will have twins in the spring." Then she patted Hamish's hand. "And you will have grandbabies."

"A grandson and granddaughter," Hamish said, as if it were his word and it would come true.

Cullum said, "I will be a great uncle. That has a nice ring to it."

Then the brothers got into a discussion about the color of their hair and what color their eyes would be.

Once the meal was through, they all moved the tables to the back walls and danced.

Even Hamish danced with Blair, forgiving her for leaving his baby son for someone to find, but understanding her fear and young age, and that she truly had saved his life.

Tamhas spent the whole time in Nelly's company. Elspeth and Magnus had eyes only for each other, as it should be. Coinneach wondered if Hamish would ever mate again. If his brother would ever mate. Blair too. If his brother and Nelly would finally be a couple. Aodhan preferred his warrior and bachelor status.

Even Alasdair had arrived with his new bride, Isobel, a Viking war maiden who had escaped her clan for a better life. Coinneach couldn't believe it, but everything that had happened in his life of late was a surprise.

"WHAT ARE YOU THINKING ABOUT, my love?" Aisling asked Coinneach. She was ready for them to run as wolves and then retire to their own chamber for some wild lovemaking.

"I was wondering if certain people would find their own mates."

"Hmm, maybe I can help with that."

"I canna believe you are still working in the kitchen."

"I like cooking, and now I am Cook's favorite assistant, as she can get anything she wants if she asks me to get it for her. Besides, I'm no' the lady of the manor until you are chief. Once that happens, hopefully many years in the future, I will be overseeing all the staff."

"Hamish wants you to do that now since he doesna have a mate."

"Well, I suppose I can do both jobs."

"Until the bairns come."

She smiled. She was so thrilled they were going to have twins and hoped everything would turn out all right. Her mother had been worried about her, given what had happened to Coinneach's mother, Orla. And both Blair and Elspeth worried that she would lose one of the twins.

"Let's slip away and run in the meadow as wolves."

He smiled at her. "Aye. Do we tell anyone we're going to run?"

"Nay, if they figure it out, they can join us." She took his hand and they left the great hall.

But they were seen right away. Once they had removed their clothes, shifted, and left the castle, several others did the same, and they were soon joined by many members of the pack.

They howled with joy.

They were glad they had gotten rid of the poison that Morag, Osmund, and Rupert represented in the pack.

Here, Coinneach thought he would get a job as one of the

warriors at the pack, but he had also become a son of the chief and mated with Aisling, elevating her own position. She couldn't be happier to have her mother and all the others who had become family to her. But especially Coinneach, who was the brawest wolf of all.

ACKNOWLEDGMENTS

I owe a debt of gratitude to Darla Taylor and Donna Fournier, whose keen eyes and thoughtful suggestions transformed these pages. This book stands stronger because you both cared enough to catch what I missed.

ABOUT THE AUTHOR

USA Today bestselling and award-winning author **Terry Spear** has written over a hundred paranormal romance novels, young adult, and medieval Highland historical romances. Her first werewolf romance, *Heart of the Wolf,* was named a 2008 *Publishers Weekly*'s Best Book of the Year, and her subsequent titles have garnered high praise and hit the *USA Today* bestseller list. A retired officer of the U.S. Army Reserves, Terry lives in Spring, Texas, where she is working on her next werewolf romance, shapeshifting jaguars, cougar shifters, vampires, hot Highlanders, and having fun with her young adult fae and vampire novels, helping with her grandchildren, and raising two Havanese.

For more information, please visit her website at: http://www.terryspear.com

Blog: https://terryspearbooks.blog/

Follow her for new releases and book deals: www.bookbub.com/authors/terry-spear

Twitter: @TerrySpear.

Facebook: http://www.facebook.com/terry.spear

ALSO BY TERRY SPEAR

Adult Titles

Romantic Suspense: Deadly Fortunes, In the Dead of the Night, Relative Danger, Bound by Danger

***

The Highlanders Series: His Wild Highland Lass (novella), Vexing the Highlander (novella), Winning the Highlander's Heart, The Accidental Highland Hero, Highland Rake, Taming the Wild Highlander, The Highlander, Her Highland Hero, The Viking's Highland Lass, My Highlander, Stolen Highland Dreams

Other historical romances: Lady Caroline & the Egotistical Earl, A Ghost of a Chance at Love

***

Heart of the Wolf Series: Heart of the Wolf, Destiny of the Wolf, To Tempt the Wolf, Legend of the White Wolf, Seduced by the Wolf, Wolf Fever, Heart of the Highland Wolf, Dreaming of the Wolf, A SEAL in Wolf's Clothing, A Howl for a Highlander, A Highland Werewolf Wedding, A SEAL Wolf Christmas, Silence of the Wolf, Hero of a Highland Wolf, A Highland Wolf Christmas; SEAL Wolf Hunting; A Silver Wolf Christmas, SEAL Wolf in Too Deep, Alpha Wolf Need Not Apply, Between a Wolf and a Hard Place, SEAL Wolf Undercover, Dreaming of a White Wolf Christmas, Flight of the White Wolf, All's Fair in Love and Wolf, A Billionaire Wolf for Christmas, SEAL Wolf Surrender, Silver Town Wolf: Home for the Holidays, Night of the Billionaire Wolf, You Had Me at Wolf, Joy to the Wolves, The Wolf Wore Plaid, Jingle Bell Wolf, The Best of Both Wolves, While the Wolf's Away, Christmas Wolf Surprise, Wolf Takes the Lead, Wolf on the Wild Side, Her Wolf for the Holidays, A Good Wolf is

Hard to Find (2024), Dreaming of a Highland Wolf (2024), Wolf Bound, Mated for Christmas (2024) , The Wolf of My Eye

SEAL Wolves: To Tempt the Wolf, A SEAL in Wolf's Clothing, A SEAL Wolf Christmas; SEAL Wolf Hunting, A SEAL Wolf in Too Deep, SEAL Wolf Undercover, SEAL Wolf Surrender

Silver Town Wolves: Destiny of the Wolf, Wolf Fever, Dreaming of the Wolf, Silence of the Wolf; A Silver Wolf Christmas, Between a Wolf and a Hard Place, Home for the Holidays, Jingle Bell Wolf

Wolff Family Lodge Wolves: You Had Me at Wolf, Wolf on the Wild Side, A Good Wolf is Hard to Find

Highland Wolves: Heart of the Highland Wolf, A Howl for a Highlander, A Highland Werewolf Wedding, Hero of a Highland Wolf, A Highland Wolf Christmas, The Wolf Wore Plaid, Her Wolf for the Holidays, Dreaming of a Highland Wolf, The Wolf of My Eye

Billionaire Wolf Series: A Billionaire in Wolf's Clothing, A Billionaire Wolf for Christmas, Night of the Billionaire Wolf, Wolf Takes the Lead

White Wolf Series: Legend of the White Wolf, Dreaming of a White Wolf Christmas, Flight of the White Wolf, While the Wolf's Away, Mated for Christmas

Red Wolf Series: Seduced by the Wolf, Joy to the Wolves, The Best of Both Wolves, Christmas Wolf Surprise

Greystoke Wolf Pack: Wolf Bound,

Wolf Novellas: Day of the Wolf, Seal Wolf Pursuit, Wolf to the Rescue, Night of the Wolf, United Shifter Force

***

Heart of the Jaguar Series: Savage Hunger, Jaguar Fever, Jaguar Hunt, Jaguar Pride, A Very Jaguar Christmas, You Had Me at Jaguar, The Witch and the Jaguar, Dawn of the Jaguar

***

Heart of the Cougar Series: Cougar's Mate, Call of the Cougar, Taming the Wild Cougar, Covert Cougar Christmas, a novella, Double Cougar Trouble, Cougar Undercover, Cougar Magic, Cougar Halloween Mischief, Falling for the Cougar, Cougar Christmas Calamity, Catch the Cougar (Halloween Novella), You Had Me at Cougar, Saving the White Cougar, Big Cat Magic

***

White Bear Series: Loving the White Bear, Claiming the White Bear, Bear of a Halloween, Protecting the White Bear

Grizzly Bear Series: Bear in Mind

***

Highland Wolves of Old: Wolf Pack, Wolf Alliance, Wolf Heir

Heart of the Huntress Series: Killing the Bloodlust, Deadly Liaisons, Huntress for Hire, Forbidden Love, Deadly Liaisons, Vampire Redemption, Primal Desire, Huntress Unleashed

Vampire Novellas: The Siren's Lure, Vampiric Calling, Seducing the Huntress

***

Comedy Romance: Exchanging Grooms, Marriage, Las Vegas Style

***

Science Fiction: Galaxy Warrior

Young Adult Titles

The World of Fae:

The Dark Fae

The Deadly Fae

The Winged Fae

The Ancient Fae

Dragon Fae

Hawk Fae

Phantom Fae

Golden Fae

Falcon Fae

Woodland Fae

Angel Fae

***

The World of Elf:

The Shadow Elf

The Darkland Elf

Warrior Elf

***

Blood Moon Series:

Kiss of the Vampire

Bite of the Vampire

Night of the Vampire

The Vampire Chronicles Series:

The Vampire in My Dreams

Demon Guardian Series:

The Trouble with Demons

Demon Trouble, Too

Demon Hunter

Non-Series for Now:

Ghostly Liaisons

The Beast Within

Courtly Masquerade

Deidre's Secret

The Magic of Inherian:

The Scepter of Salvation

The Mage of Monrovia

Emerald Isle of Mists

Tashama